"Your mother called."

Jane nodded.

"Should I not answer the phone?" Hank asked.

"Why not answer?"

"I probably sound like a man."

Jane frowned. "In Oak Harbor people pick up the phone to help out. The sheriff, the meter reader, the Federal Express driver—whoever's closest. All it means is someone's being neighborly."

"There's no such thing as that small of a town."

"Well, Oak Harbor thinks there is, so don't convince them otherwise."

Hank studied her eyes. "What about after office hours?"

Jane looked through the tall, narrow windows behind him. The glass was water-beaded from the fog, which had boiled down the Straits while they'd talked, darkening the evening. "You want to pick a fight?" she asked at last, deciding to confront him and try to put him at ease.

Faint lines deepened under his eyes, reminding her how worn-out he was. "I've lived in eleven countries, Jane. Every nation has its own rules, but there's one truth that's true everywhere. A mother may be sophisticated about herself, but she doesn't want a man answering her daughter's phone."

ABOUT THE AUTHOR

Rena Dean says that writing is more fun than any other way of making a living, and she's used that as an excuse to do many different kinds of writing, from résumés and research reports to journalism and technical writing. She loves the fact that her career as a writer leaves her free to travel with her husband, an educational consultant. Her favorite pastime is exploring small towns, especially in her home state of Washington, where each community has its own unique quality. *Public Secret* is her first novel, and she loves the way writing about a place helps her to understand more about the ways people and communities change to fit each other. She selected Oak Harbor as the setting for her first novel as a special tribute to the town's special charm.

PUBLIC SECRET

RENA DEAN

Harlequin Books

TORONTO • NEW YORK • LONDON
AMSTERDAM • PARIS • SYDNEY • HAMBURG
STOCKHOLM • ATHENS • TOKYO • MILAN

For Sue

Published November 1989

First printing September 1989

ISBN 0-373-16319-3

Chapter One

Jane stared at the TV news, thunderstruck. Sitting cross-legged on the lounge floor, she abruptly lost interest in the pot of freshly transplanted tulips on the newspapers spread before her. She saw nothing beyond the TV image of a trench-coated figure who strode with slouching grace through shadowed airport corridors, trailed by camera crews.

I'd never forget his walk, Jane thought.

People change, she told herself.

The way you walk doesn't change, she answered.

She hesitated, letting a drop of melted wax congeal on the end of the bamboo stick used to arrange the tulips. Instead of getting back to work, she dropped the bamboo stick and stared at the television.

The news camera zoomed in for the closer view, which erased all doubt. This man was Hank. His straight blond hair was longer than Jane remembered, and the unruly beard was new. But nothing else had changed, apparently. He was still very much in charge, in his enchanting way.

Jane watched him step onto the stage in the airport interview room. The voice-over announcer babbled on with professional emotion about this brave man, this hero, who'd bet his life he could interrupt the chain of ransom demands that had terrified the international business world.

"Have you been watching that?" Thelma Amstellen asked from the doorway.

Jane was glad of the interruption. "No, I've been out in the forcing sheds all morning."

Thelma clucked her tongue as if keeping up on the news was a higher duty than work, but her smile kept her disapproval from seeming serious. "They call him local news because he went to the university, but he's not from Seattle."

"What's he doing here?" Jane asked.

"He isn't here. He's someplace east, Washington, D.C., I think." Thelma plunked down comfortably on the oak and oatmeal couch. Making herself thoroughly at home, like any small-town visitor, she picked up the remote control gadget and adjusted the TV color to suit her tastes.

Jane wasn't sure the color needed fixing. Subtropical sun had bleached Hank's gold hair to straw, but his eyes were still as ocean-blue as she remembered. Surrendering to memory, Jane brushed her own heavy mass of hair away from her face. She used to keep it short, but it had always been sandy-brown, which was why Hank had called her Sandy. Five years ago. At the university.

She was tempted to tell Thelma the whole thing, even though she knew it wouldn't work. Thelma was a good friend, but people in Oak Harbor didn't talk about their pasts. They didn't need to. They'd known one another for generations. They didn't practice the get-acquainted skills city people took for granted. Jane had puzzled over the difference when she'd first moved to Oak Harbor. She was used to strangers, so she asked for a thumbnail autobiography from everyone she met. The local people always laughed and said they wouldn't know where to start. In the three years she had lived among them, Jane had gradually learned some of the details, but not by hearing their stories directly.

Mostly Thelma talked about the *Curlew*, a tuna trawler she owned with her brother. Jane answered with daily details about Dutch Bulb, the mail-order nursery she co-owned. But they never did nostalgia together. Even at their friendliest, she and Thelma didn't have the kind of relationship where Jane felt she could just turn off the TV to protect herself from shots of Hank and then say why. In Oak Harbor bittersweet didn't seem to be one of the things people felt.

What mattered in this community was reality, which didn't extend very far beyond the town limits. Everyone in town watched the TV news, but they didn't believe it, any more than they believed the soaps.

Jane wondered if she believed it herself.

After a moment she shook her head. Why should she feel surprised to see Hank on TV? After all, when they were both at the university, they had meant to change the world. They had set out, going in opposite directions, confident they both could make a difference. Hank hadn't been the usual kind of student friend.

She smiled, remembering how they had met at the Stranger Seminar. It was an innovative workshop the university ran for students in the business school. The workshop director was sure that anyone who was going to succeed in business had to be a take-charge type to start with. To him, that meant future business managers didn't need counselors because they could solve their own problems by talking frankly with someone like themselves. The Stranger Seminar was meant to prove his theory.

The university was large enough to be a city in itself, so pairing strangers wasn't hard. The director matched up students from different years and different specialties. He gave them false names to help them remain anonymous and sent them to Point Roberts, Washington, a tiny peninsula so out of reach there was nothing resortlike to do. Each couple spent two weeks in a waterfront cabin, talking out problems that might hold them back in their careers. The idea was that strangers could be honest because they'd never again see the person they swapped worries with.

It hadn't quite worked that way for "Sandy" and "Hank."

Jane was assigned to Cabin Seven. She wanted commonsense help controlling her stage fright. She had seen a picture of her stranger before they met. To be sure, she didn't know him, but she couldn't believe the athletic, confident, clear-eyed man in her photo could possibly have any kind of serious problem to discuss.

The "Hank" who joined her at the cabin at Point Roberts was an utter shock. His picture hadn't prepared her for the energy he radiated or for the tangle of thought and feeling evoked by his direct gaze. And nothing in this world could have forewarned her of his trouble.

Jane frowned at the TV, wondering what he had faced this time.

As if in response to her unspoken question, the announcer's voice recapped respectfully. "He was taken by the Hands of Allah and might have disappeared completely, since no one in the Western world knew how to contact this terrorist group. But an English-speaking Arab journalist managed to find them and interview Wandersee in captivity."

"In captivity," Thelma repeated sympathetically. "I'll bet he does feel like it's a zoo."

They watched Hank glance over his shoulder nervously. He obviously wasn't sure what the crowd at his heels would do to him.

"Reporters." Jane tried to match Thelma's casual tone, but her heart ached. She knew too well what captivity would mean to Hank.

"Let's hear that smuggled tape again," the announcer said morbidly. "Here's the hostage speaking, three months ago, when no one dared hope they'd get him away from the Hands of Allah alive. Possibly a spy, but certainly a hero, Dr.—that's doctor of psychology—Dr. Henry Wandersee."

When the secret tape cut in, Jane leaned forward as if she were alone with Hank. In spite of his desperate situation, Hank had identified himself calmly. As if his own safety didn't count to him, he went on, emphasizing the real message: "I've been blindfolded ever since they captured me. They've given me water but no food. They say I'm being held for ransom, but I think they'll kill me after I make this tape. Don't pay the ransom. Maybe that will help stop their dirty game. However this turns out—*semper fi*."

The low fidelity recording was a featureless rasp, but that didn't matter. Jane would forever recognize the voice that had teased, and confided, and laughed, and yearned, and coaxed and finally turned into her sweetest memory.

"*Semper fi*—Marines say that, not businessmen." Clinton Jarvis walked in casually, his briefcase in one hand and lap-top computer in the other. "But maybe he's both," he added when neither of his listeners responded to his observations.

Jane was glad he hadn't caught her trying to explain her memories of Hank to Thelma. Clinton liked to know everything about everybody, so he could pass it on. The whole town accepted it as part of his nature and joked that he was better than a newspaper. Glancing up at him with a hostess smile plastered on her face Jane silently admitted it didn't really matter if Clinton knew she and Hank were old friends. The trouble was, Clinton would want to know what kind of friends they used to be, and Jane wasn't sure. It was one of the questions she asked herself occasionally.

Obviously not noticing Jane's dilemma, Clinton stopped behind Thelma and set his equipment down. Adjusting his white-on-green polka-dot bow tie as if preparing for photo opportunities, he settled himself to help them watch the news.

On the TV, the announcer shut off the ransom tape and fell silent himself so they could hear as well as watch the most recent update. Hank stepped between the flags that bracketed the airport lectern.

A self-consciously glamorous reporter captured his attention. "You're *sure* it's over?"

"Why wouldn't it be over? I gave them what they want." The high-fidelity mikes brought his voice into the lounge so vividly that Jane reeled. He was hoarse, as if he'd been talking too much. That endearing detail touched her heart.

"What did they want?" an unseen man yelled.

Hank paused. Thought. Shrugged. "They're just like kids anywhere. They asked me about Disneyland."

Clinton laughed. "Would you call that brainwashed? Or is he jarred loose?"

Or maybe he's hurt, Jane added silently, keeping her protective feelings to herself. No one ever contradicted Clinton. There was no point, since he was always perfectly sure of what he thought.

Jane watched the screen intently. She could see that Hank was beginning to tire. He stepped away from the lectern, to call a halt to the questioning. He moved to the edge of the platform and leaned down confidingly.

"I want to thank you for your interest." He brushed his palm across his bearded jaw, neatening himself for what he obviously felt was the really important part of the interview. "My research shows we do our best thinking one-on-one. I've got some thinking to do—surely you see that."

He shifted his gaze through the clamoring mob of journalists. "Please help. Only one person has ever shared my privacy. I need to be alone with her."

Their reaction was predictable. They roared for her name and rammed their mikes closer to his face.

Jane smiled, imagining how surprised they'd be if they knew how innocent being alone with Hank could be. He didn't look innocent, she granted that, he looked like every woman's favorite fantasy.

He also looked hard run, she decided, abruptly sober again. She tried to read his expression as he gazed at the journalists. After a few moments, he held up one hand. They quieted restlessly.

He looked toward the nearest camera lens so that his gaze transfixed Jane and Thelma and every other woman on two continents. "Sandy?"

Oh, Hank, Jane thought, we can't go back to the past. Surely you know that.

He didn't seem to know it. He looked through the news-camera lens, not as if he hoped, really, but only as if he was struggling to resist despair.

It wasn't in Jane's nature to turn away from need.

"Thelma—" She stopped herself in time. With Clinton listening, she couldn't ask what Thelma thought she should do.

Anyway, she didn't need to ask. If she said this hero on the news was asking permission to come to Oak Harbor, it would sound the same to Thelma as if she'd claimed one of her cousins was due in from his summer home on Saturn's rings.

She shook her head, determined to get it right. She was still "Sandy," in a sort of way, for him, just as he was still "Hank" for her. The problem was, she couldn't imagine "Hank" in Oak Harbor. The man and the town were both part of her life, but not at the same time. They couldn't be.

A commotion on the TV drew Jane's attention back to the news. She watched in horror as doors slammed open behind Hank. Men in dark suits swarmed forward. They didn't touch Hank, but they cut him off from the public exit. The seething crowd of reporters struggled for last shots. Spotting a camera in the clear, Hank lifted his head in a gesture of purest gallantry.

"Don't let me disappear," he said calmly, and then he did disappear behind a human screen of federal agents.

"So there's the story," the announcer said with satisfaction. "The man's been through so much he's forgotten where he is. This is America. Nobody disappears."

"I wonder if that's true," Jane said anxiously.

"He didn't look stressed," Thelma added. "He looked glamorous."

"Surprising what inadequate lighting will do to photography," Clinton agreed scientifically.

Jane bowed her head, wondering if there was anything she could do. He had called to her. He must be counting on her. But if those men who swarmed him were the government, how could she help him? There was a number for the FBI in the Seattle phone book, but had those men been FBI? And what good could she do? She was one private citizen on the other side of the country.

Feeling helpless just made her feel angry. So she decided to get back to work as an excuse not to join Thelma and Clinton in gossiping about Hank. Retrieving her bamboo arranging stick, she dipped it into her pan of melted wax. She bent over the pot of tulips in front of her, trying to concentrate on the warm wax she was dropping into the center of each fragile blossom to keep them from closing when the light faded.

It was painstaking work, but it didn't occupy her mind. Her thoughts kept turning to Hank. It was silly to feel anxious, she decided. Hank was a hero. The TV announcer had said so. That meant whatever he had gone through was over now.

It's *over*, she repeated silently.

She refused to think about the expression in his eyes—and the blend of doubt and trust she'd heard in his voice as he'd called to Sandy. Surely that was just electronic, something in the mikes.

Except, she frowned into the cream heart of a green-gold bloom, if he wants to be alone, why did he ask them not to let him disappear?

Because he's disoriented, like the news anchor said, she answered herself quickly. Those men who had mobbed him, they were just government agents there to protect him.

She wished she could believe it, and so she tried to act as if she did. "How about some help," she asked Thelma and Clinton in a commonsense tone. "I'm working on centerpiece designs for the Festival banquet."

She held up the sample. A trio of *veridiflora* tulips was surrounded by a perky crown of the lime *sylvestris*, which she loved for their delicate perfume.

"If you were the general public, what would you think of this?"

"I am the general public, and I've never seen the use of green flowers," Clinton said.

Thelma laughed. "You know us waterfront types, Jane, if it's got something colored on one end and sticks in the ground on the other, we call it a flower and let it go."

"Which proves my point," Clinton said approvingly. "A tulip-red tulip-shaped tulip is what Oak Harbor wants."

Jane decided she shouldn't have asked.

"Speaking of Festival." Thelma picked up the remote and clicked off the TV. "You know the director's wife is always Festival secretary, Jane? Well, Dirk's been asked to be this year's director, but can you see me writing letters?"

Jane smiled.

"I told Dirk to hold off agreeing until I could dash over here. You write letters as easy as I mend fishing nets, and I figured you might be willing to do that part for me, once you knew my marriage is on the line over it."

Jane laughed. "No, it's not, but sure, let's do the letters together. It'll be fun."

Thelma sighed gratefully as she stood.

"I'm lining up Festival commitments myself." Clinton arranged his rimless glasses methodically. "Is Dutch Bulb donating this year?"

"Sure." Jane held up her hand, extending one finger to mark each item as she counted. "Banquet decorations. Sponsor the new-hybrid bulb contest. Downtown planters. Daffodil blankets for horses for the mounted cops. Desk and room bouquets for all the bed-and-breakfasts."

Clinton showed signs of intending to sit down to discuss Dutch Bulb's offerings more thoroughly in order to make sure Jane understood Oak Harbor's rules while her business partner was out of town. Jane wasn't in the mood. She set her sample centerpiece on the low table and stood to brush potting soil off her olive sweatshirt and her rugged jeans.

"I'll walk you to your cars. I'm going outside anyway."

She watched them leave, not sure whether she wanted the privacy she'd just secured in order to remember or to forget. Wandering over to a test plot she'd planted in front of the greenhouses, she bent and inspected the leaf tips pushing up through sawdust mulch. After a moment, she turned to look out across the town.

It was easy to see why the original owners of the house had chosen this site. At the lip of a bluff overhanging the port, it was high enough to give a sense of light and air, which the rest of the town missed. The old port had packed around the harbor at sea level, and as the town grew, it had bridged the lowlands across Whidbey Island's waist. It should have had the usual northwest saltwater features— long sandy beaches clogged with driftwood, and watery channels leading off mysteriously into fog. Instead, forested ridges and barrier islands protected the moorage on all sides.

Feeling oddly hemmed in, Jane lifted her gaze. Beyond the southwest ridge lay the Sound, and beyond that shimmered the snowcapped peaks of the Olympic Mountain range—home, or as much of one as she had.

Her parents were missionaries. Thinking of them reminded her again of the Stranger Seminar. They had believed the best way to raise children was to include them, not just keep them entertained. And so, Jane grew up leading sing-alongs and giving pep talks. Showing off had been fun when she was little, but it was torture in her teens. By the time she'd gotten to college, she lost her voice every time she tried to give a public speech.

When she had mentioned it at the Stranger Seminar, Hank had pretended to be appalled. Is that truly all you've got to feel bad about? he asked. Wait till you hear what's wrong with me. She almost didn't hear, as it turned out, because he'd found it all nearly impossible to confide, even to a stranger.

Jane sat on the low brick shelter wall and stared at the Sound as if it were a movie screen. Hank had said he couldn't stand the dark. Looking abashed, he admitted it sounded silly, but it was a terrible handicap. It meant he couldn't go to dinner meetings, he couldn't squire visiting bigwigs around, he couldn't study late at the library. He'd claimed what caused his trouble was his service with the peacekeeping troops. Jane had said servicemen were supposed to be good in the dark. He'd smiled good-naturedly at her joking answer, but he hadn't backed down.

She'd insisted, and so he'd dragged out details. He'd been a headquarters guard when a suicide mission drove a truckload of explosives into the building, burying everyone inside under tons of rubble. For two days, he'd lain pinned in the darkness. Too badly hurt to call for help, he'd listened to rescue crews digging out the dead. They'd grown discouraged and talked about giving up because there didn't seem to be any survivors. He'd kept panic at bay by planning what he would do when he got out. He would avoid the dark, even at night, he decided, and he would never let anything hold down his hands.

Responding to his story automatically, Jane had reached for his hand. Caught off guard, he'd jerked away. She'd insisted holding hands was fun. He'd offered to put his arm around her instead. She'd nestled against him companionably and reached for his hand again. He'd managed not to draw away. After a while it had gotten easier. And by the end of the Seminar, he'd been the one who reached out constantly to hold hands.

Would the cure have lasted through his captivity? She wondered. How could he ever bear a blindfold, dreading darkness as he did? And what about his hands? Captives were always bound, weren't they? What would that do to a man like him?

No wonder he called to me on the news, she thought, horrified. She clenched her fists. It didn't help that he looked all right, because he'd always looked all right. At Cabin Seven, even while he was reliving the very worst, he had still looked good.

She remembered walking down the beach with him on their last evening together. She'd been telling him that she'd decided stage fright was easy to handle. She was sure she could warm up even the coldest audience by reminding herself of him and the way they'd learned how fast a stranger could become a friend.

He was having trouble finding words, and so he skipped stones, putting his entire body into each throw as if the Straits of Georgia could organize his thoughts. The day had been so perfect that the water was pond smooth and the stones had ricocheted out into the channel as if heading for Japan.

When the tide set up a small chop at last, he'd turned to her with his heartbreaking smile. The ends of his cheerful mouth quirked to show that he took himself with a grain of salt. "You've saved my life."

She'd tried to turn his extravagance aside, but he'd covered her mouth with a salt-scented hand. "Face up to it, Sandy, because it's true."

OH, HANK, she told her memories, even if it was true then, it wouldn't help with this. We aren't strangers now.

"Talking to yourself?" A vigorous, gray-haired man with a cartoony red-and-white complexion stood over her.

"Hi, Corny. Pull up a chair." Smiling affectionately, Jane patted the cement-capped brick wall beside her.

"Can't stay." Corny's exceedingly pale blue eyes were fatherly. "Just checking on a rumor."

Jane sighed. Thelma and Clinton must have noticed there was something wrong with the way she had watched the news. Thelma had no doubt mentioned it as an interesting puzzle and Clinton would have reported it because he was the community bulletin board.

"I hear you may open this garden here for walk throughs during Festival."

Grateful that the rumor concerned Festival instead of her personal past, Jane nodded. "I'm thinking of it. It'll look prettier when everything's up and blooming."

"Extra traffic's more what I had in mind."

Jane narrowed her eyes against the fog-filtered sunlight. "I suppose that is the sheriff's problem, isn't it. Good. You worry about it and I won't have to."

They both looked at the residential street, which curved around the lip of the bluff. It was too narrow for through traffic if some of the drivers were tourists who didn't have their mind on their driving.

"Things sure change," Corny said. "When I was a boy, there were only three houses up there, excepting yours."

They looked along the house-lined street, visualizing Corny's past.

"I'm glad to have neighbors," Jane said. "But of course, I'm not comparing it to anything."

"Sensible." Corny lifted his index finger in a goodbye gesture.

Cheered by his tolerant chat, Jane set her worries aside and decided to get caught up on her paperwork. When she had converted a kitchen storage room into a personal office, she'd labelled the door TRADE SECRETS because she'd suspected KEEP OUT wouldn't do the job. People had laughed about the sign, but they took the hint. If she was out of sight when they dropped in, they stood in the middle of the kitchen and called out good-naturedly.

It was to be her private space so Jane had furnished the room with a battered oak desk and water-stained tables rescued from the potting shed. She felt more useful surrounded by furniture that wasn't meant for show.

She pushed thoughts of Hank out of her mind and, by the end of the week, the tables were covered with posters and charts and she felt caught up. It was slack time in the mail-order nursery, which meant there was very little to do beyond paperwork. She stretched out on the driftwood futon couch, planning to spend her evening on a hybridizing bulletin about the elusiveness of blues in tulips. The pamphlet's bludgeoningly scientific writing would keep her mind from wandering.

It worried her that Hank seemed to have disappeared. He had asked "Sandy" to prevent it, but she couldn't think of anything to do. It had probably just been a trick anyway, something to mislead the reporters. They'd leave him alone while they searched for a woman who didn't exist. And she had no idea how to reach him, if the government was holding him. And if he wasn't in their custody, they must be looking for him themselves.

Her common sense told her that whatever could be done was already happening, without her help. Still, she wished she could escape the sound of Hank's voice calling her Stranger name on the news. That was clever of him, she thought reluctantly, calling for Sandy. Sandy was a false name from the start. But she wished she knew what had become of him—just so she didn't have to worry.

She frowned as she stared at a graph. Maddeningly the lights dimmed. She looked out the window; the town was dark.

Power failures were nothing special in Oak Harbor. Pacific Ocean storms often funneled down the Straits of Juan de Fuca and smacked dead into the town. Jane groped her way along the dark hall, not bothering to grab a jacket as she left the house. She walked through the swirling rain toward the greenhouses, poking about, making sure the storm was not a danger to the plants. Her eyes gradually adjusted to the faint night loom that came from nowhere in particular.

When she turned back to the house, she saw a shadow move on the patio. She glanced toward the street. Sure enough, a strange car was standing there, its engine idling. She smiled indulgently. The guys from the Naval Air Base were forever getting lost, even when the streetlights were on. She could imagine how bewildered this one must be in the blackout.

"Need some help?" she called with small-town confidence.

"Yes."

Jane's heart stopped, waited and finally raced on in double time. "Hank?"

"I'm wired, Sandy."

Seeing him in Oak Harbor was so unreal that even thoughts of microphones were minor in comparison. "Okay."

"They'll turn me loose if you'll agree to take me in." She could hear him breathe. "I'd like to do the courtesies—ask if it's convenient, that sort of thing—but under the circumstances, I'm skipping all that."

She couldn't imagine how much it was safe to ask. Who were "they"? How long would he be wired? What did all of it mean?

While she wondered, the power surged back on. The patio was flooded with blinding light.

Jane was stunned. Hank's face was startlingly gray; she remembered how Thelma had tinkered with the color control to make the TV image warmer. His posture was hunched, as if his muscles didn't work. He had looked exhausted on the news, but now he looked unbelievably worse.

"I could come back tomorrow, when it's light," he said.

She remembered how he felt about the dark.

"I can wait at the Base, if you'd prefer that."

"The Base?" she whispered. "Is that who's got you?"

"The Navy flew me in," he said in a normal voice.

Jane wasn't deceived. He'd always acted undisturbed, even to his friends. But at the Stranger Seminar, she had managed to break through to the complex man behind the charming self-control. She knew that must be what he was counting on—he wanted her to see his truth again.

"Is it all right, Sandy?"

She dreaded the thought of surveillance, but he must hate it, too. He hadn't been given a choice, but even so she saw he was trying to protect her right to choose. She hurried her answer, before tears could clog her throat.

"Of course it's all right," she said clearly so the wire would pick her up. "Come in."

Chapter Two

Hank turned back to the car and his guard got out. They stood talking quietly. Jane thought it was taking too long, though she had no idea how long it ought to take. Finally Hank flipped up the collar of his trench coat to remove the mike hidden there. He had warned her he was wired, but seeing the proof was disturbing anyway.

Hank reached into the car for his luggage and came up to the house. The car didn't drive away until after Jane held the door open, and ushered her guest inside.

In the shadowy entrance hall, Hank set his suitcases down. "I'd like to crash, but should we say hello first?"

"I can't quite believe you're here."

"I hope this isn't just another fantasy. For months, I've been telling myself if I could make it this far, I could make it."

Another fantasy. Jane's mind shied away from what the words implied. "Are you okay?"

"I am now."

His electrifying gaze was the only part of him that still seemed like Hank. The changes made their situation seem impossible. At the Stranger Seminar, he had never looked tired. Even when he talked about his troubles, she had believed he would never reach the end of his strength. But now, his ashen face told her he had used up his last reserves.

"Show me around?" he suggested.

His habit of politeness wrenched Jane's heart. In spite of his own desperation, he was taking responsibility for easing their awkwardness. Trying not to sound as formal as she felt, she pointed to the panel doors on one side of the hall, separating the dining room and the public office. She didn't need to tell him what the office was for because they had kept in touch over the years since the Seminar. He knew her rambling old house was also Dutch Bulb, Inc.

He knew that after she left the university, she'd bought a partnership in a flower shop on the verge of bankruptcy and helped to convert it into a mail-order nursery. At first the partnership money had gone toward debts. When the ledgers first turned from red ink to black, every penny had gone toward expanding the greenhouses. But recently, finally, there'd been money for luxuries like refinishing. She pointed out the beautiful old leaded glass in the lounge doors on the other side of the hall.

Hank stepped into the long room. "This is public?"

"Yes, not that it matters. Oak Harbor's a small town. People walk in anywhere."

The sample centerpiece she had left on the coffee table caught his eye. He bent to inspect the delicate blooms. No one ever believed the endless patience it took to create the fragile blossoms. She didn't mind Oak Harbor's scoffing remarks, but she couldn't face the same sort of misunderstanding from Hank. She suddenly wanted to grab the pot away from him and hide it behind her back.

"You've got to go to Turkey." His voice deepened heartrendingly. "I've seen whole hillsides of these little stars so thick you'd think the Milky Way had fallen down."

"You recognize them?" she asked in disbelief.

He reached out and touched one of the dainty petals meditatively. She remembered how much it meant for him to be able to use his hands.

"I've never seen quite this color."

"They're mine." She might have been confessing a mortal sin. "My hybrids, I mean. And you're right—I did start with Turkish bulbs."

He turned to look at her. "You're doing patent work? Developing new blossoms? Why didn't you tell me?"

"Around here, everyone thinks I've done something unnatural to get blooms like this. I was afraid if I wrote to you about it, you might say something I couldn't forgive." She hesitated, wondering if it was all right to answer back, as she would have done at Cabin Seven. "Why didn't you tell me when you went to Turkey?"

Obviously remembering something, he laughed, disconcerting both of them. "Oh, Sandy, it's good to be here."

He reached for her hand as he would have done five years ago. The chill of his fingers was alarming.

"Hank—" She tightened her grip on his hand. "One of Dutch Bulb's local clients is a doctor. If I phone, he'll skip the awkward questions and just check your temperature. And he won't stand on his dignity about office hours."

"No, thanks." Hank freed himself from her grasp and plunged both hands into his trench-coat pockets. "They did a million medical routines before they let me go."

"They? Do you mean the Base?"

"No." He glanced suspiciously toward the uncurtained windows. "They have initials, mostly—government agencies. You don't realize how many federal employees have nothing better to do than disassemble you after you've been in touch with what they think of as a hostile political group."

Jane was dismayed. His angry tone was totally out of keeping with the Hank she remembered. He had faced ordeals before and had come through them strengthened, not destroyed. Would that be true this time? she wondered.

"Is there stuff I should know?" She sounded guarded.

"You can probably imagine it well enough not to need the grubby details."

That wasn't an answer. She remembered how hard it had been for him to admit his needs. That was the problem he'd brought to the Stranger Seminar, even though he hadn't realized it at the time. He still didn't know, she decided. But she did.

"I asked a perfectly reasonable question, Hank, and you didn't answer it."

He nodded, looking worn to a thread. "The hardest part is remembering to use my hands. I got used to the chains."

He pulled his hands out of his pockets and rotated them as if to show her they could move. Shackle marks across his wrists had barely begun to heal. Instinctively she cupped her palms protectively over his wounds. His breathing quickened.

She looked up at him, alarmed by his reaction. After a moment, she released him and stepped back. As if having to think about what came next, she headed for the kitchen, leaving him to follow or not, as he chose.

Hank was charmed by the ordinariness of her confusion. It had been so long since anyone had worried about hurting his feelings. Or leading him on. It seemed worlds away since any woman had looked at him just as a man. He knew what his ordeal had done to him; it would take a true friend to let him enjoy the wholesome sense that he was still attractive, in spite of everything.

Smiling tenderly, he followed her down the hall, amazed at her ability to sweep him into a reality so seemingly normal as to include a kitchen.

"Would you like some Dutch chocolate?" she asked. "It's what people around here use instead of chicken soup."

"Sure."

He didn't care what she said, as long as she kept talking in the low voice that brought back the safe past. She seemed unbelievably fragile, as everyone did when he compared them to the Hands of Allah. But fragile or not, she was trying to protect him. He was confused by the evidence that a world still existed where people were kind. Not that it mattered, he admitted wearily, because it couldn't apply to him. From now on, his world included terrorists.

Still, she was his link to a remembered, saner world, and so he wanted to keep her talking. He lounged against the kitchen door frame to watch her pull ingredients out of one of the old fashioned cupboards. "The Navy calls Oak Harbor 'Little Holland.' Is it really?"

"Yes, except maybe the other way around would be closer to the truth—we're a bit more Dutch than Holland is."

"You aren't Dutch."

"No, and neither are my Turkish tulips."

They both laughed.

After a short pause, Jane went on. "People here are tolerant, and really, a small town anywhere isn't much different from a small town anywhere else. At least, not when you've grown up the way I did."

He thought about the childhood memories she had shared with him at the seminar. Her parents were Africa specialists. They'd worked with nations who resisted missionaries but wanted developed-world benefits. Her parents had accepted risks for themselves, and they had trusted that the people they served would never hurt a child. So Jane had played on beaches washed by the Mozambique Channel instead of Puget Sound. It hadn't mattered to a four-year-old. Besides the sea, most of her early memories were of the dark. She had shared countless recollections of waking up in a stranger's arms, being carried along a rough path to a camp to join her parents. Her experiences had taught her to trust everyone in a completely uncivilized way.

Thinking about Jane's past and present reminded Hank of other changes. Her hair curled around her shoulders now, but it used to be a rich cap that teasingly exposed her earlobes and emphasized her emotional dark eyes. "Why did you let your hair grow?"

She measured sugar into a saucepan elaborately. "Oak Harborites think you're a boy if they can see your ears."

His shrouding beard half hid his smile. "How much fitting in do you have to do?"

"People don't care. Most of them."

She lowered the heat under the saucepan, staring at the sugar mixture as if daring it to boil. Amused, charmed by anything normal, he remembered how glad she had been not to do her half of the cooking when they were together before. Apparently that was something that hadn't changed—she still hated to cook.

"Clinton insists it costs Dutch Bulb local business for me to dress and act the way I do," she added, trying to correct her too-simple first description of Oak Harbor. "He's forever shaping me up with these little remarks. But he treats everybody that way. It's his idea of conversation."

"Sandy. It occurs to me I may have walked into more than I thought. You didn't mention your botanical experiments. Did you also not mention men?"

She turned to stare at him, a second saucepan in one hand. "Did I do something to provoke that? Or are you just getting too tired for this conversation?"

"Clinton."

"Oh." She set the saucepan down on the stove. "He's the accountant for half the town. He does our books."

"You can keep your own books."

Pouring milk into the pan distracted her so she answered carelessly. "I can, but my partner can't. And if she gets dependent on me, I'll never be able to pull out."

The kitchen filled with a tense self-consciousness. Jane was puzzled until she realized Hank had applied her caution to himself instead of to her business partner.

"Hank, look. This is going to be a mess if we have to keep being so careful of each other." Her hand trembled as she adjusted the heat under the milk. "Maybe staying with my folks would work out better for you. When they quit traveling so much, they set up a training camp for missionaries, you know. It's over on the Peninsula, in a mountain valley. It's truly beautiful. Peaceful. And they're equipped for people who've gotten hurt, or lost their ideals, or need a fresh start. Shall I give them a call?"

His face was utterly expressionless. "If I'm an inconvenience, say so and I'll leave. Where I'll go isn't your concern."

"Yes, it is."

"I'm sorry, Sandy." He looked around the room as if trying to orient himself. "If you can put up with me for a while, I'd appreciate it—that's what I was trying to say. No one else on this continent seems real to me."

"I can't imagine that."

"I don't really want you to," he said protectively. "Time is all I'm asking for, if you can give me that."

She nodded. "When you took off that wire, was that the end of it? Or are you still being watched?"

"They said they'd leave me alone if I'd cooperate."

"That contradicts itself," Jane protested.

"They don't worry about what you and I call logic."

His anger worried her. "Are you supposed to lie low?"

"I got them to accept that I'm going to tell the truth when anyone figures out who I am. So that covers you, too. In return, I promised not to make public appearances. That's no problem because I wasn't going to."

Alarmed by the evidence that he wasn't free, she gave herself time to think by watching the spiral of light mixing with dark as she combined her heated mixtures. "The TV said you might be a spy. Is that what the government thinks?"

"I'm not sure what they think."

She filled two mugs. He carried them to the old kitchen table she had kept as part of the decor; its well-scrubbed surface was as gray as driftwood. They sat down across from each other as they used to do at Cabin Seven.

"*Are* you a spy?"

"My terrorists said I could earn my freedom and I took them up on it. That doesn't make me a spy, does it?"

My terrorists. Jane tried not to react to the telltale word. "Did they make you do something slimy?"

"No. Just my usual work—consulting. The Hands of Allah are tired of being unknown. They asked how to get respect. I told them to release hostages in a way that looks merciful, instead of killing them, and to help prisoners with culture shock. Americans miss their dental floss and their fried foods. But if their prisoners came home swearing they'd been treated like guests, the Hands of Allah would get more publicity than they can use. The Hands of Allah kept their bargain—they turned me loose after we worked out how they could get publicity doing it. And they promised I'd never hear from them again if they got lots of coverage on the *Evening News*."

"They ought to be satisfied," Jane said, remembering how he had filled the news for days.

"I'm sure they are. But it infuriates the feds."

He curled his fingers around his mug of chocolate, savoring the heat. The small gesture of distress roused her protectiveness.

"Then maybe you should have waited to be ransomed."

"No. You can't imagine how it feels to wait. You get to the point you'll do almost anything to take control."

She looked at his distressed blue eyes, wondering if "doing almost anything" included betraying his country.

"Waiting wouldn't have helped anyway. I was already under a cloud," he added, his voice bitter and resigned. "I was working for Options. They're an importer specializing in media, anything that comes from a society where you can't get the other side here in the States. Options wants the full spectrum—books, magazines, tapes, videos, anything they've got. It's hard to get good coverage unless you open foreign offices, so they hired me to knock on doors for them. My first contact was this African nation where the U.S. sent a lot of famine relief and couldn't understand why it didn't help."

He didn't say which nation, but Jane decided not to demand details like that. Getting him to talk about his feelings rather than just facts would be struggle enough.

"It turned out the farmers are women, and our government sends money only to men," he went on. "So money for seeds, machines, irrigation—all of it went astray. The men didn't know what to do with it, and the women couldn't get hold of it. The U.S. was out the money, and the people kept on starving. Options wants everybody to have a chance to know."

"Is it illegal to import information like that?"

"No, but sometimes it gets tense. That's why I haven't written since I started working for Options—if anyone came after me, I didn't want you in my address book."

Jane frowned. "But if you weren't breaking the law, why is the government upset?"

He sipped his chocolate while he decided what to say. "When the Hands of Allah picked me up, I'd been in their area long enough for them to know I was learning their language and their politics. I was trying to arrange an export edition of a magazine they publish. I wanted their language on one page and a translation on the facing page. You've seen literary translations like that."

She nodded.

"I went to meet with a translator and was kidnapped instead."

"You were set up," Jane whispered, dismayed.

"Apparently."

Even in the midst of so dire a story, he was obviously determined to be fair, not to accuse anyone falsely. Jane sighed. "But our government thinks since you made the appointment, it wasn't really a kidnapping, is that it?"

"That's what they said until I stripped."

Involuntarily she looked at his injured wrists. He drew his arms deeper into his coat sleeves to hide the wounds. She was bewildered by the gesture. Could he really believe she expected him to pretend everything was ordinary?

"If the Hands of Allah wanted your help, why did they hurt you?"

"I resisted at first."

"But you finally gave in," she half whispered.

"No. Eventually they asked for something I could do honorably. That's when I cooperated."

She stared at him silently.

"You believe me, don't you, Sandy?" His tormented gaze told her no one else in two hemispheres had believed him.

"Yes." She answered unhesitatingly and she was surprised to find it was the truth. What did the TV news know? Or the government? Of course he was telling the truth.

She reached across the table to touch his hand. His fists were clenched. The coldness of his skin was a shock, but she held on to him until he relaxed. Finally he laced his fingers through hers as if they had never left Cabin Seven.

"How can you keep from hating them?" she asked.

"Hate doesn't help. Besides, it worked out well. I can design a better program for negotiating in situations like this, now that I've been through it. The feds ought to be glad, but all they can think of is that I worked with terrorists."

"You sound like you hate the government instead of hating the Hands of Allah."

"Of course I do." He looked annoyed, as if she had been cruel to him or wanted to misunderstand. "The feds like to call themselves the Pulsing Heart of the Free World, but somehow that doesn't apply to me. They swarmed me in the airport. For my own protection, they said, in case the Hands of Allah weren't through with me. I told them I'd run the risk of being free. So they locked me in a military hospital. They were worried about my health, at least that's what they said. I promised to take care of it privately. So they finally admitted I was in protective custody. Do you realize what they meant by that?"

His dark blue eyes narrowed. "They stick you in jail without a hearing and they can keep you there for as long as they want."

"They have to say why, don't they?"

He shrugged in a way that reminded her of how long he had lived in Europe. "For debriefing, they claim."

"That doesn't take long, does it?"

"Not usually." He looked abashed, to show he wasn't bragging. "But they use a debriefing program that won't work if you know what the questioner's going to do. And that's the trouble—I wrote the program while I was still in the service, so I did know."

"Why not just explain that to them?"

He laughed edgily. "I *did* mention it."

Taking advantage of his renewed confidence, Jane briefly tightened her fingers around his and then withdrew her hand. When he acted as if her retreat was a rebuff, she realized how desperate he was, for all his pretense of feeling safe at last.

"I offered to write down every detail of my captivity, if they'd let me come here. They finally agreed because they figured you'd throw me out and I'd have to come crawling back to them."

"Why would they think that?"

He studied her face methodically. "They take a very elemental view of women," he said at last.

She narrowed her eyes. "I suspect I'd get mad if I knew exactly what you meant by that."

He laughed.

"I wish I could see your face properly," she said.

He neatened his beard with the same gesture she had seen him use on the TV. "It's hard to shave with your hands chained behind you. And I decided to leave this on as long as I might be photographed. Shaving won't be a real disguise, but it ought to keep me from being spotted in the grocery line."

"You're running from the TV news, as well as the government and the Hands of Allah?" she asked, dismayed.

"It does sound like quite a list." He stood. "How about calling it quits for tonight? I can't tell you how long it's been since I felt safe enough to sleep."

He retrieved his luggage from the front hall and followed her upstairs. "Your partner lives here, too?"

"Not anymore. We bought the house next door as soon as Dutch Bulb was doing well enough to earn us a line of credit at the bank. Fran moved over there last year. We get along, but we both prefer being neighbors instead of housemates."

Jane was surprised when he stopped at the landing. He set down his luggage and waited a while to catch his breath, but he tackled the last half flight before she could think what to say.

"That's the spare bedroom in front, and here's the bath." She turned on the bathroom light.

He dropped his suitcases in the hall and crossed over to the bathroom mirror, which hung at the right height for Jane. Stooping for a better look at himself, he sighed and ran both hands through his unruly mop of sun-bleached hair.

"Would you cut this for me?"

"I don't know how."

He glanced at himself again and then shot her a demoralized look. "Could you give it a try?"

"If you're afraid of shocking the barber, don't bother. Fishermen come in there looking every which way, and nobody minds."

"It's so hard to know I'm here." He paused. "I wanted to be as much like myself as possible before I try to sleep."

"I'll get my scissors. They're downstairs." Jane trotted back downstairs, glad for a moment alone to compose herself.

She couldn't imagine the horror that had become routine to him. Believing he was there, in her bathroom, seemed unreal enough. And yet in some ways it seemed perfectly natural. He had never stopped being a part of her life. And where he was had never mattered.

She pulled her scissors out from under a stack of papers and went back upstairs. Hank had sat down on the edge of the tub to wait. When she came back he stood, smiling. She dragged her ladder-back dressing chair into the middle of the room. Hank draped his rumpled trench coat over the hook that held her bathrobe. Standing in front of the giant wicker basket she used as a clothes hamper, he skinned out of his natural wool sweater.

Casually dropping it into the basket on top of her clothes, he unbuttoned his gray shirt. "If I'm your first customer, I'd better take this off, don't you think?"

He dropped his shirt into the wicker basket, too. She grabbed a bath sheet off the lower shelves of the linen closet and held it out. Royal blue, not exactly the color of his eyes, but close enough. She told herself it was silly to feel constrained by the sight of his body, after their casual, almost familial relationship at Cabin Seven.

She let her gaze sweep downward. She was amazed at how familiar every detail was, in spite of his weight loss. The muscle ridge across his shoulders. The body hair like gold dust. The sight of his heartbeat escaping under the edge of his ribs.

She frowned. His heart was beating much too fast. All he had done was climb one flight of stairs.

"More than just the climate change is bothering you," she said fearfully.

"A little bit more."

He reached for the bath sheet and swirled it around his shoulders like a bullfighter's cape. Her dressing chair suddenly looked spindly as he settled on it, adjusting his cape and propping his feet up on the bathtub rim.

"This is the finest barbershop I've ever patronized," he said, determined to sound playful. "Are you going to talk to me about baseball?"

Jane smiled obligingly, hoping to mask her worry. He had set his shaving kit beside the sink. She dug into its orderly contents. The search was disturbingly personal. By the time she found his comb, she felt thoroughly confused.

His hair felt slippery from heavy conditioners meant to compensate for months of neglect. "I'll leave it long enough so a real barber will have room to even it up after."

She cut slowly so she could adjust mistakes before they became severe. He closed his eyes and the contented gesture tugged at her feelings disconcertingly. For the first time in years, she remembered how close they had come to being something more than friends.

They were different from the other strangers at the Seminar. He had assigned himself to take part in the project because he believed researchers couldn't evaluate what the subjects said unless they had been through the experience themselves. Since he was the director, he had seen her history, and so he had wanted her to see his. He didn't think it would matter, since they were all strangers, but he had wanted to be fair.

It had mattered somewhat. For one thing, he wasn't a business student, as the rest of them were. He was majoring in psychology. The Seminar was his PhD research.

What had mattered more was his military status. After his peacekeeping hitch, he had signed up for the reserves. And then he was being called back "for the convenience of the government," as he had grimly quoted. He had special skills with languages. The government hadn't cared that he needed three more civilian months to finish his education—they had wanted him at once. He would have to leave the country right after the Seminar.

If it hadn't been for that, Jane and Hank might have said "call me," on their last day. Instead they had walked down the beach together one last time, struggling with a self-conscious silence because of all the things they couldn't say. They couldn't say they'd never felt so close to anyone before. They couldn't say what a high it was to fall half in love with an attractive stranger. They couldn't promise how the two glorious weeks were going to change their lives.

The problem had been, he couldn't ask her to give up her own career and follow him from post to post. And she couldn't pretend she was willing to sacrifice her own work in order to trail him to posts around the world, whenever the Marines changed their plans.

And so, at the end, they'd only said, "let's write."

It was meant to sound friendly, even though neither of them really thought the other would actually write. When they both did write, after all, they'd decided it made sense to keep the friendship going since they were both living among strangers and facing loneliness at first. By the time they had found new friends, writing had become a habit they both enjoyed. Sometimes months had gone by between letters. Sometimes only days. It didn't matter because they didn't keep count, they just wrote.

His letters were travelogues while he was in the service. After he was discharged, he'd stayed in Europe as a freelance consultant, and his postmarks had become even more outlandish. Her letters were mostly business yarns—horror stories of the sort she could tell in a funny way.

But as the years passed, Hank had stopped seeming like someone she knew. She remembered how he looked at Cabin Seven, but she knew he must have changed, and so she stopped thinking about his face while she wrote to him. Eventually he became just a series of unreadable postage stamps and odd-sized stationery, and quirky stories about strange ways to live. The warmth never faded, but the physical memory had.

He had lived so long abroad that he couldn't still be the same man. So how could he be sitting in her very American bathroom getting his hair cut? He couldn't be.

She stepped behind him and pushed his head forward so she could study the contours of his nape. His shaggy mop looked as if his captors had hacked it off with a dull ax. The quiet way he sat was a reminder that he must have gotten used to being handled.

Comb in one hand and scissors in the other, Jane let her arms fall to her sides. "Does this bother you?"

"A little bit." He looked up at her with stress-hazed eyes. "The feds kept throwing counselors at me. They wanted me to come apart so they could put me back together in a way they like better. I swore I'd stay glued until I got out here to you. I knew you wouldn't try to make me over because you've been a participating counselor all your life."

He interrupted himself to reach down and clasp her hand, scissors and all. "I know you don't call it that, but it's what you are. You're what I need, and no one else helps."

She remembered that most counselors seemed like do-gooders to him because they risked nothing in a one-way relationship. He had good reason for his belief. His parents had died in a skiing accident when he was fourteen. He had loved them and hadn't known how to give them up. His grandmother had been too frail to make a home for a teenage boy, but she'd promised to keep him out of foster care if he would consent to boarding school. It had been hard for him to learn that the best way to show his love for her was to stay out of her life and convince her that he was glad to do so.

She'd sent him to an expensive school which could afford plenty of counselors. They'd pitied him and wanted him to turn to them, but he clung to his memory of family life. And so he'd learned to use his remarkable charm to persuade them that he'd accepted his loss. Whenever they tried to stir his demons, he'd politely told them life was good and he felt fine.

It had worked with the counselors. But by the time he was of an age that he could send them away, he had convinced himself it was cruel to open up to anyone who liked him. As a man, he knew that idea wasn't true. The trouble was, he could persuade his mind, but his heart wouldn't budge.

At the Seminar, Jane had managed to get inside his guard because she was a stranger and because she was risking herself along with him. For her, it was easy—she had grown up the opposite way, trusting everyone.

"I don't know if our being together will work for you, now that we're friends." She didn't realize how sad she sounded.

His feet crashed to the floor and he reached to draw her between his knees. It was the sort of friendly invasiveness he had learned to offer at Cabin Seven. His hands slipped down from her waist to curl naturally around her legs.

Disconcertingly her knees turned to jelly.

She stepped free of his hands and frowned. She knew he wanted a friend, a sort of sister. Unfortunately neither of them had ever had a brother or sister, so they weren't quite sure how it ought to work.

But one thing was clear, even to an only child—her body's unexpected response to his touch wasn't sisterly in any way. Bewildered, Jane tried to keep him from sensing what was happening to her. He had enough troubles to face without her adding to them.

She struggled to focus her attention on finishing the haircut so he could bathe and get the rest he so obviously needed.

Chapter Three

Hank's presence roused feelings Jane wasn't prepared to face. She decided it would upset her to lie down in the bathtub in a room still steamy from his shower. It was too intimate. Instead she went downstairs to the stall shower that was off her private office.

She took her time showering, standing under the hot spray until she stopped feeling that something impossible had happened to her life. She went back upstairs quietly, thinking Hank might be asleep. His room was dark. Slipping out of her robe, she listened tensely. Nothing. Was that all right? she wondered.

She grabbed a knit sleep shirt out of her top dresser drawer. When she was dressed for bed, she stopped to listen to the small-town night silence. Distant foghorns groaned, but there were no closer signs of life.

Giving in to a nameless dread, she went barefoot down the hall to Hank's closed door. "Hank? May I come in?"

He didn't answer. Alarmed, she opened the door.

He had been sitting in bed in the darkness, one knee drawn up to support his folded arms, his back curved forward so he could rest his forehead on his arms. When the light from the hallway spilled into his room, he lifted his head.

It seemed to take him a moment to realize who she was. Finally he lounged back on the pillows stacked against the pine bedstead. He moved uncomfortably as if unnamed segments of his body hurt.

He had rearranged the room in a way that warned her his horrors had returned. Both windows were wide open, and he'd shoved the bed up close to them. Tired as he had been, he'd still needed to do that to ease his claustrophobia. He surely didn't expect to jump out of a second-story window, but he apparently couldn't hope to be able to sleep unless he had extra exits from the room.

"I couldn't hear you in here and I got afraid."

"Don't be afraid."

She perched on the edge of his bed. "You mentioned doctors there in Washington, D.C., but you didn't say what they thought was wrong."

"I know you'll be amazed. After evaluating thousands of dollars worth of tests, they decided I've been under stress, and I haven't been eating right or getting enough exercise."

Laughing was the last thing she had expected to do. "You're supposed to eat and sleep and walk around?"

"You make my recovery sound so homey." His eyes shone in the light. "I *told* them you could help me without sticking me full of needles first."

She wondered if he really was all right. She let her gaze linger on his chest before wandering to the bands of muscle across his waist and belly. His blanket was pulled up modestly.

"If you're looking at me, by all means go ahead, but if you're looking for symptoms, don't worry about it, truly." His tone was disturbingly tender.

"You'll tell me if you need something?"

"I need to remember there's such a thing as normal life. Seeing you takes care of it—you don't have to do anything except be yourself."

Her heart ached at his bravely understated words.

"I keep deciding you're a dream." He smiled heart meltingly. "Could you stay with me, do you think?"

The simple-sounding request called up a world of memories. Their first night at the Seminar, Hank had warned her his dreams were so intense that he didn't usually sleep where anyone could hear him. She'd been casual about it when they said good-night, but there was nothing casual about the blood-curdling yells that had awakened her later on. She had raced to his room to find him on his feet, his sleepwalker's gaze horrifyingly empty, his back to the wall as he fought something unspeakable with a pillow and a chair. She had stayed out of reach and called to him gently until he woke. He'd been embarrassed about the nightmares, but not about her discovery that he slept nude.

She'd offered to sit with him while he slept, on the condition that he would tell her why he needed her to. It had been hard for him to agree and nearly impossible for him to talk. She'd sat up all night on a camp chair, watching him struggle and dream. By morning, she'd looked so exhausted he'd tried to cancel their bargain. When she'd refused, he'd asked her to share his bed so she could rest. She told him he was too attractive for that, and so they dragged a twin bed from her room into his.

It hadn't helped much at first, because his yelling kept her awake. But finally she'd made out a few frantic words. "You keep saying they're alive," she'd said. "Who are they?"

He'd managed to answer, even though it was a long time before he confessed fully. It was his parents he dreamed about. He had been with them when they died in a cross-country skiing accident. The snowpack had weakened during a long sunny day. It had come down in an avalanche and swept his parents to the bottom of the mountain. He had been lagging behind, so he'd escaped. But he'd watched helplessly while his parents died.

He'd never escaped the memory and the guilt. When he'd been buried alive, himself, by the bomber who'd attacked the peacekeeping troops, it had seemed like fate. The bomb had seemed somehow deserved since he had not saved his parents—and not died with them.

Jane had asked hard questions until he'd forced himself to remember that his parents had died instantly and that he hadn't abandoned them. After a long struggle, he admitted the bomb had been nothing more than rotten luck. It wasn't a cosmic punishment meant especially for him.

Telling her the whole story had left him able to sleep peacefully at last. He'd called it a miracle. But it had worked only as long as she held his hand across the space between their beds.

Back then it had been easy to know what to do. But now he had been through so much, she couldn't imagine what might help. She was touched by his polite attempt to hide his torment. Could *anything* help? she wondered half despairingly.

Holding his hand would surely remind him of captivity. But she could guard him, if that would help. She dragged a rocking chair toward his bed and turned on his bedside light.

"I'll sit here and read so you can see me while you fall asleep." She went to her room to get her bedtime book—a text on organic treatment for plant diseases.

"What's that?" he asked, obviously dreading sleep.

She explained. "I'm up to the chapter on nematodes."

He smiled, pleased to find himself in a world where the worst danger was to plants. "This is kind of you, Sandy. I'll keep thanking you until you get tired of hearing it."

"Don't even start." She opened her book.

Pretending to read, Jane watched him settle down to sleep. She felt a stab of possessiveness, of hurt, as she watched him make small nesting motions, as if someone were cuddling him. It was too vivid a reminder that his life abroad had included more than torment. His letters had never mentioned women. But of course there had been women, she told herself sadly. He charmed the world without intending it. Of course there were women.

I'm a friend, she reminded herself. That's a very different thing. She wasn't sure she believed herself.

Hank distracted her by groaning softly. After a moment, he turned his head away and gasped. "Let's get out of here," he muttered in an excited tone. He repeated it loudly in French. His legs thrashed, as if he were running, taking his own advice.

Abruptly he yelled in a language she couldn't understand as he lunged to his knees in bed, his right arm swinging like a club while his left arm shielded his shockingly empty eyes.

Jane didn't move. "Hank."

She spoke quietly, using the tender, intimate voice he would remember from the Seminar. "Hank. You're here with me, Hank. Speak English, Hank. Wake up, Hank. Hank. Hank."

He froze, as if trying to hear. Jane continued to call his name in her gentlest voice. His chest rose and fell desperately, as if all the oxygen in the world had disappeared. Seeking Jane's voice, he turned awkwardly, using muscles that barely worked. Intelligence slowly seeped back into his blank eyes.

His body glistened with sweat. "Sandy?"

"I'm here. You're in Oak Harbor. Remember?"

He lay down cautiously, as if unsure of his balance. He didn't pull his blanket up in time to keep Jane from seeing the sickening mosaic of bruises that covered him from waist to knees, almost like clothing, as if he weren't really nude.

"What were you dreaming?" Jane asked gently.

"Oh, God." He blinked slowly and looked at the ceiling. "I was back there. I heard your voice. But that didn't mean anything because whenever something got to be too much, I pretended I could hear you, the way you were at Cabin Seven."

Her heart nearly broke at that trusting confession. Jane sighed. "Can I do something to help now?"

He nodded. "Stay with me, if you can stand it."

"Are you trying to hurt my feelings, pretending you have to ask for that?"

"Thanks." He used the sheet to wipe sweat from his face. "Would you read aloud?"

"Glad to. She took a deep breath. "'It is its versatility which makes the nematode so successful a pest,'" Jane began in a soothing monotone. "'Basically an active, segmented roundworm, it consists principally of a needlelike mouth part...'"

As she read on, Hank's body slowly relaxed. He watched her fixedly. His eyes gradually blurred with sleep, but it was a long time before he drifted off.

When she was sure he was asleep, Jane stopped reading. She shifted to a soothing monologue that told him where he was and reminded him how safe he finally was and urged him to sleep peacefully.

Compassionately she studied the changes in his face—the deeply marked lines, which emphasized the gray smudges beneath his eyes, the disturbing pallor. She watched his breathing slow and deepen, and slow again. Profoundly asleep, he reached his hand toward her. Wondering if her touch would keep dreams at bay, she nested her hand inside his. It had been a simple gesture at Cabin Seven, but she had changed since then.

He'd changed, too, she realized. His fingers were thin as well as cold. His wrists were bruised and scraped. She could see medical damage to his bare arm—signs of blood draws, injection sites.

But neither the Hands of Allah nor the federal government mattered, she realized. When he held her hand, discomfort drained from his face, leaving him as sweetly undisturbed as a cherished little boy whose summer vacation had just begun.

Oh, Hank, she asked silently, what are we going to do about all this, without a seminar to tell us when to quit?

She hadn't a clue. But one thing was clear. Holding his hand was disturbing enough to her feelings without also watching him sleep. Self-protectively she bent over her book and forced herself to concentrate on nematode habitats.

SHE WASN'T AWARE of falling asleep, but she woke up with a start. Could she really have overslept sitting up in a rocking chair? she wondered, staring at Hank's travel clock.

Instead of hurrying out, as she should have done, she inspected her guest. Hank was sprawled on his stomach, his face burrowed into his pillows, his blond hair scuffed into an unruly rooster tail. He obviously felt safe at last.

Jane sighed, wishing she didn't have to leave him. Then she tiptoed to her own room to dress. Since she was due to sit in for her partner at a meeting of the Festival Board, she couldn't wear her usual jeans. She put on wool pants and pulled a bulky sweater over a natural linen shirt. Running quietly downstairs in her stocking feet, she paused in the middle of the kitchen to stomp into her boots.

She scribbled a quick note on the fridge door message pad: "Breakfast meeting at the café—Festival Board. Back for lunch."

At the back door, she remembered the neighbor who came every morning to clean. She could imagine Betty's shock if she walked in on a sleeping Hank. Ripping a page from the message pad, she wrote quickly: "Overnight guest—front bedroom. Late sleeper. Skip the upstairs."

She clothespinned the note to the porch door at Betty's eye level and left at a run. Jumping into her green Sentra, she raced down the hill toward the Dutch Café.

Being late wasn't the best way to endear herself to the descendants of the original settlers who made up the Board, but it wouldn't improve matters if she looked flustered when she finally got there. She slowed down across the sea-level parking lot, which the city had provided by filling a marsh between Old Town and the harbor. Leaving her car, she strolled sedately toward the weather-battered wooden stairs, which gave rickety access to the harborside business district.

The Dutch Café was built on creosoted piers like harbor pilings. Its waterside wall was glass so customers could enjoy the view. As Jane stepped through the Café's blue door, she gave a quick wave toward the window table, then went to the counter to serve herself coffee in the casual way of a small-town regular. As she crossed the room toward the meeting, Corny gave the only empty chair a slight, inviting push.

"Well, then," Dirk Amstellen said, his squarish face unsmiling as he assumed his director's role.

As harbormaster, Dirk was used to responsibility of a rough-and-ready sort, but the dignity of Festival was a change for him. His self-consciousness made Jane's role easier. She knew they didn't think of her as Dutch Bulb; they thought of her as "the newcomer." Her partner should have been the one serving on the Board, but until Fran was back from her Holland bulb tour, Jane was standing in. She had promised herself she would lie low as a way of helping everyone handle the shock.

The weather was Dirk's first agenda item. So far spring had been one long rainstorm. The rain had turned the famous Skagit Valley bulb fields to mud and threatened outdoor growers with rot. Even if the rain stopped soon blossoming time would be delayed, which meant the prop-plane pilots would lose the income they counted on from spring color flights.

"One of my Mount Vernon retailers has been talking about that," Jane said, when no one could think of anything to do about the rain. "We've got a rocky base here on the island, and Skagit Valley isn't really land, it's just a silted-up estuary too flat to drain."

Thelma smiled at her across the table. "Maybe that's what it is to you college types, Jane, but for us who've always lived here, what this seems like is a wet spring."

Jane and Thelma both laughed. The rest of the Festival Board joined in tentatively, but they hadn't come to the Dutch Café to joke, and so Dirk cleared his throat. Sounding official, he read his list of assignments for the Board to endorse. Minnie, the mayor's wife, would judge the new blossom contest, as usual. Thelma, as director's wife, would be in charge of paperwork. Clinton, as always, would keep the Festival books.

There was only one surprise. Dirk apologized for being innovative. He wandered off into a description of how he had attended one of Jane's small-business workshops so he could check out her presentation skills. And then he announced his nomination for publicity director—their newcomer, Jane Woodruff.

Jane was shocked. It had to be a mistake—Dirk's kindly gesture toward his wife's friend, but still a mistake. She frowned at Thelma. Unhelpfully, Thelma smiled.

Corny patted Jane's thigh reassuringly, keeping his own hand tactfully out of sight under the table. Not pausing to confuse herself over what Corny's action would mean in a more urban situation, Jane looked into his fatherly blue eyes.

"I'm stunned." With her usual forthrightness, she looked at every member of the Board. "I'd love to do it. But only if you all are sure."

She couldn't tell if all of them were sure, but the vote was unanimous. Afterward, the meeting was adjourned and board members drifted away in gossiping pairs and groups.

"Have a last cup of coffee, Jane." Clinton moved down the table to take Corny's empty chair.

Jane hesitated. If she loitered she wouldn't be home for lunch, as her note had promised. But being added to the Festival Board carried obligations, too.

"I'll make a quick phone call. Be right back."

Crossing to the cash register, she reached over the counter to pick up the phone on the bottom shelf. Punching in Dutch Bulb's number, she smiled at the cashier, hoping Bernice wouldn't ask why she was calling home. When the phone kept ringing, she wondered how long she should wait.

She glanced toward Clinton. A waitress was keeping him occupied while she cleared up after the meeting. Her billowing blue polished-cotton bloomers, white blouse and starched lace cap were more quaint than comfortable, but she seemed used to the uniform. She clattered around in enameled wooden shoes, gossiping as she stacked dirty dishes and brushed crumbs off the blue-and-white checked table cloth.

The phone was obviously going to ring forever. Jane hung up and went back to the window table. She sat down by Clinton as if her missing guest didn't worry her.

"This is a wonderful morning for me, Jane." Clinton popped a piece of butter roll into his mouth.

Jane was startled. She had never thought of Clinton as having ups and downs. "Why is that?"

"When Dirk put you on this year's Festival Board he proved I'll be next year's director."

Jane was so obviously perplexed by that observation that he laughed smugly. "Can't follow it?"

Clinton gestured with his butter knife. "It's dangerous to open the door to a newcomer, even in something as lowly as the publicity slot. So adding you to the board means the director has to be utterly old settler. Otherwise we'll drown in change."

"I see." Jane smiled accommodatingly. "For Oak Harbor, old settler means 'Jarvis.'"

"What else," Clinton answered as if her answer had been boringly obvious.

He was only a silhouette against the bright window, but the set of his shoulders proved his claim. She saw he was going to explain it to her in detail. Wanting to seem attentive without really listening, she gazed past him toward the parking lot. A strange car pulled a Jartran trailer into end-to-end parking spots. While Jane watched, the sun broke through the dissipating clouds, turning the last of the rain into a glittering silver shower.

"Dirk's right about one thing," Clinton summed up grandly. "We've outgrown the amateur volunteers Festival used in the past. This town needs professionals like me and you. We make quite a team, and I'll help you fit in."

"Hi. Have you given your instructions to the weather service yet? Either wet or dry would be better than change-able, I'd think."

The familiar voice was so out of place that the room seemed to shift. Like any small-town citizen, Jane had been absorbed in the unidentified Jartran and in trying to figure out what Clinton was saying without going to the extreme of listening to him. She had been too fully occupied to notice Hank as he came in.

He stood beside the table holding a thermal carafe of coffee. The change in his appearance was astounding. His tweed jacket was more expensive than anything for sale in Oak Harbor, and his banker-gray trousers were obviously the product of European tailoring.

But his behavior had changed even more than his clothing. His face was alive with optimistic energy, as if an undisturbed night's sleep really had been the only medicine he needed. He radiated an amiably in-charge feeling, which blanketed everything within a hundred feet. A cashmere sweater under his jacket indicated he was having trouble keeping warm, but nothing else about him revealed that he had ever faced a difficulty of any sort.

"You people were so intent on your conversation, you ran out of coffee. I brought refills since I was joining you anyway." He set the carafe near Jane and waited cheerfully.

"Oh. Clinton, this is Hank," Jane said doubtfully. In the confusion of Hank's arrival, she had forgotten her first belief that he and Oak Harbor couldn't possibly adapt to each other, even if they tried.

Apparently they were going to try. Clinton got to his feet immediately and Hank held out his hand. Jane worried that Clinton might wonder why Hank's hand felt cold, but she saw nothing special in his face. The men sat down with Jane between them, and Hank poured himself a cup of coffee the Dutch Café considered famous.

"You're a friend of Jane's?" Clinton asked in his usual busybody way.

Hank seemed utterly unaware of being inspected. "We met at the university."

"University," Clinton said assessingly. "I went to Washington State, myself, so I must have met you somewhere else. I never forget a face."

He suspects, Jane thought. She wondered if it was worth the trouble to try to confuse him. She decided not. He never paid enough attention to anyone else to become confused in a normal way. And Hank didn't seem concerned.

"Remembering faces—that's an excellent skill," Hank said easily. "Have you thought of going into politics so you could put it to work?"

Clinton chuckled. "There's time for that."

Irritated by the masculine taunting that never seemed friendly to her, Jane inspected Hank more carefully. He had obviously found a barbershop. And without the beard, no one would immediately recognize him from the TV news. She decided Clinton was just gossiping.

"What do you do for a living?" Clinton asked, going on with his homey inquisition.

"I'm in psychology, research applications. You're in business here in Oak Harbor? I'm going to need services of various kinds."

Clinton took a business card out of his card case and began to describe his accounting firm. Too late, Jane wondered if she should have warned Hank that the whole town was fanatical about the news. He had walked into a local publicity buzz saw by coming to the Dutch Café.

"You're planning to stay awhile?" Clinton asked.

"I have to do some writing, and Oak Harbor looks like the right kind of place."

"It can be, for the right kind of person. You'll have a lot to learn, of course, but people are glad to help."

"I'll count on it," Hank said.

"I wouldn't rely on Jane too much," Clinton said in his ponderous kindliness. "She's a newcomer herself."

"Maybe her friends will take me in hand."

"Good thinking. Now. Where are you staying? We have a number of very pleasant guest houses. I do their books, of course, so I know which to recommend."

"I'm presuming on our long-standing friendship—"

Jane broke in. "Out at Dutch Bulb. I have that spare bedroom, now that Fran's moved next door."

When Clinton turned an interested glance at Jane, Hank distracted him with his most persuasive man-to-man look. "She assures me her neighbors won't worry, but she's such a kind friend that I'd like your opinion on it. I've always lived in big cities where people neglect one another. This smaller town social structure is extremely interesting to me, but I need advice. Were you born into it?"

"Fourth generation," Clinton said like a man who knew he would be excused for a justifiable pride.

Hank looked as if he were counting it up, but Jane suspected he was hiding amusement. In Europe he must have become used to families who had lived in the same place for a hundred generations. Clinton's proud claim of four couldn't seem like much.

"Four? That makes you a founding family, I expect," Hank said, inviting a discussion.

"Jarvises *are* Oak Harbor," Clinton agreed. "My great-grandfather moved our family branch out here and we took root. Granddad watched the town grow up around him as the natural squire, but my father was a black sheep. He insisted on being an accountant, and I followed that path."

Jane knew Hank was trying to charm Clinton—no doubt he would charm the whole town—but she couldn't bear to watch. She was glad of her new Festival responsibilities. Worrying about that would take her mind off Hank and give him the space he needed. "Did you just happen on us here, Hank, or what?"

"I figured you couldn't get home for lunch, no matter what your note said, so I'd do better to join you rather than wait." He turned disarmingly to Clinton. "I checked three cafés, but I should have known this was the place."

It was an invitation to describe the town. Under cover of listening to Clinton's methodical analysis of how Oak Harbor worked, Hank watched Jane. He had never before seen her deal with anyone except himself. It was disconcerting to see how much at home she felt here—comfortable enough to let her jitters show.

What was she jittery about? he wondered. Clinton didn't seem hostile toward him as a man or as a stranger, and she had said Oak Harbor didn't cold-shoulder newcomers.

He watched her glance around the room. Each of the lunch customers smiled at her and nodded or waved. It was clear she had made a place for herself in this community. What was his arrival going to do to that? he asked himself belatedly.

That's why she's jittery, he realized sadly. He considered himself thoughtfully and then compared himself to Clinton. The difference was so total. He saw that he was probably an embarrassment.

But Clinton didn't act as if he were. Hank was relieved that his listening skills still worked; it has been months since he'd held a normal conversation.

And maybe that was what Sandy noticed, he decided affectionately. She was simply bored. He looked at her face to check. She flashed her dark eyes at him very reassuringly.

When Hank smiled in response, Clinton reminded them all he had a job to do and so he would get on with it, after one last reminder that Hank was welcome to his friendly town.

"I don't like things to dangle, Hank," he said as he stood. "And you asked two questions but I only answered one. About Jane's reputation, no problem. You go ahead and stay at Dutch Bulb. I'm in and out all the time, what with the bookkeeping and all, so even if this town were dirty minded, which we're not, people know I'll keep an eye peeled." He flourished his umbrella as if in salute.

Then Clinton was gone.

"I'm afraid he's recognized you," Jane said, revealing what had worried her.

"Probably." Hank smiled easily. "But the rest of the conversation was meant to reassure me that he's not going to make me talk about it. That's the most you can ask."

Almost carefree, he changed the subject quickly. "That sweater's a perfect color on you. Cocoa. Makes your eyes intense, like an emergency."

His heart surged at her thank-you smile.

"I *feel* like an emergency. They've appointed me publicity director, and I wasn't expecting it."

"Congratulations!"

"I'm afraid not. Clinton sees it as a reason to lecture me on my newcomer traits. I can't answer back because he and Fran are sort of courting, I think, and I don't want to get in their way."

"Sort of courting... what are the symptoms of that?"

Jane laughed. "He isn't very good at it, and Fran gets disgusted, I think. Maybe you could give him some pointers."

Instead of answering playfully, as Jane had expected him to, Hank looked thoughtfully at the exit, as if Clinton's image still filled it. When he smiled radiantly at someone behind her, Jane realized Bernice had caught his eye.

Understanding his campaign to charm the town, Jane waited indulgently until his attention wandered back to her. "What's in that Jartran trailer?"

"Office equipment. I've had a busy morning. My room is plenty big enough to be a study and still let me sleep there."

Buying furniture sounded long-term, but the Dutch Café wasn't the place to question him about his plans. "If it's all right, I'm going to run a few errands for Festival publicity before I come home."

Responding to her domestic explanation with a nod Hank drowned her in a smile before approaching the cashier. Bernice had been gazing at them with small town fixity. Jane watched Hank chat with her in his affable way while he took his time finding his wallet. Bernice thawed much too thoroughly. Had she spotted him as a celebrity? Jane wondered uneasily. Or was it just Hank's usual charm?

Jane dug her appointment calendar out of her purse and considered the rest of her day.

Chapter Four

The sprawling courthouse perched precariously on the lip of its cliff, its cream stone brightened by orange lichen in the moist spots. Jane trotted up the cement steps happily. Genuinely fond of the mayor, she looked forward to her courtesy call on the fatherly man everyone called "Boss."

"Not because I'd ever be so foolish as to tell anyone what to do," he had explained when he first met Jane. "But a name like Bostetter doesn't look like much on a handbill, so I use just the front half. People can think what they want."

His secretary smiled and waved Jane in.

"Now, Jane." Boss thumped his feet down off his desk in the way that annoyed everyone in the engineer's office downstairs. "I know you're rampaging to talk Festival, but we'll take a rain check. Here's an old friend, Don Maguire."

Jane wondered what was wrong. Maguire was nothing special: medium height, squarish build, short brown hair, dark eyes that were observant but not intent.

"Pete Shaw, here, is my assistant." Maguire's imitation of the mayor's friendly patter was not convincing.

Assistant at what? Jane wondered. He was slim, fresh from a tanning salon, his smooth face highlighted by long-lashed light eyes. She decided Pete Shaw was unpleasantly handsome.

The two men held out federal ID. Horrified, Jane saw that Hank's arrival had let her in for a great deal more than a visit from the past.

"What are you doing to me, Boss?" she asked, betrayed.

"Making my office available so you're among friends. After what happened at Festival Board meeting this morning, everybody knew you'd drop in on me. And, as for my part in this, you know when it comes to getting anyone in trouble, I'd rather be shot." Boss gave her shoulder a friendly squeeze as he passed her on his way to the door.

After the mayor was gone, Maguire took charge. "If you would sit down, Miss Woodruff?"

Maguire touched the mayor's chair invitingly. Jane scooped a stack of papers off an oak conference chair instead. Following her lead, the men cleared guest chairs and left Boss's comfortable leather chair respectfully empty. Jane was offended by their pretense of letting her control the interview. She was indignant that a dumb hunk and a grampa had been paired up to see which cliché she responded to. She was terrified because they had arranged to be sponsored by someone she liked. She gritted her jaw to keep herself from giving them the advantage by anxiously speaking first.

"Your houseguest," Maguire began at last. "He's here, and we're here, because he had the mother wit to say on camera that he didn't want to disappear."

Jane frowned. "Surely you aren't going to announce where he is. He needs privacy. Rest."

Pete Shaw flattened his full lips. "Don't be taken in, Jane. The man is in total control."

"You can't possibly believe that," Jane said angrily.

"Wandersee does seem like an odd choice," Maguire agreed, as if the discussion were friendly. "He's noticeable, and not just to women, whereas a courier is usually more like me."

When she automatically looked at him, he smiled. She closed her eyes briefly in disbelief.

"What's a courier?" she asked grudgingly.

"In this case, it's someone who carries messages and materials for subversive foreign groups."

Jane didn't explain Hank's view of his work for Options. He must have told them, and evidently it hadn't helped.

"He probably wants you to think he's brainwashed," Maguire went on.

"He isn't brainwashed," Jane contradicted automatically.

"I'm glad you see that. He's extremely clever at using every situation to his own advantage."

"*None* of this is to his benefit!"

"I understand your feelings, since Wandersee's been your only information source up until now. He's skillful at changing what behavior means. That's why we're here—to show you the other side."

"He's a genius," Pete Shaw added, not admiringly.

"There isn't any other side," Jane said flatly.

"Yes, well, there always is." Carefully factual, Maguire explained their side of the evidence. "When the Hands of Allah released Wandersee, they called all major U.S. TV networks because they wanted news cameras on the spot to show their hostage coming home unharmed. They didn't tip off the government until the plane touched down, so federal agents wouldn't have time to prepare strategy. They hoped the TV news would show armed guards whisking Wandersee off against his will."

"That's what the news *did* show."

"Possibly."

Jane suddenly saw she mustn't answer. Hank had told the Hands of Allah how to release him in order to get maximum publicity. They had followed his advice and it had worked as they wanted it to. If Hank had explained that to the government, he might be in serious trouble.

She wished she knew what he had said. But after a moment she realized it didn't matter. Regardless of everything, she wasn't going to betray him.

Maguire leaned forward as if confidingly. "Miss Woodruff, we've checked you down to your vaccination scar. We know every detail of what Dr. Wandersee is to you. We also know how you feel about your country. Talk tough if you need to, that shows up on your profile—an independent mind. But when it comes down to it, you're loyal to America."

Pete Shaw nodded. "We trust you."

I don't want to be trusted by slime like you, Jane thought.

"This is the kind of disgusting mess you hear about but don't believe." Struggling against the complex feelings that interfered with her thoughts, she looked out the window. Spring buds greened the black branches of a sprawling oak that was older than the building. Which was unreal? she asked herself. Nature, with its reassuring cycle? Or these repellent questioners, these abnormalities?

"I don't know what Wandersee's been telling you, but I assume he's been persuasive." Maguire sounded sympathetic. "He's subjected us to quite a bit of charm these past few days."

"Are you really as cynical as you sound?"

Maguire sighed. "Eventually you've seen it all, Miss Woodruff. I can't say that's good, but it happens anyway."

Jane's mind filled with a vision of Hank at bay, gallantly trying to reason with narrow-souled inquisitors like these. Helpless protectiveness left her feelings raw.

"He kept asking to come to you." Maguire smiled. "But who ever heard of a woman who'd let a man from the past just show up the way he expected you to? There were two ways to go with it. He might really be talking about some woman he used to know—you can never throw that out entirely—but your partnership seemed like a better possibility. Dutch Bulb might be a code name for some group we hadn't picked up on yet. Subversive, maybe. Or else drugs."

"Oak Harbor doesn't have drugs."

Maguire's cynical gaze was worse than a slap.

"The closest we ever came was when a crabber took too many No-Doz once and felt weird for a while," Jane insisted. "It made the newspaper police reports, which ought to tell you what you need to know about drugs around here."

They both smiled, as if she had tried to joke with them. She clenched one hand unconsciously.

Apparently satisfied, Maguire moved to the next topic as if checking things off an unseen list. "We also wondered about Dr. Wandersee's fantasy picture of you."

"We ran a character evaluation, which has to include a person's parents, if it's going to be any good," Pete Shaw said. "And yours are interesting, for sure."

Fear made it hard for Jane to breathe. Missionaries could usually get away with trips other people weren't allowed to take, but she knew her parents had been questioned occasionally over the years. The government had thick files on them. Had she gotten them into new trouble by agreeing to help Hank?

"Leave my folks out of this."

Maguire shook his head. "As much money as you spend on phone calls home, they're not out of anything you do."

"You can't look at my phone bills!"

"We're talking your government's right to know, Miss Woodruff," Pete Shaw said.

Maguire went on as if no one could doubt the government's rights. "Given parents like yours, the kind of compassion Wandersee was counting on from you—it might make sense."

"The bottom line is we need your help," Pete Shaw said, obviously trying to soothe her by using business terms.

Jane could hardly breathe. "I won't hurt Hank! And don't say you'll hassle my parents if I don't! They'd disown me if I hurt anybody in order to shield them."

"Miss Woodruff, please. We expected loyalty from you, but it's been five years since you saw Dr. Wandersee."

"Yes, we know—you wrote." Pete Shaw patted the air to silence Jane. "But Wandersee doesn't write the kind of letters that keep you current on changes in his personality."

"How do you know about his letters?"

They both looked at her.

She gave up on privacy and battled the other part of what they claimed. "Personalities don't change."

"That may be true in general, but when a person's isolated and tortured—" Maguire gazed at Jane with no expression in his eyes.

She remembered the shackle marks on Hank's wrists. The terrible thinness. The bruises.

"He refuses hypnosis," Maguire went on. "You're a hypnotist, so you know how that can be."

The reference to her skill was meant to show they really did know everything about her. Jane shook her head.

"I learned to hypnotize for stress control. Just to calm yourself so you can do your best under pressure. I teach it to business managers at my workshops sometimes."

"You also hypnotize for pain control," Pete Shaw said.

Jane flushed at his presuming, invasive, insulting tone. "I help my neighbors, sure, but I *never* invade someone's privacy, so don't bother asking me to."

"Our medics tried drug-assisted questioning," Maguire went on as if he hadn't noticed her anger. "Unfortunately Wandersee's allergic to everything, if they give him enough to overcome his resistance. One thing they tried, he was barely breathing, much less talking. Something else made him vomit pretty well forever, which interfered."

"Don't go on." Jane's voice broke.

"Our best bet is to get him comfortable in a trust situation and let it unroll from there."

Jane squared her jaw. "I won't do anything to him."

Maguire didn't seem to hear. "He says he'll cooperate if we leave him on his own. We've decided to go with that because we've tried everything else. He'll be doing some writing for us. All we ask is that you watch him."

"Watch for what?"

"Anything weird," Pete Shaw said.

"I have no idea what seems weird to you."

Maguire didn't quite suppress a smile, as if he wanted her to believe the put-down pleased him, too. "Watch for compulsions. Secrets there aren't any reasons for. Emotions that aren't quite right."

"Also, who he gets in touch with," Pete Shaw said.

"Oh, I see." Jane's eyes narrowed in disgust. "It's one of those horrible sting operations. I *despise* that stuff. I *won't* entrap him."

"Okay." Maguire nodded. "We'll go pick him up for you and stick him back in a psychiatric ward. That's probably for the best, so don't blame yourself."

Jane recoiled from his trap. "I'm the one the sting's against."

"If words matter to you, Miss Woodruff, call it something else," Maguire answered. "Call it a request for help."

"We have to put you on the spot this way because we need someone he trusts to take him in, and he doesn't trust anyone but you, apparently," Pete Shaw explained. "It's *pathetic* how he counts on you."

Jane let herself hate his oily disbelief. "I've always thought I couldn't be blackmailed. I believed a person could live up to their values and escape all that."

"Life gets more complex as we get older, Miss Woodruff," Maguire said reassuringly.

Believe me, Jane thought in despair. "Is he still wired? Or whatever you do?"

"No. And he won't be, if you cooperate."

"Okay," she said bitterly.

Maguire seemed to misunderstand the stressed whiteness of her face. "Try not to be afraid of him. He'll sense it if you are. He's very alert."

"Afraid? Of *Hank*?"

"He's been living with terrorists," Pete Shaw said. "Making deals with them."

It was true in a way, even though Pete Shaw obviously misunderstood. Jane decided he couldn't be set straight.

Both men stood.

Maguire held out a card with nothing on it but an 800 number written in pencil. "Here's where you call."

She didn't reach for the card.

"Miss Woodruff," Maguire urged her in a patronizing tone.

It was too small a battle to waste energy on. She took the card and crammed it into the pocket of her pants.

"Am I supposed to *believe* this?"

Instead of answering, they walked her to the door in a solicitous way, which offended her. She nodded to the secretary as she crossed the reception room, but she couldn't manage a smile.

She left the building in a daze, walking slowly downhill to the strip garden that bordered the recreational boat marina. Sitting on a blue park bench, she watched a red-sailed Blanchard round the breakwater light while she tried to decide whether to tell Hank about Maguire. If she didn't tell him, he might sense that she was hiding something. But if she told him, he would leave Dutch Bulb in order to protect her.

She remembered his reaction to her offer of her parents' missionary camp. Even a friendly alternative had seemed cruel to him. And, thinking of his nightmares, she knew why.

A huge sea gull perched on the end of the bench, asking for a handout with a sudden shriek. Jane looked at its arrogant button eyes and sighed.

It wasn't fair to tell him, she decided. If he sensed a lack of openness, she would just have to convince him otherwise.

Satisfied with her decision, she headed for Old Town Mall. She needed to collect some Festival stories to talk about so Hank wouldn't find out how she had really spent her afternoon. A visit to the mall would give her an endless supply of anecdotes.

It wasn't really a mall. An old port warehouse had been refitted instead of being torn down. For the sake of atmosphere, it hadn't been painted, except for bright blue trim around the windows and doors. Completely rebuilt inside, it housed four stories of individual shops that opened onto balconies overlooking an air shaft. Dutch Bulb had donated plantings to make the open space into an atrium.

Jane smiled as she stood beneath the skylighted vault. The small-business owners leaned over their balcony railings, calling gossip down to her to liven up their afternoon.

"What's this about your boarder?" the yarn shopkeeper asked, after everyone in the mall had told their news.

Jane knew she shouldn't be surprised by the question. Clinton must have mentioned Hank at every business where he kept the books, and Bernice would have discussed it as the Dutch Café's customers paid their bills. At least two hours had passed since Hank had appeared downtown—that was plenty of time for the news to have spread.

"Are you hiding him?" the paper-craft owner asked when Jane didn't answer quickly enough.

Wondering if the question meant they knew who he was, Jane wasn't sure how to answer.

"Who from—us?" the candle shop proprietor asked.

All the women laughed.

Jane laughed with them, suddenly seeing she could use their teasing to protect herself as well as Hank. "Is this fair? It's a lot of work—finding outsiders. I'm not talking until you've got something to trade."

As soon as they started discussing it, she knew her plan would work. They were sure to tell her about any new strangers in town. Maguire might have her or Hank watched, but he couldn't keep it a secret in Oak Harbor.

"My wife's brother-in-law is here from South Dakota, does he count as a stranger?" the man from the scrimshaw attic called.

"How strange is he?" Jane asked.

The whole mall laughed. Feeling protected, Jane waved goodbye cheerfully. She could count on Oak Harbor—they were too decent to let one of their own come to grief.

The foghorns began their haunting lament as she strolled back to the city parking lot. Stepping into her Sentra, she gunned up the face of the bluff. She parked by the shelterbelt and went to the potting shed to check on the high-school girl who helped out every afternoon.

Jane had hired Nyla temporarily, to fill in while her partner was away, but she had decided to keep her on after Fran returned. Nyla was fascinated by plants. Barely sixteen, she already knew she wanted to learn the business, and Jane enjoyed watching her abilities develop.

Nyla looked up earnestly when Jane's shadow in the doorway darkened the potting shed. "I thought I'd get these pots sterilized. We'll need everything we've got for Festival, won't we?"

"We sure will." Jane loitered a few minutes, giving Nyla a chance to talk about school while she scrubbed clay pots, setting aside anything showing the least crack, which might harbor disease.

"Boy! Am I going to be popular tomorrow!" Nyla brushed her dark hair off her forehead with the back of one wet hand.

"Why's that?"

"Well, I went in the house looking for you and met your boarder. Everybody wonders what he's like, even Miss Timmans in sixth-period math, and now I can say how nice he is."

"Is that going to surprise people?" Jane asked.

Nyla's narrow face lighted up. "Well, you're going to get a lot of job applicants."

They laughed together in a purely womanly way.

"I'll remember you have seniority, if you'll tell me anything interesting you hear," Jane promised.

She knew she should go to the house and change her clothes, but she dreaded it. Meeting Maguire had cast a pall over her thoughts of Hank.

So she went to the species greenhouse instead. Walking slowly down the aisle, she stopped at a lighted glass hood over an in-the-ground bed. Kneeling in the sawdust without giving a thought to her wool pants, she lifted a glass panel away. She leaned inside the humid box, sharing earthy air with the experimental tulips as she checked them.

"Is that the sick bay?" Hank asked from behind her.

Jane sat back on her heels. He had been shopping for himself as well as for his study, she saw. His jeans and sweatshirt were pure northwestern, and his quilted fisherman's coat would keep him warm even on the open sea.

"This batch looks dilapidated, but they're healthy," she said, glad to talk about plants. "They don't set seed very well, though." She pointed to yellowish seedpods that had begun to soften and droop. It was obvious they wouldn't ripen, so there would be no new generation.

"It's an experiment. There's a botanist in Oregon who did this with corn. He put the plants on double days by controlling their light cycle, and stress made them develop backward toward what they used to be. He started with table corn and turned it back into a sort of spindly Indian corn."

"And because of that, what did he know?" Hank's interest sounded genuine, so it was easy for her to answer.

"A lot of things about growth. I'm doing it to see if the books are right when they say all tulips originally came from species bulbs. I wondered if you could take Holland bulbs and drive them back."

"Stress does that?"

She nodded and fitted the glass panel back into place. "I'm getting plants that are pretty weird for Holland, but they aren't species, really. I'm not sure what they are."

"All this stress I've been facing, what's it likely to turn me into?"

"A cook, I hope."

He grinned. "Supper is ready and on hold."

"Good." She stood, brushing sawdust off her pants.

"I was coming out for a walk when I saw you over here." The words were casual, but his voice was suddenly tense.

"You're welcome to inspect, is that what's bothering you?" Jane asked in her forthright way. "And I know I don't have to protect Nyla from you, if you're worried about that sort of thing."

His smile preceded his confession. "I want the townspeople to accept me, if possible. So sure, I was working on it with your helper. But all I did was ask how much botany you can study here in Oak Harbor. A week's unit in ninth grade general science is it, apparently. That's why she likes working here with you and your experiments."

"She's a natural-born green thumb," Jane said.

As they stepped outside into the early twilight, Hank finally explained what had distressed him. "I was going to walk around for a few minutes. I know it isn't enough to count as exercise, but it's more than I've done for months."

Jane pretended not to notice how hard it was for him to admit he had lost strength. "What about the grand tour? That wears everyone out."

She led him through the greenhouses at a tactfully slow pace. By the time they reached the potting shed, Nyla had cleaned up and was shrugging into a green wind shirt.

"I'll mix extra potting soil as soon as you get the ingredients." She spoke to Jane, but she looked at Hank.

Jane couldn't repress a smile. "I'll go down to Feed & Seed tomorrow."

"If it's just a matter of loading up, why don't I drive Nyla down?" Hank said. "I was going to return the trailer and rent a car, but I could make it a truck instead."

"Terrific. I'll be by for you about three." Nyla waved and set off across the yard.

"Is that okay?" Hank asked. "She can introduce me around without feeling confused over it." He glanced at Jane but after he had explained, she wasn't sure which of them he'd meant to protect. "I noticed it was awkward for you this morning in the Dutch Café. I don't want that, but

I do want the town to think it owns me by the time your partner comes home and disapproves.''

''Fran won't say anything, she's a friend. We met at one of my workshops and liked each other by the end of the first coffee break.''

Jane decided not to say his new plans created a different kind of problem. Her supplies came in hundred-pound sacks. In his present condition, he wouldn't find it easy to lift that much weight. But involving him with the ordinary world was a good idea. The workers at Feed & Seed would load his truck for him if he asked and between them, he and Nyla could probably figure out some way to manage the unloading.

Casually silent as they crossed the patio, Hank stopped in the enclosed back porch to take off his fisherman's jacket. Jane noticed he had moved one of her jackets in order to empty a coat peg for himself.

It was a warm day, by Oak Harbor standards, in spite of the drizzle, so Jane hadn't worn a coat. She went on ahead of him and stopped abruptly, shocked by the appetizing aromas. The kitchen was fragrant with the scent of Middle Eastern cuisine.

How could he possibly want his captor's foods? she thought in dismay. What have they done to his mind?

Chapter Five

Hank seemed disarmingly normal as he followed Jane to the lounge and handed her a glass of *kokinelli*. Frightened, she set the wine on a small table beside her favorite leather chair. Was it going to increase his stress to face the changes in her life? she wondered. She decided the best thing to do was to ask.

"I don't drink," she said cautiously. "I know I did at the seminar, but it's a hassle for a woman. Every time you have a meal with a client, you can't be sure if they hope you'll make a fool of yourself. Is it okay for me to tell you this?"

"Makes sense. It's a hassle for a man, too. Why shouldn't you tell me?"

"I don't know if it bothers you that I've changed."

"We've both changed." He picked up her wineglass. "I noticed Tehuacan water in the pantry—is that what you like?"

She nodded.

"Will it bother you if I drink?"

She shook her head. "It's a business decision, not morals. I can't risk getting fuzzy."

"I promise not to sing off-key, or fall down, or do anything else embarrassing. The hospital gave me enough tranqs to mellow out Seattle, but I don't want to get into that. Wine does the job for me."

"They want you to take tranquilizers?"

"It's nothing much." He met her gaze sincerely. "You're not afraid of me, are you? I can ask the hospital to call and say I'm not dangerous, if you'd like."

She couldn't bear to look into his guileless blue eyes and tell him they had already gotten in touch so they could warn her that he *was* dangerous. "I was worrying about you—not about myself."

"No, don't worry. I had trouble eating, but I think it was just the food. Have you ever confronted what they serve at—" He stopped abruptly.

Protective feelings overwhelmed Jane's fears as she remembered Maguire's description of his ordeal. She answered quickly, as if she had no idea what he had left unsaid.

"You lost your appetite for public food? No problem. The world's best cook has moved in here at Dutch Bulb."

He smiled and rested a hand affectionately on her shoulder before going down the hall to exchange her drink.

She sank into her chair and let her head loll back. Propping her feet up, she wondered if there was some perfectly wholesome explanation for the Middle Eastern food. He seemed so much like himself, it was hard to believe in his nightmare world. And it was even harder to know how to help.

He came back with a glass of Tehuacan and lime. Setting it down at her elbow, he returned to the spot he had chosen for himself on the couch. He rested his feet on the coffee table, as if he had lived in her house for years.

"You'll ask for help, won't you, Hank?" she asked wistfully.

He smiled, seeing she needed to be reassured. "I already have. Why would I stop?"

She rubbed her forehead, admitting tension, which concerned him. "I can't bear it that you've been hurt."

He nodded soberly. "Is it too much, Sandy?"

"You know I didn't mean that."

"Yes, but I also know you're too polite to tell me if I've ripped your life to shreds."

"Could we kind of agree on something?" She caught her lower lip between her teeth, steadying herself to get it right. "Could we say I'm glad to have you here, and you're glad to be here, and we'll *trust* to both sides of that?"

He smiled as if she had described Santa Claus. "Okay. I'll go first. Clinton barged in this afternoon."

"He drops in every day to do our books."

He watched her eyes. "He's quite possessive of you."

"He owns the world. He keeps books all over town so he can butt in everywhere. Nobody minds. It's just his way."

Hank sipped his *kokinelli*. "Tell me if that changes."

"I won't have to—he'll tell you himself."

Hank smiled and stood, holding out his cool hand to pull her up from her chair. They walked down the hall side by side like old friends. Hank seated her in the dining room and served the meal. It was delicious, but he had trouble eating it. Jane talked about Oak Harbor and Festival to slow herself down and keep pace with him as they idled through their Basmati rice and spring lamb.

"Your mother called," he said when she ran out of stories about Festival. "I said you'd get back to her."

Jane nodded.

"Should I not answer the phone?" he asked.

"Why not answer?"

"I probably sound like a man."

Jane frowned. "In Oak Harbor people pick up the phone to help out. The sheriff, the meter reader, the Federal Express driver—whoever's closest. All it means is someone's being neighborly."

"There's no such thing as that small of a town."

Jane allowed herself to sound grouchy. "Well, Oak Harbor thinks there is, so don't convince them otherwise."

He studied her eyes. "What about after office hours?"

Jane looked through the tall narrow windows behind him. The glass was water beaded from the fog that had roiled down the Straits while they talked, darkening the evening.

"You want to pick a fight?" she asked at last, deciding to confront him to put him at ease.

Faint lines deepened under his eyes, reminding her how worn-out he was. "I've lived in eleven countries, Sandy. Every nation has its own rules, but there's one truth that's true everywhere. A mother may be sophisticated about herself, but she doesn't want a man answering her daughter's phone."

"That's not fair to my mom. She'd *expect* me to take you in. Compassion is the top of her value list and nothing else is even close."

He thought about it, then nodded. "That's good to know. If it won't bring a lecture down on you, I'm going to tell your parents who I am. When I get going on my own work, I'll need to test some ideas. Their missionary trainees would be perfect for it."

"No, Hank, please. Leave them out of it."

Feeling attacked by her abrupt change in attitude, he sat utterly still. "Surely you don't think I'd do anything to hurt anyone you love."

"Not everything that happens is something you plan."

He reached across the table to cover her hand with his own. She laced her fingers through his, admitting they both needed the comfort.

"If you're worried about your parents, that means what really worries you is the feds." His voice was gentle.

She was relieved to be able to admit it without having to say why.

"Will it help if I talk about that?"

She nodded, not trusting herself to speak, for fear he might figure out what had happened this afternoon with Maguire.

"Their trouble is, they have a simple explanation for something complex," he said in the confident way that reminded her psychology was his work. "When you live abroad, you start seeing the U.S. for what it is—a big country with problems like anybody else. That's the point of the corporation I was working for. Options imports media so Americans can see more than one side without leaving home.''

Jane nodded to show she followed his explanation.

Encouraged, he went on. ''Government agents in the U.S. are like government agents everywhere—they don't want to hear alternatives. If you say this country isn't perfect, they like to believe your skull has been zipped open, your brain taken out, and a microchip and wires put in to replace it.''

She remembered Maguire.

''I'm still running on original equipment. Want to check?'' He bowed his head and ruffled up the blond hair at the back of his neck.

It would have been easy to reach out and stroke his exposed nape as if checking for surgical scars by touch. But he had enough to cope with already. It wasn't fair to let him know how confused her feelings were. She let it go with a mock-inspecting glance.

''Looks good to me.''

He smiled supportively. ''It's ridiculous, but it's just something I have to deal with. I won't let it spill onto you. I promise. I wouldn't have come here if there was any danger to you.''

Jane was profoundly grateful she hadn't told him about Maguire. ''It was just a small fit of jitters. It's gone.''

''I'll believe that later on.''

She managed to smile. Using their original work-sharing rituals to change the subject, she cleared dishes onto a tray. ''I load the dishwasher so the dishes don't sit around, but one of the neighbors does the rest. Hiring a housekeeper has been my goal since I was old enough to say 'scrub.' ''

''I saw your note on the back door this morning. Does it mean I can toss my clothes into the hamper and wait for them to come back?''

''Like magic,'' Jane agreed.

He followed her to the kitchen and poured decaf, setting her mug conveniently between the sink and fridge before settling down at the kitchen table with his own mug.

"Since Clinton was here anyway, a while ago, I asked him about the local rate for bed-and-breakfast. And I'll cook, like I used to, and do the groceries. Does that sound fair?"

Jane splashed water in all directions as an excuse not to answer while she tried to decide why she was annoyed. "If you talk to people about me, they'll think you don't know me well enough to ask *me*, and that will make them wonder why you're my guest."

"Makes sense." He didn't say anything for a few moments, but she could feel him watching her, as if looking at her back would tell him what had upset her.

"It was myself I talked about," he said eventually. "Options offered me a split of what they'd have paid if they ransomed me. I wasn't going to take it, but they swore I was doing them a favor because of the grief I saved by not getting killed. It's a big enough lump I've got to figure out an investment strategy. I thought Clinton might have theories about it. He's an accountant."

"You're not broke?"

The corners of his mouth moved. "No, I'm disgustingly rich, apparently, but it's not going to wreck my life."

The phone rang. He reached to answer it without getting up, looking distractingly appealing as he tipped his chair back precariously and stretched to reach the phone above his head. Disturbed, she watched him wait, frown, say hello again.

"No one there?" She turned back to scrub at the baking pan before it went into the dishwasher. "That's funny. We hardly get nuisance calls here in Oak Harbor."

"You get this kind everywhere," he said with a tiredness that was not resigned. "I'm treading on someone's turf."

"*Turf*? Forget it. I'm nobody's property."

"Introduce me to him anyway. I'll work out something, but that kind of negotiation needs to be face-to-face."

"What *exactly* are you talking about?"

"If a man answers, hang up. Oldest signal in the world. Or at least, as old as telephones."

Jane shut off the splashing water so she could turn and face him. "I thought you came here because we're friends."

There was a turmoil in his eyes that made her wonder if he was having problems with his feelings, just as she was. If that was it, she wanted him to know how she felt. But she'd have to tell him in a way that didn't commit them to anything. And she didn't know how she was she going to do that.

"You're talking about Europe, Hank. In Oak Harbor, if a man calls, he talks." She smiled wryly, to soften the contradiction. "There's no such thing as a secret here. If you're interested in someone, they're discussing it at the Dutch Café before you've finished your first kiss."

"Who are you interested in?"

She shook her head. A week ago, she would have answered frankly that she wasn't interested in anyone, but now, looking at Hank, she couldn't be sure that was entirely true.

"In that case, why did they hang up when they heard my voice?" he insisted.

Jane turned back to the sink so he couldn't see her sudden dismay. "Someone's probably annoyed because I'm on the Festival Board. You can't imagine how important Festival is around here. It must be someone who's not too involved with it, if it took them this long to call."

The phone rang again.

"Will you answer this time, Sandy?" He looked grim. "It's the only way to see if you're right."

Trying not to seem anxious, Jane crossed the room and picked the phone off the wall with a soapy hand. "Jane."

The answering voice sounded disguised. Artificially high, but clearly male. An uninflected chant: "Get the dirty boyfriend out of town."

Shaken, Jane hung up quickly.

"They spoke, didn't they? What did they say?"

"Nothing."

"A threat?"

She leaned against the sink. "Not exactly."

"Tell me the words." His voice was horrifyingly harsh.

"Don't yell at me."

He crossed the room slowly, trying not to threaten her. He leaned against the counter beside her and gently locked her shoulder in one big hand.

"Sandy, let's not fight with each other. There's plenty of others to fight."

It was easier to shut her eyes than to bear the devastated look in his.

"If that call was about me in any way, tell me. I want to stay here, but not if it messes up your life."

Jane bowed her head, annoyed at herself for craving his help when she was supposed to be helping him. Anxiously, she repeated the threatening sentence.

Startled by the difference between what she said and the horror he had expected, Hank laughed. "You must have an unknown admirer. Or did you recognize the voice?"

Disconcerted by his jarring change of mood, Jane turned back to her dishwashing tasks. "He sounded halfway down a well. He must have had a rag over the phone."

"That doesn't work anymore. Electronics are just too good these days. Even throwaway phones pick up anything."

"Then it must be a stranger."

"Can't be."

She stepped around him to slam the dishwasher and set the energy-saver dial. "Why not?"

"He's utterly gone or he'd be ashamed to say anything so ridiculous."

She frowned.

"I mean it," he insisted. "Suppose some dizzy blonde showed up on my front porch. You might call me up and discuss my character faults, but wouldn't it embarrass you to say what he said to you?"

His logical analysis helped Jane to deal with her shock. But what helped more was his apparently unconscious suggestion that he thought they were more than friends.

She tried to echo his light tone. "Sure you're blond. But I never thought of you as dizzy."

He smiled, but he didn't yield his point. "Give me a list of the men you've noticed looking hungry when you walk into the room. I'll do the interviewing. That's fair—I caused the problem by moving in on you."

"*List!* I can't imagine what you think my life here is like."

"That's just it." He watched her dry her hands and turn off the light above the sink. "You've got a public role. If your friends can't accept me, I need to know it. I'm not willing to get you crosswise with your community."

"My friends, the people I work with, they won't care."

"I do." Instead of following her to the lounge, Hank started up the stairs.

Jane watched thoughtfully. There was no question that he was tired, but if he was going to bed, he'd have said good-night. It had to be something else.

Worried, she trotted up the stairs after him. His bedroom door was open. She stopped in the doorway. He had rearranged his furniture again, this time to make room for a pine computer table and filing cabinet. Then she noticed the open suitcase on his bed.

Her heart raced at that proof of how much he cared. He was so determined to protect her that he was willing to turn himself in to the government merely because she'd gotten a rude phone call. What they shared wasn't what most people would call mere friendship.

His actions put her on the spot. It was fine for him to offer to go, but she couldn't let him actually do it.

"Stop it," she said.

He continued folding shirts into the suitcase. "Military hospital is easier to face than threats to you."

"You don't have to face them. They're *my* threats." Hoping to slow him down until she could think of some argument that might persuade him, she grabbed a shirt out of his suitcase and jammed a discarded hanger into the sleeves.

He pulled a stack of sweaters off his closet shelf. "I provoked them."

She scooped a handful of red briefs out of the suitcase and turned toward the campaign chest. "My dirty boyfriend provoked them. I didn't know that was you."

He dropped the sweaters into the suitcase and looked at her in discouragement. "If you won't tell me who has claims on you, I don't think I can handle this."

"Claims?" Hoping a womanly argument might shift his attention away from himself, she tried to sound offended as she grabbed up a sweater. "You have weird ideas about what goes on between men and women."

He straightened the stack of sweaters she had toppled over. "Look, Sandy, can we be frank? Maybe it's different for you. Maybe it's different for women generally. But when I'm involved with someone, I don't want her sharing her home with another man. So whoever's feeling that way about my being here, I can understand his point."

Dismayed by his skill at expanding the topic she had set for him, Jane didn't answer. She just handed him his sweater.

He accepted the sweater unthinkingly. "Am I making this clear enough? Here's what I mean—if I thought you were in Clinton's bedroom making a mess of his suitcases, I'd go mad."

"If you knew how to go mad, you'd have done it for the Hands of Allah." She wanted him to know how he made her heart leap. "Besides, why imagine me doing this with anyone else? I'm here with you."

He tossed the sweater to the floor. "Sandy?"

She looked at him without trying to hide the truth, even though she wasn't sure what he could see in her eyes.

He sank slowly onto the bed. "I've been afraid I'd just seem needy to you."

She looked down at his upturned face. "We're friends. I worried I'd fail you if you wanted to live in the past."

He drew her down beside him as if his hands touched insubstantial dreams. "I suppose I do, in a way. At least, I want to build on what we shared, to start."

She locked her arms around him with a strength that surprised him. "That'll do for the past. But whatever this new stuff is, we'll face it together."

Chapter Six

Hank was settling in fast.

Jane closed the door to her private office behind her. His doubts had been easy to deal with, compared to the struggle she now faced with herself. She didn't pace, exactly, but she moved idly to different parts of the small room.

Who had made the crank call? she asked herself. She was still insisting to Hank that it was someone upset over her appointment to Festival Board. And it might even really be that. But it could be someone offended by Hank's arrival. They had both happened at the same time.

But why would anyone object to Hank? His theory that it was a man friend of Jane's absolutely wasn't true. Jane was always friendly to everyone, and everyone was friendly to her, and that was where it had stopped. Most of the men she knew were married, and the ones who weren't behaved like the rest. It was what she preferred, and everyone accepted it.

Could it be someone's husband, irritated by such glamorous competition? Bernice was friendly at the Dutch Café. Jane laughed, embarrassed at the thought of accusing Bernice's husband, Marvin, of making crank calls.

Could it be something about her work? If people had recognized Hank, they might think she had called in a top-level consultant. But, no! Surely no one thought she couldn't run Dutch Bulb! And they couldn't worry about

competition since there weren't any other nurseries here to
ie hurt by her success.

What else could it be? No one could be rejecting Hank
just because he was a stranger. The Festival Board meeting
had proved how kind Oak Harbor was to newcomers.

She noticed the topic of her thoughts had shifted again.
Why *was* she on the Festival Board? Accepting the assignment implied roots, which she'd never thought of as her
style. She gazed around her office, feeling unreal. It was
beautiful, with its pine worktables so scrubbed that the
grain in the wood was raised. She loved this place but she
had never meant to really belong here or anywhere else.

She preferred the way she had grown up—able to say her
name in thirteen languages before she was old enough to go
to school. She remembered talking about it at Cabin Seven.
Back then, she and Hank had seemed a lot alike. Enough,
at least, to keep them writing to each other, over the years.

Was that why they had written? she wondered. No. She'd
known from the first that Hank was special. And apparently he had thought she was special, too. That's why
they'd written.

Okay, she told herself. It's harder this time because we
don't know when it will end. But now we know each other
better, after all the letters. Maybe we can handle it.

She had no idea how Hank had come to terms with their
situation, but the crank call had obviously been a turning
point for him. After their talk he'd settled in as if for life,
involving himself with everyone he met. He'd hired Jane's
housekeeper to teach him how to choose northwestern
clothes. He'd charmed a neighbor into explaining the
walking trails through the woods behind Dutch Bulb. He'd
provided the mail carrier with a coffee break when she
asked about his subscriptions to the New York and L.A.
Times.

Now Jane sat in her private office on Thursday—delivery day—and listened to him make friends of Bare Woods's
delivery men. His amiable voice drifted across the kitchen
as the men muscled a table up the stairs. She couldn't hear

Hank's words, but he was answered by what she'd always thought of as men's room laughter. She smiled at the proof of Hank's effectiveness.

When the deliverymen had left, she went upstairs to help. Jane took one end of his new worktable as he swung it around to join his computer desk in a work-station L.

"Did you tidy up for me in here?" he asked when they stepped back to judge the effect.

"I don't do housework," Jane teased.

"Okay." He grinned at her.

"But my stuff's been moved," he added after a moment.

"Not by me."

"Must have been the housekeeper."

"Couldn't be. Betty knows she'd lose her job if she touched paperwork." Jane frowned at the manuscript beside his computer, wondering if he was just being paranoid. It was possible, but he had seemed so much more cheerful, even after only a week of Dutch Bulb's peace.

Could what he suspected be real?

"What's wrong exactly?" She tried to sound only curious.

"Someone checked through my notes. My clothing. That sort of thing." He shrugged. "Probably kids who saw the news and decided to see if their local evildoer carries a gun."

"When kids here want to know something, they ask."

"Then who could it be?"

"This is Oak Harbor. Nobody would get into your stuff."

"Good, that narrows the possibilities." He smiled calmly and seemed ready to let it go.

Jane wasn't sure. "Maybe it's the same person who made the phone call. It's probably something about me, not you."

"My clothes," he said logically. "My computer."

"My house," she answered firmly, keeping her anxiety out of her voice.

It took him a moment to smile, which told her he wasn't convinced, but he yielded the point with his usual grace. "I'll password my computer files so only I can read them, and that will take care of it, whoever it is and whatever they want."

He watched her stare at the dark computer screen. "If you want to know anything, Sandy, surely you'll ask?"

"You can count on it that I won't snoop."

He had expected her to be angry, but he had needed to say it anyway. She sounded sad, instead, which worried him.

"Do me a favor?" he said to make amends. "Come with me on my walk? I'm working on a handbook for business people, besides this government stuff, and I want to try something out on a business type."

He didn't comment when Jane left the house unlocked, although her carelessness disturbed him. She strolled to the end of the street, chatting about the neighbors as if the need to suspect them never crossed her mind. Entering the forest, which enclosed the town, she followed a deer trail to a nearby lookout, obviously a favorite spot. He rebelled at the thought of her walking alone in such dense woods.

She gazed inland across regrowth forests, admiring the snowcapped Cascade Mountains as if nothing closer was of any concern. Hank watched Jane instead of the view.

"Would you role-play for me?" he asked.

"Sure." She looked at him, waiting.

"Pretend you're hungry and thirsty and you've been blindfolded for a week and your hands and ankles are in chains."

The plunge into his nightmare was too sudden. She wanted to discuss it in order to back away. "Is that what happened?"

He ignored her question. "An innocent teenager of the opposite sex from you comes to your cell and releases your chains and offers you a meal. He can't speak English, but he's gentle and his eyes are big and compassionate."

"A girl, in your case, but a boy for me?"

He watched her eyes. "You move around to be sure you remember how. You eat your supper slowly because you haven't eaten for a while and you're afraid you'll throw up if you eat too fast. Just when you start feeling human, you hear a child scream. It cries for a while and then starts screaming again. It screams and screams."

He paused, studying her face. "What do you do?"

"Make the teenager take me to the child."

"He won't. He'll act like he doesn't understand."

"Then pound on the door. Find somebody who talks a language I can understand. Bargain." She went on to the important part. "Is that what they did to you?"

"If you're a man, they use a woman, begging and crying in the distance. If you're a woman, they use a child."

"They *can't*! That's too *dumb*!"

"It works, so it's not totally dumb."

She tried to imagine it. "Is that what they'll do if they come after you again?"

"No. They're proud people, so they don't repeat themselves. Besides, trying new things interests them."

Her horrified look caused him to shake his head. "Sorry. I answered the wrong half of the question. You wanted me to say they won't come after me, didn't you. It's true. They won't. They promised."

Disturbed by his trust of the terrorists, Jane didn't know how to react. If she said it was sick to trust his tormentors, he would cloak himself in charm and refuse to talk about it. But she couldn't pretend it wasn't sick to trust them.

"I wish I could make it not have happened." The ache in her voice made it easier for him to talk about it.

"That's what my business handbook will be for. You want to change the past. The advice we give now works only for people who just hope to forget."

"Passives?" She frowned.

"Government types call it not getting killed." The hurt look in his eyes told her she had insulted him, but he went on calmly. "Like many terrorist groups the Hands of Allah are clever. They know you'll do as you're told if you're unnerved, so everything they do is meant to kill your sense of yourself."

"Hank, are you all right?"

He didn't answer. "Their method works. They find a threat you think you can withstand, and then they prove you're wrong. Death, in my case. I thought I didn't care."

She had always hated situations that called for bravery. The TV news had said Hank was brave, but she hadn't expected to have to hear exactly what they meant.

"They live in a sandy country. They make you dig a trench," he said, no longer referring directly to himself. "You accept that it's your grave. They stop your digging before it's deep enough. You think it must be something else. You're glad. They make you lie down in it. You think about the birds your body will attract if you're buried so shallowly. You try to believe it won't matter after you're dead, but it's an ugly thought, and you're sorry it's your last one, and you wish they'd hurry up. They take a break instead. Tell jokes. Enjoy themselves. Finally they drive an empty truck back and forth across the trench. The crust from windstorms holds the sand in shape well enough so you aren't crushed. You see they're having fun watching you hate the exhaust in your face. You think that's all it's for, and you feel saved again. They start loading the truck so each trip over you it sinks deeper into the sand."

Jane shuddered. "When I think of terrorists, I think of bombs. Armaments. *Equipment*."

"Their favorite piece of equipment is your own mind."

She glanced around the woods before she spoke. She hated to add to his worries, but it had to be said. "Maybe they turned you loose so it would hit harder when they come after you again."

"No. They're through with me."

"How can you be sure?" She needed reassurance, for both of them.

"I understand them." He sighed and went on bitterly, "You don't have to be a traitor in order to understand."

"Of course not." Contradicting her firm tone, her eyes were fearful. "Should you hire a bodyguard?"

"Are you offering?"

"Sure."

Not bothering to decide if they were trying to joke, she wrapped her arms around him, clinging fiercely, trembling. Sensing how appalled she was by what he'd told her, he held her close, his feelings wrapping her even tighter than his arms. His intensity shocked her to the heart. For one wild moment she needed to escape. But she knew letting go of him wouldn't help.

And anyway, it wasn't necessary. One-sided love was what she dreaded, after all, and this was something else. Shared trust. Mutual listening. She wasn't sure exactly what.

Not that it mattered. She let her mind stop groping. She didn't have to find a name for it. She knew how it felt.

Chapter Seven

Hank's stories made terrorism so real for Jane that horrors seemed to lurk behind every door. She tried not to let Hank see how worried she was, but she took to spending her spare time, when she wasn't with Hank, in the greenhouses where the clear plastic walls would let her see who might be creeping up on her.

Enjoying her work in spite of everything, she filled a pot with forcing mix and alternated bulbs for reds and whites in the open circle preferred by the Forty Winks guest house. Absorbed in preparing the centerpiece, she didn't notice Hank cross the yard. When he opened the greenhouse door, she greeted him with a small shriek.

"Sorry." He smiled. "Someone named Thelma is on the phone. I said you'd call back, but she says it's urgent."

Jane washed her hands quickly and hurried to the house.

"It's Bobby, Jane," Thelma said, when she heard Jane's voice. "That skateboard of his. Why did they invent those things? Nothing's broken, thank goodness, but there's gravel everyplace he ought to have skin. Doc Brussel left a bunch of capsules, but Bobby's not going to get hooked on downers. Doc swears I'm a cheapskate and gave me free samples. I said not for my Bobby and I flushed them."

Jane was grateful for the normal-sounding emergency. "Is he okay?"

"He hurts, Jane. Would you hypnotize him for me?"

"Be right there."

Jane found her hourglass-style egg timer and hurried to her car. Hank kept pace beside her. Jane explained patchily as she backed out of the parking lot.

"How well do you know these people?"

Jane was startled by his somber tone. "Thelma's my dearest friend."

"The son's injuries, are you sure they're accidental?"

"What else could a skateboard be?"

"If everyone knows Thelma's your dearest friend, someone could have attacked the child to get at you."

Jane drew up to a stop sign and looked at him in horror. "You said the Hands of Allah hurt children when they want women to cooperate with them."

"It's not the Hands of Allah. If terrorists were behind this, they'd say so."

Not reassured, Jane turned onto a downhill street, plunging them into fog as thick as cotton batting. "Maybe they're making it mysterious so we'll start to hope it isn't them."

He reached one big hand to her shoulder, stroking her back. "You were upset before you thought it might be terrorists, Sandy. And somebody obviously *is* on our case. We're more likely to make sense of it if we work on it together. Tell me what's bothering you."

She didn't want to tell him, but keeping secrets wasn't fair, since she dug into him whenever he acted mysterious.

"I don't like to hypnotize," she admitted.

"Why do it then?"

"It started by accident." The fog was terrible. She slowed to a creep, slow enough to give the right of way to dogs and gulls. "A while back, I did a workshop in Spokane on cashflow management. Doing workshops gets me out of town." She paused to look at him.

"I met this guy who was making a lot of money but was still in trouble with his bank. His loan officer told him his income wasn't his until after all the bills were paid. He was furious—he hated the whole idea of net profit."

Disconcertingly Hank laughed. Jane nodded guardedly.

"He didn't have enough money to sign up for my course, so I agreed to trade workshops with him, and now he's doing great. He sends me a thank-you card with a copy of his balance sheet every year when he files his income tax."

She turned on the fog lights. "I learned from him, too." She paused. "He teaches hypnosis to professionals. Mostly dentists. And cops. But it helps in business because you can use it to make stage fright go away."

She stopped talking and thought about it a long time before she could get herself to tell him the rest. "Everybody pitches in around here, so I offered to hypnotize as my community service."

Her knuckles whitened on the steering wheel. "One day a local fisherman got horribly beaten up. Somebody wanted his boat, so they boarded, beat him up and threw him overboard. Puget Sound's so cold you don't last long, but he got lucky and washed ashore. A shell picker found him on the beach at the high tide mark. The sheriff called me."

She took a deep breath. "I hypnotized the victim. We got details he couldn't face remembering on his own, and they sent those three monsters to jail."

"Why does that bother you?"

She glanced at him with horrified dark eyes. "It doesn't. They were vile and deserved worse than they got. But he's a big tough guy and it took a lot of beating to do the job. His attackers were having fun. If you're the hypnotist, you listen to it."

She gnawed at her lower lip. He gently touched her mouth. She struggled to relax.

"There are other ways to be useful," he said.

"That's what the sheriff said."

She parked in a two-track driveway, which was almost invisible in the fog. "I help friends—this is the third time I've been down here for Bobby. But people here are good about it. They don't ask for what I can't stand."

They walked together through the moist air. Jane realized her distress had drawn Hank out of himself—he was a psychologist, after all, so he was trained to respond to others in distress. But it felt like more than that. It felt genuine. She set it aside to think about more when there was time. Concentrating on what she had to face now, she opened the back door and called out as she entered the kitchen.

Bobby was explaining before they reached his room. "It's not my fault, Jane, I was coming down the hill behind VanderWerff's where the sun gets in your eyes and then you hit this fog bank, it's neat, but I smashed into the curb."

"Plus a few trees?" Hank said.

Bobby turned a bandage-swathed head to squint at Hank through blackened eyes. "I turned three somersaults before I landed," he said with a friendliness that embraced willing strangers. "I counted."

"Good idea—counting. Keeps your mind off landing," Hank said.

"Dad told Doc he would give me a lickin' if he could find a spot that wasn't bruised," Bobby added.

Jane laughed comfortably. "Your poor dad."

Hank was surprised. She had been extremely distressed, talking about her skills in the car. He had expected that tension to remain in her voice, even if she could summon a reassuring smile. Intrigued by the depth of her self-control, he moved aside to where he could be inconspicuous while he watched.

Jane sat down on Bobby's bed and rummaged in her purse. "I brought my hourglass again, Bobby."

"I'm glad yours doesn't take an hour, but if Mom uses one, the eggs are still gross when the sand's gone."

Jane nodded seriously. "I like my eggs well-done, too, but I think three minutes will about do the job for you."

Bobby's gurgling laugh was infectious. Jane set the timer on his bedside table where it was slightly awkward for him to see it.

"Can I hold your hand?" He suddenly sounded as young and upset as he was.

"I'm in your dad's spot, Bobby, I don't know where it's safe to touch."

He made a scoffing noise. "Forget it, nothing's going to hurt more than another second, now you're finally here."

"That's true."

Jane looked him over carefully. One of his arms was entirely wrapped in gauze, but surgical cling left most of his other grubby hand free. Jane gently slipped her hand under his and locked their thumbs together reassuringly.

"Okay, mister." She reversed the hourglass and thumped its top. "This gadget may not do for hours of eggs, but it's a good Bobby-timer. Give it a look."

He responded with a gap-toothed grin and stared at the running sand. Hank watched the small suffering body relax. Coaxed by Jane's murmur, Bobby's brash energy eased.

Hank was surprised to find himself reacting to her reassuring patter, even though Jane was concentrating on the pale child she was talking to. Bobby's round blue eyes lost focus. His desperate grip lost strength. Hank felt his own breathing slow as trust flooded through him.

"What hurts the most?" Jane asked softly.

"My knees, ugh, Doc said I ripped holes in my jeans just so I could leave my skin on the sidewalk."

My wrists, Hank thought. Friction wounds take forever to heal.

"I'm thinking about your knees, Bobby. Tell me when they quit hurting."

Bobby grunted scornfully. "That's dumb, Jane, they felt fine the second you said 'knees.'"

Hank smiled and looked at his wrists. It doesn't completely work unless she holds your hand, he thought.

"Good," Jane said quietly. "What shall I say next?"

They worked slowly through the inventory until every body part Bobby had a name for was crossed off his pain list. He finally insisted he felt good everywhere. Jane roused him from his trance and sat listening to him talk.

When Hank realized she was waiting to be sure Bobby was fully alert, he joined in. "Can I talk you into shooting baskets with me sometime after school, Bobby? When you're off the sick list, that is."

Bobby's bruised face brightened. "You bet, this won't slow me down."

Jane laughed and stood. "Nothing slows you down."

"Isn't that the truth," Thelma said as she walked them to the back door. "I don't know why I worry, that kid's got more lives than an octopus has arms." She turned to Hank without a pause. "And you must be Jane's new friend."

Hank held out his hand. "Was it all right to ask your son to help me get some exercise? Games make it more fun."

Thelma's scoffing laugh was an amusing copy of Bobby's. "Depends on how much small boy you can take."

"It *is* different from cities, here, then? Everyone keeps telling me so."

Thelma clucked her tongue disapprovingly. "Which is why we live here instead of Seattle. Everybody sees everything here, so even if a stranger is creepy, which you're not, it won't matter more than a minute, and kids can hold out that long."

Hank grinned enchantingly. Thelma looked amused as she turned to hug Jane by way of thanks.

"You're good at that," Hank said as they got into the car. "I've never seen an approach like yours."

"Have you been hypnotized?" She tried not to sound as if she already knew the answer.

"The feds claim I resist," he said easily. "I was surprised when it didn't work. But watching you, I see what was wrong. They wanted power games, which make it hard to cooperate."

"How you go about it matters to the hypnotist," Jane agreed. "But I don't know if it matters to the subject."

"You bet it matters. After the feds gave up, they tried to insist it meant the Hands of Allah got to me first. But if that were true, I'd be easier afterward, wouldn't I?"

"Not really. Well, no, you're right, you might be."

He watched her face assessingly. "If you'd quarrel one side of this at a time I could follow you better."

"One side is the theory—if you've been hypnotized before, you know what to expect so you help it along. It works that way with Bobby."

He smiled. "I noticed."

"The other side is, you have to trust your hypnotist. And that's hard for adults because the world gets mixed in."

"Tell me about the world."

She was grateful for the humor in his voice. "If the government hypnotists tried dominance, naturally it didn't work—I can't imagine what it would take to dominate you. But they would have to admit they failed, so claiming you're under a posttrance suggestion gives them an excuse. They'd say your captors did it to keep you from being debriefed."

"This is why the feds won't let go of me?"

"Probably." She pulled into the parking lot and turned to watch him. "If they can't break you down it hurts them in their macho, so they cook up some heroic explanation."

The gradual blankness of his eyes betrayed his thoughts. He was seeing the debriefing room again, with its cynical guards, drug-assisted therapists and hostile hypnotists.

"I don't mean you aren't heroic, of course," she said to break into his painful meditations.

"Naturally." His wry smile faded quickly. "Is there some way to tell if I'm just hard to hypnotize?"

She nodded. "Physical tests. I don't use them. They seem like a battle of wills, so anybody resists."

"Like what?"

"Oh, I could have you stand and then try to talk you into losing your balance. The trouble is, I'm supposed to catch you if you do."

"One squashed hypnotist," Hank said.

They both laughed unconvincingly.

"We don't need tests, Hank. From what I see around the house, I don't think you'd ever accept a trance."

"How do you judge?"

"You have this charm," she said slowly. "You act open and obliging. Everybody falls for it. But underneath—"

She rubbed her forehead to help herself think. "What's the polite term for 'iron will'?"

He looked wistful. "Is there one?"

"What I mean is, you never surrender your control."

"That's not true."

She smiled to show his contradiction proved her point.

He shook his head. "If it were true, I wouldn't be here, Sandy. I came here because I absolutely trust you."

She reached for her keys, shying away from the emotional extravagance that roused her yearning but didn't seem to cost him anything. "If you dominate me over surrendering, which is that? Dominating? Or surrendering?

"You choose."

Jane was glad to laugh in answer to his mock-submissive smile since it gave her a way to break off the conversation before he noticed the questions he hadn't asked. She wouldn't be able to tell him whether their shared memories might make it possible for her to get him into a trance. And she couldn't guess whether he was in the grip of posthypnotic suggestion. If he was, then he was dangerous to everyone he met. She rebelled against the thought.

On the other hand, posthypnotic suggestion would explain a great deal quite efficiently. But the very fact that it was such a good explanation made it seem false—she was suspicious of simple explanations for behavior as complex as Hank's.

Fortunately Hank seemed satisfied. He went on with life and recuperation. He put up a basketball hoop in the patio without discussing it. And when Bobby arrived on his bike at the end of the week, Hank greeted him as if nothing concerned him but exercise. Jane heard them agree on their rules as she checked inventory in the greenhouses. When they began to play, their thumps and laughter reminded her of how much her life had changed.

"It's really nice of Hank to give Bobby something to do where he won't get hurt," Nyla said in the doorway.

Jane was touched by Oak Harbor's explanation of Dutch Bulb's new basketball hoop. "Hank's a friendly fellow."

Nyla zipped her wind shirt. "Fran's getting in soon?"

"After supper. Corinne's meeting her at the airport."

Nyla fidgeted with a trowel. "I really want to keep on working for you, Jane. Is Fran going to object?"

"No." Jane dangled her clipboard at her side to give Nyla her full attention. "She agreed before she left."

"But only for while she was gone."

"Okay, and so now she'll agree for the rest of your life."

"But her dad doesn't exactly adore my granddad."

"And Dutch Bulb isn't hiring either one of them." When Nyla didn't smile, Jane went on soberly. "I'm sure Fran will agree, but if she doesn't, I'll hire you myself. I've gotten so I count on you around here."

Nyla's narrow face lighted up. "It isn't what you pay me, you know. What matters is being with the plants."

Jane scowled. "It's *both*. Don't sell yourself short."

Jane touched Nyla's elbow. "I'll call you as soon as I've talked this over with Fran, but if waiting starts seeming too awful, you call me."

Nyla gave a small wave and headed home. Jane thought about her partner's return while she zigzagged through the dormant rooms with a stack of orders. Counting cool bulbs into mesh sacks that she closed with a label band, she dropped the filled orders into appropriate boxes on a handcart. When everything was gathered, she dragged the cart to the shipping room.

She sealed boxes and taped preprinted address labels as she listened to Hank thank Bobby for the game. Bobby yelled goodbye as his bicycle sprayed gravel in the parking lot. And Hank went inside to start dinner. The neighborhood settled back into its usual quiet. Jane smiled happily.

When a car turned into the parking lot, she looked through the plastic wall. Fran got out of the car carrying only an overnight bag, and waved goodbye to the driver. Jane sprang to the door, ready to meet her with a hug.

"You look great! You must have had a gorgeous time."

Fran's broad face had rounded during her Holland tour, and her corn-silk hair did nothing to minimize the change. A less confident woman might have gone on a diet, but Fran made her comfortable size work for her. It supported an exuberance that a smaller person couldn't have carried off.

"Aren't you early?" Jane added as she coaxed Fran back toward the shipping room. "Or did I get confused?"

"My plane was on time, which still happens in Canada, so I caught an earlier connection, which I could do because I sent my baggage airfreight."

"I was going to have all this done before you got here." Jane tapped the pile of order sheets. "Everybody's bulbs rotted in all this rain, and they figure, why call the weather an act of God when they can blame Dutch Bulb? I'm re-shipping for the sake of goodwill instead of arguing."

"Can we afford it?" Fran asked sharply.

"Listen to the world traveler pinch pennies."

Fran had the grace to look ashamed. She perched one generous hip against the wrapping table and fiddled with the overhead roll of UPS tape while she launched into a high-energy description of Holland. Finishing her last package, Jane vaulted onto the table, drawing her legs up and curling her arms around her ankles to rest her chin on her knees as she listened. Affectionately she watched Fran decide against getting more comfortable. It was all very well for Jane to sprawl in jeans, but Fran's European dress was a big geometric print in shades of red. It demanded dignity.

"So what's your news?" Fran asked at last.

"Same old stuff." Jane described her Festival plans.

"Jane," Fran interrupted. "When I left, there wasn't a man in your house. Now there is."

"Oh. True. Hank."

Fran's face was ideal for frowning since its squarish shape contrasted intriguingly with a downward turning mouth. "Tell me if that's a clear and complete explanation because I wouldn't know it otherwise.'' She sounded a bit exasperated.

Jane giggled, delighted by Fran's prickliness. "Hank's an old friend. I don't know what else you've heard.''

"I heard you've decided to break your own heart to see what's inside.''

Jane's smile faded. "It's kind of you to worry, Fran, but it isn't true.''

"It must be.'' Fran's forthright tone showed she knew her advice was unwelcome but she wasn't letting that stop her. "You claim you like to live alone, but then you take in a magnet for the TV news. You say he's sick and confused, but the people who've seen him around town don't think so.''

"He pretends he's recovering faster than he is.''

"However sick he is, I'm not prepared to go partners with an international spy ring.''

"Nobody thinks he's a spy.''

"No, they think he's lovesick. You know how sentimental this town is.''

"Lovesick.'' Jane laughed in order to pretend the description didn't hurt.

Fran shook her head. "Here's the point. You're not turning this business into an outlet for the international drug trade.''

"Fran, what *is* this! I'm still working on the same bottle of aspirin I brought with me when I moved here three years ago, you know that. And as for Hank, he won't even take the tranquilizers the government gave him.''

"Funny you mention the government. Why do you think they're still interested in him?''

Jane tried to keep her face from showing that she was worried about that, too. "For debriefing. It's routine.''

Fran's mouth hardened frighteningly. "Your charming boyfriend was all over the druggy part of the world for *months*. Add it up.''

"Amsterdam is a landmark city in the drug trade, Fran,'' Hank said affably.

Startled, both women turned. Hank stood in the doorway of the shipping room, looking unconcerned in a way
that made it clear to Jane he was willing to fight.

They'll have to settle it themselves, Jane thought. If
Fran's going to be blunt and Hank decides to be a reality
therapist, heaven help them both, but I'm not going to
choose between them.

"You're the expert on that," Fran said harshly.

"Then I wish you had consulted me earlier. It wasn't fair
to Dutch Bulb's reputation for you to go to Holland after
the Netherlands drug situation was written up in the *Wall
Street Journal*, where the whole world would read about
it."

Fran breathed out angrily. "Talk smart all you like, Dr.
Wandersee. But don't try to drag Dutch Bulb into your
muck."

"I wouldn't dream of it," Hank said formally. "And I
have to ask why you don't expect me to feel like that."

Fran stared at him instead of answering.

"You assumed the worst before you even saw me," Hank
insisted. "Why?"

"Your looks are supposed to change my mind?" Fran
asked, brutally looking him up and down.

"Not if you've already judged me."

Fran flushed. It was as close as she could come to admitting Hank had a point. Her reaction satisfied Hank.

"If the town thinks I'm dangerous, I wish you'd explain
what they see. I've had trouble finding out, because everyone's polite, and your partner protects me."

"No doubt." Dismay rearranged Fran's flushed face. "If
Jane were a mother hen she'd have grown five dozen wings
by now."

Hank's startled laugh helped to dissipate the tension.
Obviously misunderstanding, he held out his hand to Fran.

Jane watched sadly, knowing the conflict in their values
had put them on the spot. Hank would never dream of
joking with an enemy about a friend. But to Fran, a joke
had reasons of its own and needed no excuse to exist. Pre-

dictably Fran stared at Hank's hand. Typically Hank waited confidently.

At last Fran offered a businesslike grip. "You came to the wrong place if you meant to lie low, Dr. Wandersee."

"I'm more comfortable with people who call me Hank."

Fran ignored his appeal. "You'd have done better in Amsterdam. In a big city anyone can blend in."

Hank shook his head. "The best way to lie low is to ask a generous small town to make you their public secret."

"That *is* why you came to Oak Harbor, then?"

Hank smiled. "You know why I came."

Fran flushed, resisting an answer that could mean anything.

Chapter Eight

Falafel was Hank's favorite vegetarian meal, but that night he played with his portion as if he had lost his appetite.

"You were good with Fran," Jane said to try to help out.

He set down his fork. "I wish she'd stayed for dinner."

"We rarely share meals. It wasn't because of you."

He inspected his tabbouleh salad without much interest. "What part of the work around here will she do, now that she's back?"

"Local contacts. Including Clinton. I suppose it's natural for women friends to be annoyed by each other's tastes in men." She hoped it was an explanation that would soften the shock of Fran's rudeness toward him.

"If Clinton's her man, why didn't he go out to the airport to pick her up?"

"He's not into recreational dating."

Hank's automatic smile didn't reach his eyes.

It was something else to worry about. Fran didn't mention her feelings again, but her silence when she came to work destroyed their peace. Hank tried to ease her rejection by involving her in his routines. He asked her permission to continue running errands with Nyla. He apologized for the noise of his rowdy games with Bobby. He tried to talk to her about European travel. Nothing helped.

Jane blamed their personalities—Fran was too stubborn and Hank too civilized for them to find companionship easy. Even so, she was mystified when the tension went on for longer than a week. After spending the morning with her species experiments, she made up her mind to talk it over with both of them, beginning with Hank.

She went to the house. As soon as she entered the kitchen, she knew something was wrong. Hank was gone, but the house felt occupied, somehow.

She called. No one answered. She began to prowl—not wanting to find the kind of person who wouldn't answer, but not wanting to find the house mysteriously empty, either.

The house was empty.

She stood in her private office, where the sense of an invasion was worse. What *is* it? she thought. The worktable clutter looked disturbed. Her pot of *turkestanica* hybrids was too close to the edge of her desk.

When Hank came in from his walk, Jane was glad to have someone to tell. "Remember when someone went through your stuff? Apparently they came back."

He stood protectively close while she explained. "Could it be the government, do you think?"

"Why suspect the feds?"

She tried to smile. "Because you hate it when I suspect the Hands of Allah."

It wasn't a joke to him. "If terrorists came, there'd be nothing left."

When she stopped trying to make light of it, he saw how frightened she was. "I don't know what happened the first time, Sandy. But this time, I did it myself."

She was so shocked she decided she couldn't have heard correctly. One glance at his face told her she had.

"I had to search Fran's house. I was careful. I don't think she'll notice. But if she does, I wanted you to be able to say you'd been searched, too, so I rumpled our house up a little bit."

"Why?"

"Something's wrong about Fran. She was angry before she met me, and nothing I do helps."

"Not everybody has to think you're God's gift."

"You know that isn't what I meant." He sounded affronted. "You're much too kind to Clinton, for her sake. Why doesn't she return the favor by putting up with me?"

"Compared to what she feels like, she's being kind."

He shook his head. "You didn't expect her to react this way. I worried about it, remember, and you just insisted she's a friend."

His logic didn't help Jane feel less invaded.

"I've tried to think of some harmless explanation for her attitude," Hank went on relentlessly. "Maybe someone talked to her before she met me. Who's this Corinne who met her flight home?"

"A kindergarten friend. I irritate Corinne by liking my career—she doesn't think women ought to work for pay. But that isn't new. It wouldn't cause this."

"Fran works," Hank objected reasonably.

"Fran inherited Dutch Bulb. That excuses her."

"Okay, cross off Corinne. Did someone write to Fran?"

Shocked by the whole situation, Jane could barely concentrate. "Fran was gone only two months. No one wrote."

"Did they call?"

Jane covered her eyes with a trembling hand. "A lot of people here have relatives in Holland. Sometimes they call."

"If they call, they gossip."

Jane bowed her head, not bothering to answer in words.

"You ought to be glad." The sympathy in his tone softened the coldly rational words. "The only other explanation is the obvious one."

"Nothing's obvious to me."

"Drugs."

Jane lifted her head furiously, but before she could rage at him, she remembered that Fran had accused him of the same thing. Trapped between them, she sat down at her violated desk and propped her head on her fists.

"You trust everybody, and you *blindly* trust your friends," he said gently. "It makes you a perfect partner for a drug importer. Fran could use Dutch Bulb as a cover and you'd never suspect, but she'd have to get rid of me fast."

Realizing he had found a way to force her to choose between them, Jane looked up despairingly. "Hank. You can't live here and talk like this. I won't accept it."

He sat on the corner of her desk. "I won't mention it again. Anyway, Fran's house is clean."

"Is mine?" Jane asked bitterly.

"I didn't search our house," he said as if he were the one being tormented.

She couldn't control her voice. "I can't bear to think of you getting into Fran's dressers and closets. *I've* never looked in them."

"Do you think I enjoyed it? I felt like a pervert."

"You should."

As if he finally realized how profoundly disturbed she was, he stopped sitting on her desk. "Can you think of any other way to explain her attitude?"

"She thinks you're invading my life."

"We invaded each other's."

"That's what I told her," Jane admitted.

He looked at her bowed head, wondering how to deal with her shocked recoil. "I want to be fair about it, Sandy. I want to be checked out. For Fran's sake."

"Ask her, then."

"No, she can't do it. You'll have to."

Jane shook her head. "I can't do any such thing. Searching Fran was vile and it told you nothing. Learn from it."

"Hypnotize me."

Jane's heart lurched into double time. "No."

"I'd go to a commercial hypnotist, if that would work. But you said I'm probably difficult to hypnotize, which means you're my only chance."

"You're not difficult. You're probably impossible."

"You owe it to Fran to try."

"I can't hypnotize you! I can't even look at you, now that you've pawed through Fran's—" She stopped.

"Stop sounding like this is a lover's quarrel." He had folded his arms but he sounded merely rational not quarrelsome. "The problem is either Fran or me. Fran checks out, so that leaves me. Maybe I'm posttrance, controlled by the Hands of Allah. I know you don't think so, but we've got to check. Just like I had to check Fran's house."

It was blackmail, Jane decided. If she refused to hypnotize him, he would claim she was afraid of what she'd find. To prove he was as much her friend as Fran, she had to comply. The trouble was, he no longer seemed like a friend, exactly. If she told him so, she'd have far more to face than just a failure to hypnotize.

But she knew it was hopeless. He was the worst possible subject for her because of both personality and experience. He was used to being in charge. What was worse, he was pragmatic and brilliantly impervious to suggestion. Worst of all, he had recently been brutally mismanaged by government hypnotists.

On the other hand, he trusted her. It might make enough of a difference to him.

But it didn't help her. She didn't want to involve her spirit with his. He might see the truth.

What truth? she asked herself irritably. She had gone a little bit overboard about a charming, handsome man who was staying in her house temporarily, and who had been her friend for years. That was normal enough and nothing she needed to be ashamed about. Maybe he even felt slightly sentimental toward her.

She glanced at his face to see. He looked almost as agonized as he had the night he first arrived.

She had to help, whether she could or not, and so she faced their situation squarely. If he was in the grip of posthypnotic suggestion, it *would* be safer for them to know. And it might even spare them horrors yet to come, if she could find out what the Hands of Allah had planned for him to do.

Working on her own nerves first, she resigned herself. She didn't stand until she felt at peace.

"Let's go upstairs where we can get you comfortable."

"Do you need the egg timer?" He sounded anxious.

She shook her head. "It's just for kids."

"Will my academic training get in our way?"

"We'll just think about Cabin Seven. Our education didn't get in our way back then."

It was the technique he remembered from watching her work with Bobby. Like the professional he was, he couldn't keep himself from analyzing. She would reassure him. That was the stage they were in as they went to his room.

Next, she would establish physical trust. He lay down on his bed. She bent over him, untying his running shoes and slipping them off in a ritual way. She suggested he loosen his belt.

"Are you chilly?"

He shook his head. "Just right."

She hooked her fingers inside the crew neck of his sweater, feeling to be sure his shirt collar was unbuttoned.

He grinned. "This is more fun than I realized."

She smiled and sat beside him, her hip warmly pressing against him. Her confident silence blanketed his mind.

"Are you going to swing a coin?" he asked, jittery.

"Do you want me to?"

She had done the same thing with Bobby, he remembered. She had accepted little-boy aggressiveness so Bobby would feel in charge and relax for her.

Hank didn't want her to play games with him. "Just do whatever works."

She looked him over one last time, to be sure he was comfortably arranged. "All right, then. Look at my eyes."

"I've been doing that for weeks."

"I know. You put me into a trance every time."

The uncharacteristic flirtatiousness was meant to make him feel in control, he knew. But, distressingly, it worked the opposite way. Instead of pouring her soul into her eyes, as she sometimes did, she held him at a worrisome distance that kept her spirit out of his reach. Her murmur was encouraging, but not soothing in the way he had counted on.

He suddenly realized how totally she was a woman to him. He had taken her generous spirit for granted and accepted her openness casually. It had never crossed his mind that her lack of reserve was a voluntary act.

The discovery was unbearable. If she opened up to him because she was willing, she must also be able to make the opposite choice. She could shut him out.

She's doing that to me now, he thought resentfully—maintaining herself as separate in order to stay in control. It felt the same as if she were slamming her door in his face.

"I don't *want* to resist," he said distractedly.

"I know."

His rapid breathing told her how hard he was fighting. "Let's just talk for a while." As casually invasive as if he were Bobby, she stroked his cheek, resting her fingers gently beneath his eyes. "When you stop feeling self-conscious, we can try some things."

He shook his head, wanting to savor the feel of her hands as he moved his head beneath them. "It's worse than that. You're good at this stuff. You had me ready to respond there in Bobby's bedroom. But just when I'm ready to give in to you, something tromps in."

"That's normal. You should have seen Bobby the first time." She traced the distressed line of his mouth, trying to comfort him. "He lay there like he was in a wrestling match all by himself. He yelled that I was full of baloney until his mother got so mad at him I had to ask her leave so he could insult me in peace. He worked his way up to calling me a bossy biddy hen, which is going quite a way for Bobby."

Hank's mouth moved gamely beneath her hand as he tried to respond to her soothing story. "How did you win?"

"I didn't win. When he ran out of things to call me, I asked if he wanted some help. He couldn't really argue, because he was badly hurt, that time." She drew a line along Hank's jaw. "He fell off the neighbor's roof and laid his chin open all along here. I forget how many stitches."

"This is different, though, because I don't feel aggressive. But when you relax me, I lose track of who you are, and then I protect myself."

"For some people, it just doesn't happen."

His gaze wandered over her, comparing every inch of her body to the pattern he held in his mind. She waited patiently until he looked at her eyes again.

"It doesn't mean anything, Hank."

"I wish I believed you." He rolled to the opposite side of the bed and stood to move away, as if his staying close might damage her. "What kind of posttrance suggestion could I have? Besides one to keep me from cooperating with you?"

"I don't think that's true." Her compassionate tone shook his self-control.

"But what if?"

"Hank," she said thoughtfully. "If you write debriefing programs for the government, you must know all about this."

He crammed his hands into the pockets of his jeans. "Yes, but my analysis looks so grim that I hoped you might have some better ideas."

"I won't daydream nightmares with you."

He looked bludgeoned.

"Let's talk about the process," she suggested. "When someone I'm trying to hypnotize resists, I have them free-associate."

"It doesn't work for me. I get hung up on the theory. Maybe you say 'guilty.' I try to decide whether to say the opposite, 'innocent,' or a synonym, 'criminal,' or an application, 'vile,' or a context, 'law,' or give an example, 'myself.' I end up discussing it instead of responding."

She saw he had responded, even in refusing to respond. "You aren't an example. You aren't guilty."

He studied the floor. "I wanted this trance for proof."

"People care too much about proof. It's better just to know. You and I *know* what you're like. We don't need proof."

She hoped her argument reassured him, since it didn't help her. She *knew* why he resisted—it was his nature. But, as he said, what if...

"When I was over there in Fran's house—" He stopped. "In her closet—" He stopped again. "I couldn't believe I was doing such a thing."

His eyes darkened in misery. "They always say people in a trance won't do anything against their nature. But if I could search Fran's house, then I could do anything. All it takes to get someone to do something against their will is to make them look at it from an angle they'll accept."

Jane shook her head. "I'm sorry, Hank."

Chapter Nine

Dealing with Hank's fears drew Jane into a world of shadows that made Dutch Bulb's routine unreal. She sat in her office after the failed attempt to hypnotize him, struggling with a press release. But unless she could convince herself that Festival was the center of the universe, there was no point in trying to write anything. And there was no chance of that.

The phone rang. Hank answered since he was in the kitchen, starting a lamb roast. Without really listening, Jane heard his excited low laugh. He began talking in rapid French, his voice alive with pleasure.

You can go back to breathing, Jane told herself silently. It's nothing you didn't suspect.

She couldn't translate fast enough to be sure of all he was saying, but she didn't have to understand the words in order to realize what was going on. The rhythm of his speech was playful, musical, electrified. Every time he paused to listen, his silence ended in an enticing laugh.

It continued forever. Finally he tapped on her door. "Cooperate with this, Sandy. It's a call from Paris."

"I can read French, but I haven't spoken it in years."

"She speaks English."

How nice for her, Jane thought. Picking up the phone, she grudgingly said her name and then stood listening. At first, she noticed nothing but the voice itself. Throaty.

Breathy. A midnight voice. Just enough accent to make her English tantalizing.

Jane's heart splintered at this glimpse into Hank's real privacy. No wonder he resisted hypnosis from her. If he had someone to share his very center, it was perfectly right for him not to offer himself to anyone else.

She forced herself to focus on the lilting words as a way to distract herself—from what? Nostalgia? Jealousy? Now wasn't the time to try to figure that out.

"A Zurich trust fund assures you the prize will continue," the seductive voice said.

"Prize?" Jane repeated, realizing she had missed the point of whatever this voice from Paris had to say.

"My donation, yes. A large prize for newly developed tulips makes your Festival contest international because growers everywhere wish to compete, this is so? The same amount of money looks even larger in the desperate countries where Turkish bulbs grow. A few winning novelties convince the world how many different kinds of blossoms there can be. It is good for tulips. I know you join me in wishing this."

"I am interested in species tulips," Jane said unhappily. "And, yes, you're right—there should be new patents to encourage species breeders."

"*Henri* says how large a prize to offer." She named a figure in francs and did her math aloud as she changed it into dollars. "It is enough?"

Henri. Jane's mind ached.

"Yes, you're very generous. It's more than enough."

The voice laughed thrillingly. "Then we work together, you and I. I support the prize. You publicize."

"I can, I guess. I'm in charge of Festival publicity."

"There is a string."

"String?"

"The contest name. I choose it."

"All right, sure, that's a donor's privilege." Even to herself, Jane's voice sounded monotonously American in comparison to the other woman's.

"This prize is called—The Hands of Allah Competition."

The Hands of Allah? Hank's terrorists? Horrified, Jane slapped her pencil down on the counter by the phone.

"No. I'm sorry, no. Is this some kind of— Whatever this is, no. Leave us alone here. All of us."

A delighted laugh answered her. "The bank in Zurich will send you papers. It is my joy to meet you, Sandy."

The international connection was broken as casually as if it had been an old friend calling from across the street. Jane turned uncertainly to Hank. His eyes gleamed with pleasure.

There were too many questions. She started with the easy ones. "How did she find you?"

He grinned. "Sylvie knows all about you."

"Is she one of the terrorists?"

"No. She's a friend."

Jane frowned. "Then they've gotten to her, haven't they. They're coming after you, and this is the first step."

He shook his head, smiling. "She has safety zones, bodyguards, total security. There's no danger."

"A friend wouldn't honor your terrorists."

His smile widened. "She's celebrating. My being a hostage was grim, but this prize turns it into a joke."

"That's sick."

"To her it's not." He laughed. "Don't worry. She's got more money than she can get rid of and, poor gal, she learned early you can't be generous if you're rich because all you'll ever meet that way is leeches holding out a hundred hands. So she's got a rule—no presents. Dreaming up ways to work around that handicap gives her something to do."

Poor gal, indeed. Jane resented the uncomplicated pleasure in his eyes.

"People send flowers when you're recovering from a hospital stay," he added. "So, fostering new patents in my honor is Sylvie's way to send me flowers."

"Your trip to the hospital wasn't the main point."

His happy glow dimmed slightly. "Sylvie knows that."

His affectionate confidence made the larger pattern stunningly clear to Jane. The Hands of Allah had put him on a plane to the U.S. When he landed, he was swarmed, first by the media and then by the government. The federal hospital had released him only on condition that he would come to Oak Harbor. Making sure, they flew him there on a Navy plane.

He'd never had a chance to say where he actually wanted to go. Of course he would have preferred to return to Europe, where his friends were. But since that wasn't allowed, he made the best of a bad bargain. Ashamed, Jane realized she hadn't behaved better than anyone else—she had taken advantage of him by believing his gallant lie.

When she noticed he was watching her, Jane shook her head. "I'm sorry. I have no right to feel any of what I was thinking. I'll try to quit."

He seemed surprised by her distress. "Can you tell me?"

Could she? She couldn't confess that jealousy was slashing her to ribbons because she was the one who kept trying to make it true that she was merely a friend.

She decided to tell him the other part. "I was thinking that this proves you're fine. A phone call can trigger post-hypnotic suggestion, but if that's what this is, you wouldn't be happy. You'd be blank or distressed."

"Why even think of that, much less believe it?"

"This prize—the name she wants to use is *sick*."

He shrugged. "Not to her. Her world is games."

"And you like it?"

"To an extent, sure. It's her way."

"Then I'm sorry, Hank. I wanted to give you what you needed so you could heal and get on with your life. But I don't do games. For that, you'll have to go back to Sylvie." She wasn't able to keep the hurt out of her voice.

His jaw set. "If any other woman talked like that to me, I'd assume she was demanding I choose. But that's not you. You can't be possessive because you think love is therapy. I saw you doing it with Bobby. He needed affection so you gave it. And you do the same with me when I'm suffering—you're *so* tender. But you take it all back as soon as I get hold of myself."

"I don't take it back." It panicked her to say so, but that didn't matter because he was too busy quarreling to notice her distress.

"Yes, you do."

She decided to fight the less damaging part of his accusation. "Don't cheapen my feelings! I *like* Bobby, and he knows it."

Responding to her rage, Hank straightened formally. "Maybe you are annoyed, come to think of it. Sylvie called me from halfway around the world, and you don't like competing with that. You want Dutch Bulb to be the only shelter available to me."

"Competing!" It took a lot to raise Jane's temper, but that did it. "Dutch Bulb isn't available to you, not any longer. You're not dragging me into your sick games."

She stomped toward her office. A knock at the back door stopped her. It had been so long since anyone had knocked on her door that she looked blank. When she called, the sheriff walked in.

"Corny. How come you knocked?"

The sheriff's pale eyes were apologetic, and his sigh seconded the impression. "Official business, I'm afraid. Want to introduce me to your friend?"

"Oh, sure, haven't you met Hank?" Jane nodded toward Hank, though she was too angry to look at him. "Hank, this is Cornelius Postma, our sheriff."

Hank stood cordially.

"You know, Jane," Corny said, "I have a last name, I heard you mention it. Wonder if this young fella has one?"

Jane paled abruptly. No one in Oak Harbor had ever asked for Hank's last name. Utter silence filled the room. Jarringly, the refrigerator switched on.

As if the domestic sound were a signal, Hank nodded. "I'm Henry Wandersee, Sheriff Postma, but obviously you know that already. What can I do for you?"

"I'm supposed to hand you these papers."

Hank held out his hand.

Corny sighed gustily. "Glad that's over."

He walked over to the cupboard and chose a cup. Ignoring the tension that filled Jane's kitchen, he poured coffee for himself and sat at the table like a welcome friend. Adapting quickly, Hank sat down across from Corny like a cordial host.

Jane watched anxiously. "What is it, Corny?"

"Federal subpoena."

"What for?"

"Some mix-up there in the other Washington. No doubt intended to inform us of how much trouble they give themselves wasting our tax dollars."

Hank glanced at the papers. "When they told you to serve me with these, did they say why?"

Corny swirled his coffee and gazed at the whirlpool he had created in his cup as an excuse to avoid looking at Hank. "Some committee in the Congress wants to talk about terrorists. They seem to figure nobody gets loose on their own, so either you might be a spy, which they probably don't really think, or a drug runner, which there's no evidence of, or else what's more likely, you've got some secret method of walking away, which they want to patent and sell at an exorbitant price. I said the government's already watching every breath this boy draws, and hasn't he been through enough? But they said, never mind expressing an opinion. If I didn't serve this subpoena, some stranger would. So here I am, which I hoped you might prefer."

"Yes. Kind of you." Hank's voice was tense. "I'm being watched, did you say?"

Neighborliness didn't quite mask the embarrassment on Corny's honest face. "I was under that impression. When somebody's subject to a federal watch, quite often the locals know, but not always of course."

Hank narrowed his eyes as if they hurt. "Do you know who's watching me?"

"Small town like this, everybody pretty much knows everything." Corny's fatherly smile softened his refusal to answer. "Nothing to worry you."

"I've had a feeling that someone was on my trail. It never occurred to me that the government might be hiring them."

Corny scratched the short gray hair above one ear. "Oh, I wouldn't say anybody's taking money for it."

Hank turned to Jane. "Did you know that I was being watched?"

Jane nodded reluctantly. She wished they hadn't just been quarreling. Leftover anger made his questions sound brutal instead of reasonable. And she suspected her admission sounded cold to him instead of protective.

"Why didn't you tell me?"

"You'd know I'd hate it. You'd feel you had to leave, to protect my privacy. I thought you had enough to face."

"I see." He blinked as if his eyes wouldn't focus. "I should apologize." He rubbed his forehead. "It was selfish of me to lose my temper. Of course you're under a million kinds of pressure. I should remember it."

Pity softened the look in Corny's pale eyes. "Go ahead and blow your stack, both of you. Do you good."

Hank looked at Jane with a desperation that told her his weeks of healing were fast coming undone. His struggle for control was painfully obvious when he turned to face the sheriff.

"I could use some advice, sir. I'm ordered not to talk about myself until I turn in a debriefing journal the intelligence agencies will accept. If I break that agreement, I'll go to jail in protective custody. But here's this subpoena. It says if I don't bare my soul to Congress, I'll land in jail for contempt."

"Nice little crossfire they've fixed up for you," Corny said companionably. "Sounds an awful lot like jail whichever breath you draw."

"I can fix the subpoena, Hank." Jane stood up and reached for the papers.

He looked blank. "How?"

"They gave me a number to call if anything happened."

"They?" Hank asked in a dead tone.

Instead of answering, Jane turned her back and tapped numbers into the phone. She hadn't tried to memorize the number Maguire had written down for her—she hadn't needed to—it had insinuated itself into her mind without her choice.

"How've you been?" Maguire asked cheerfully.

The social question was disorienting. Jane decided to ignore it. "You said I could call if we needed help."

"Muscle is on the way. Where are you, home?"

"No, wait! Hank's the one who needs help."

"Sure, we knew that when we let him loose. We hoped he might keep a lid on because of the way he felt for you, but sometimes that works the other way. Is he listening?"

"Yes." She would have liked to ask what feelings they thought Hank had for her, but she knew she wouldn't believe them, whatever they said.

"Then don't let him read your face," Maguire said calmly. "Can you leave the room?"

"What kind of world do you live in?" Jane asked. "You said you'd help. Let me at least tell you what we need."

There was a pause. Finally Maguire said, "Go."

Jane explained the subpoena. There was another pause. At last Maguire laughed. "You sound so plausible, Miss Woodruff, I'm tempted to take this call at face value. That's disconcerting."

"It *is* meant to be taken at face value. Can't I call you about this?"

"Sure. It lends variety." He laughed again. "I'll have the subpoena quashed, is that what you're asking for? Tell Dr. Wandersee to forget it. Everything else okay?"

"We're both fine," she said evasively.

"Let me talk to the sheriff if he's still there. And thanks for calling, Miss Woodruff. Boss told me you have a good head on your shoulders, and I see he was right."

Irritated by the social-grace note, Jane held out the phone toward Corny. When the sheriff's attention was absorbed by the phone, Hank looked up at Jane with the same gallantly at-bay look he had turned toward the TV cameras the day she first saw him on the news.

"This means you're my jailer?" he asked neutrally.

"No, Hank. I'm not."

Unstoppable as always, he asked the same question a different way. "The sheriff said I'm under surveillance. Are you the watcher?"

"They think I am, but they're wrong."

"How many others?"

"So far as I know, I'm the only one," she said laboriously.

"No wonder you were so ready to coax me not to leave. You're good at it—you seemed so openhearted that I took it personally. I felt liked. But I suppose acting is easier if you feel you're serving your country. And no doubt they've convinced you that I serve the bad guys."

The total lack of heat in his voice made the accusation worse. Jane sat down across from him. He divides the world, she thought. He trusts one part—Sylvie. The rest of the world, including me, is out to get him.

Maybe it's true. She stared at the work-worn tabletop.

No, of course it isn't true! she decided angrily. He's not going to undermine my confidence.

She frowned at him assertively. "I know you feel betrayed, but I do, too. Please don't make a battle out of this. I don't deserve it."

"You don't deserve it? Does that mean I do?"

"Come on, Hank. You're not the kind of person who makes himself feel better by smashing someone else."

He ran a finger across his ear as if wiping her words away. "I'll clear out."

"Stop it!"

He looked at her with a cold, expressionless gaze.

"Don't you see what's happening? You were a hostage. You got into the habit of being a victim, so the whole world looks soulless to you. Sylvie's sick humor—if it *is* a joke—

you relate to that just fine. But if somebody really cares about you, you think they're haywire.''

Corny hung up the phone. "Well, sir, now that's more like it," he said in the friendly voice he used to break up street fights. "I like to hear young people getting it out in the open where anybody can spot its stingers and horns."

He waited until Jane and Hank both turned to stare sullenly at him as they tried to make visual sense of the image he'd described. "I met my wife at a wedding when we were both ten months old. You can guess that whatever there is to say about the sore spots a relationship works up, we've gotten around to in all this time."

"Oh, Corny, you and Hilda are happily married and you know it," Jane said in a defeated voice.

"That's what I said. I was sharing our secret of how to accomplish happiness while staying friends."

Some of the distress faded from Hank's eyes. "No doubt it helps to be married."

Corny nodded comfortably. "I've always thought so."

The two men looked at each other, negotiating without needing words for it. Jane felt shut out. In a few seconds, Hank will smile charmingly, as he always does, she thought painfully. And Corny will fall for it, like everyone else.

As she expected, Hank's shoulders relaxed. The set of his mouth softened. He matched Corny's fatherly gaze with a slow smile. Corny grinned and stood.

Jane felt drained.

"Now then, that's all settled?" Corny asked. "I've never held with leaving the house in the middle of a row, but I've been ordered to invite you downtown, Hank."

"What's wrong?" Jane's voice didn't sound like her own.

"Can't amount to much, I wouldn't think," Corny said.

Hank barely glanced at her as he stood. "You don't have to go on pretending you're in the dark, now that I know what your protection amounts to."

"Hank, you *don't* know," she insisted.

"But *you* do." Hank followed Corny toward the back door. "After all, you've been briefed."

Chapter Ten

Jane thought the whole thing through, trying to be fair. She had called Maguire because it was the only way she could think of to help Hank. Maybe she should have known Maguire would try to turn it against her and Hank, but she couldn't have known Corny would go along with him as if Hank's freedom were no big thing. And Hank had no right at all to join the plot by leaving so eagerly.

Repelled by the overwhelming male unity, she decided to give herself credit since no one else was ready to. She had rescued Hank from jail. And from the ordeal of congressional testimony. Good for me, she thought. She didn't allow herself to think about who ought to be saying that to her.

As always when she was disturbed, she went to the greenhouses. She trailed along the aisles, gaining composure from the scent of growing greens. By the time she reached her species tulips, her jangling nerves had eased.

She stopped to inspect a *saxatilis* hybrid she was working on. She hoped to breed its original lavender toward a luminous gray that would look like ice. Each plant grew inside a plastic hood to prevent random pollination. Seven of the plants from this generation had finally bloomed.

She brought her culture diary and a sterilized camel-hair brush from the workbench. Removing the hoods, she made her plans. So far, her crosses had paled out every trace of warmth from the blossoms, but the gleam had disappeared as well. Choosing the new generation's best glow, and the palest color, she hand pollinated the blooms.

When each plant was back in its protective hood, she wrote up culture notes. Contentedly she moved on to the dormant room. Hugging herself against the cold, she stopped at her bin of *saxatilis* lavenders, wondering how many generations it would take to change the blooms to ice.

As she ran her mind back over her three-year-long effort, she noticed that the bin label was gone. She had come to the correct bin by memory, so the tag didn't matter, but its disappearance was puzzling.

She glanced down the row. All the labels were gone.

Feeling even colder than the room, she inspected carefully. Nothing had been disturbed except the tags. Stepping outside, she walked around the area, looking for discarded labels, or signs that children had built a play fort, or tracks in the sea-sand path, or crushed spots in the invasive moss. She saw nothing out of order anywhere.

She decided not to mention it to Fran. If Fran knew anything about it, she would have complained, and she was already angry enough without being given a reason. But the neighbor on the other side might have seen something. Jane went to the house to phone next door.

Well past eighty, Edna sounded frail, but her spirit hadn't given an inch. "I did wonder, two nights ago," she said with trembling briskness. "Old ladies don't sleep, so I was in the kitchen about three, considering a glass of warm milk. I saw a flashlight in your greenhouse. I couldn't tell who it was, and I hadn't turned on the kitchen light, so they didn't know to wave to me."

"Weren't you going to mention it, Edna?"

"If us old ladies reported every light we see and can't explain in the middle of the night, there wouldn't be time to talk about anything else."

"That's no loss." Jane waited for Edna's pleased laugh. "If you notice anything else—"

"I sure will," Edna interrupted. "I never saw the kind of troublemaker who could stand up to a neighbor on the watch."

Jane went on with neighborly gossip a little while before telling Edna goodbye, and then she went to her private office so she could concentrate. Why would anyone take her labels? If someone wanted to enter Festival's new bulb contest without doing the work themselves, they'd take experimental bulbs, not her tags. And they'd take only one.

She tried to think of anything else that made sense. It couldn't be someone wanting to spoil her experiments because she knew the order of the bins, even without tags, and everybody knew she did.

There was one good thing, she decided, this time there was no possibility that the Hands of Allah were to blame. She smiled at the thought of terrorists flying halfway around the world just to steal greenhouse tags.

The crazy vision left her relieved, but it also showed her what was left. Her prowler must be the same local person who had made the crank phone call. And whoever it was, this invasion of the greenhouse proved they were angry at her, not at Hank. It confirmed what she had believed from the start.

She discovered she was grateful for this new mystery. It was such a silly, harmless act—stealing greenhouse tags—so she didn't have to worry anymore. And puzzling over it would keep her mind off Sylvie.

Or at least it helped. She curled up on her futon couch with a botanical history of Turkey and refused to let herself think beyond each page.

When it got too dark to read, she realized she had skipped dinner because Hank wasn't there to cook it. She ate an apple. Disturbed by the sense that the house was empty, she went to bed, remembering how peaceful her life used to be and missing Hank.

He might not come back, she realized as she turned out the light. She hoped that if he didn't, it was because he chose not to. It would hurt, but maybe it would be for the best.

She liked her work, and yet Dutch Bulb had certainly taken second place since Hank arrived. She quieted her mind, and forced her body to relax, muscle by muscle, and finally fell asleep.

IT WAS WELL AFTER MIDNIGHT when Hank was driven home by a Navy airman. He wasn't sure what reception Jane would give him but he regretted leaving her the way he had. He wanted to set that straight, even if she didn't want to hear it. He crossed the yard wearily, scanning the dark house. He knew he had no right to wish Jane had been too worried about him to sleep.

Using only the moonlight to find his way, he entered the unlocked house and went upstairs. Her door was open. He stood beside her bed and looked at her. Completely uncovered, she lay on her stomach in front of the open window like a neglected child.

At Cabin Seven she had told him that the least covering kept her from cooling off enough to fall asleep. He had been intrigued, wondering how a normal man would spend the night with a woman who felt drowsy only in an ice chest. During his captivity, it had given him a puzzle to work on as a way to shut out the unbearable reality around him. Their friendship hadn't gone that far at Cabin Seven, but he had never seen any reason why it couldn't, given time. And so he had lightened his imprisonment by imagining how she might lie on top of him. If they slept blanketless, her back would be exposed to the night cool so she could sleep. Her sleeping body would cover him with as much warmth as any man could need.

It should have been ideal for both of them—he still thought so, even though they'd faced mostly trouble since they'd met again. But why didn't trouble bring them together? he wondered.

She looked so trusting, uncovered in her unlocked house. She trusted everyone in the world but him.

Her sleep shirt was barely long enough to do its job. He studied the way the superfine knit rumpled, not quite covering her curves. Moonlight poured in through the open window, silvering her body. Charmed, he sat on the edge of her bed. She adjusted without rousing, rolling onto her side and curling against him. He watched her firm breasts strain the fabric of her sleep shirt as she breathed.

Moonlight reflected off his weatherproof jacket, and revealed her face. She was smiling, not from amusement but simply because she liked to be alive. A tendril of her long hair trailed across her cheek and clung to the corner of her mouth. He brushed it away and tucked it behind her ear. Reflexively her eyes opened. Vacantly they drifted closed again without any hint of focusing. He watched her long lashes settle against her cheek.

Does she know I'm the one who touched her? he wondered.

Of course she does, he answered, his heart surging protectively. If she'd given anyone else the right, she'd have told me.

After a moment, his lips curved down at the very end of his smile. She wouldn't need to mention it, he assured himself, because I'd know.

Warmed, he laid a gentle hand on her shoulder. Her already relaxed body eased further at the touch. Her responsiveness left him breathless.

But it also maddened him. I could be anyone, he thought. A drunk coming home to the wrong house. A drifter needing to crash. An ex-hostage on the run.

He sighed. He had no right to sit here looking at her when they'd been quarreling. Shielding her eyes with one hand, he reached to turn on the bedside lamp. She was slow to wake.

When she finally focused her eyes, she groaned. "Hi."

He watched her rub her eyes. "Doesn't it even startle you to wake up with a man sitting on your bed?"

"Sorry. I suppose I should have screamed." Reminded of his angry parting words, she pulled her sheet up to her chin.

He tried to ignore the defensive gesture. "Cooling my heels out at the Base gave me a chance to see how all this must look to you. You could have waited till breakfast to hear me say that, but I'd like to get some sleep myself. I know I won't be able to sleep as long as I feel guilty."

"It's all right." She scooted up in bed. Her voice sounded touchingly rusty with sleep. "What did they want?"

"They said they've been wanting a medical check, to be sure I'm recovering, and your call gave them an excuse."

"That's nonsense."

He nodded. "What they really wanted was to know why the town is worried about Fran's attitude toward me."

"Who told them about that?"

"Maybe the sheriff." He touched her knee to quiet her protest. "His job means he has to talk, if they ask."

"Should I tell them it doesn't matter?" She yawned gigantically. "Or maybe they know, since they let you go."

"It's why I woke you, Sandy. They think the same thing I do about Fran—her reaction doesn't make sense. I said I searched her house, but they don't accept that as proof of anything."

Jane closed her eyes. "I doubt they care. They probably just want you to dislike yourself."

He had expected anger again, but she only looked sleepy. Her total lack of self-consciousness was more disturbing to his senses than flirtation would have been. Her sheet slipped down to her waist, ignored. He watched it rumple around her, unable to curb his imagination.

"They wouldn't release me until I promised to watch Dutch Bulb. It felt like a just punishment because I was brutal to you for accepting that same bargain. I'll leave if you tell me to."

She shook her head. "That's what they want. You know—watching makes us feel like we have secrets. Tattling means we've betrayed each other."

"You didn't betray me by calling Maguire. I betrayed you by getting angry about it." He reached for her hand. "Now that I see the real situation, I'd like to start again."

"No. We've both been doing the best we can." She lifted his hand to press his knuckles against her sleepy frown. The innocent gesture seemed more intimate to him than the most blatant suggestiveness from someone else.

"Good. Provided we change one thing."

She sighed and looked at him.

"I want dead bolts on every door in this house. Anyone could have walked in here while I was gone."

She shook her head. "Dead bolts don't work in a small town. My friends will go right on walking in."

"Is everyone in town your friend?" he asked, not seeming to realize how brutal the question was.

"Yes. Sure," she answered loyally, but the expression in his eyes shook her confidence.

Chapter Eleven

After a week passed without event, Jane stopped looking at everyone as a possible greenhouse burglar. She stood in front of a women's mirror in the Island Mercantile as optimistically as she would have done last year. Like everyone else in Oak Harbor, she had come downtown for the spring clearance sale.

"Choose that stripe, Jane, the one you've got on is much too plain." Minnie Bostetter's pleasantly round face broke into a hundred creases when she smiled.

"Thanks, Minnie, I hate deciding for myself." Jane shrugged out of the ivory jacket and put on the first one she had tried. The simple tailoring was similar, but this one gained interest from broad stripes in four shades ranging from cream to a brown that matched her pants.

"That's it. Real good with your coloring."

Jane smiled. "What about you?"

Minnie held a dress against herself, its silver-and-blue print reminding Jane of dimes cast over a summer sky.

"Emphasizes your eyes," Jane said. "Is it for judging the bulb contest?"

"It's handy you mentioned that, Jane. I'm going to just do what I enjoy, which is play hostess, and I'll beg off what I don't like, which is getting everybody sore at me."

"What does that mean, exactly?"

Minnie looked into the mirror to meet Jane's eyes. "You can invite this Canadian judge to be my houseguest. If she stays with Boss and me, everybody'll know I approve of her.''

"There's no Canadian judge, what are you talking about? *You're* the judge.''

"That's what I'm saying, and you'd hear it if you'd listen. With this big new prize, there are bound to be at least Canadian growers. Maybe even Europeans will get interested, except I don't know if there's time for them this year, although maybe, if they get a wiggle on.''

"So what? Nothing's changed really.''

"You perfectly well know *every*thing is changed. The new publicity you got out made me notice what had come creeping up on my blind side. Boss always says I act like an ostrich just to prove I've got the rear end for it.'' Minnie patted her ample behind in a charmingly satisfied way.

"There's a lot to choosing. I never minded too much when it was just between Pauline, up in Lynden, with those red-and-yellow virus parrot tulips of hers, or else Maxine, over in Mount Vernon, if you happen to like more black in the red every year. But we were getting a little too famous for me, even before this new prize. Last year, if you remember, a contest bulb came clear from Michigan, I forget the name.''

"Don't desert me," Jane said pleadingly.

"No, now, think about it. I love those star clusters of yours, you know I do, you gave me some for Christmas when I asked for them. If a star like that showed up for the contest, I'd give it the prize, and then what kind of pickle am I in? There's going to be plenty of the other kind, and people might wonder how I failed to notice them. Ruth there in Anacortes—Clinton's already seen her entry, and he says it's going to be the best. Brick red. That easy shape kindergarten children draw.''

"Clinton doesn't know anything about bulbs.''

"Of course not, but he knows what he likes, and he's likely next year's Festival director, so there's no point in offending him this year, which is what I'd do if I judged the way I feel. And I couldn't pretend I didn't know any better than to pick the prettiest, because Clinton's good enough to express his views before you talk yourself into a jam by accidentally saying what you think and contradicting him."

"His bark's worse than his bite."

"Really?" Minnie's eyebrows rose, to express wonder. "There now. I've known Clinton since his grandmother was a girl, and I never knew he bites."

Jane laughed, amused as always by Minnie's homespun canniness. But she decided not to let Minnie lead her away from the real question.

"Is the new prize causing trouble?"

Minnie looked disgusted. "It's more these phone calls."

"What phone calls?"

"Everyone's getting interviewed. They don't know how they feel about it, and to tell the truth, I don't, either."

"Were you interviewed?"

Minnie patted her hair stagily. "As last year's judge, they said, but I had my doubts. I didn't say anything to worry a person—just rambling is the best way to make people give up plaguing you without quite knowing why they did."

"What's going on, Minnie?"

"Sometimes a person has to be brave enough to accept a little help, which now seems to be your turn. Nobody's doing anything that everybody else isn't doing, so I wouldn't worry. And now I'd just as well go find Boss," Minnie said, expertly moving the conversation along before Jane could ask more questions she wouldn't answer. "I suppose that young man of yours is around here somewhere, too?"

"He's looking for sweats," Jane said, still thinking about the phone calls Minnie wouldn't describe. "He's on an exercise program. He's worked his way up to jogging."

"While we've been standing here, I've been trying to spot some stranger who isn't from the Base."

"Do an about-face and open your eyes."

Both women laughed and turned around.

The mayor had collected Hank from unisex sportswear. He took care of introductions in an amiably high-handed way which showed that Hank didn't need a last name. Jane went to the dressing rooms to change back into her jeans, thinking about the obvious conspiracy. Whatever was going on, it seemed to be something Oak Harbor thought it could handle.

Leaving the dressing room, Jane was touched to see the mayor and his wife blocking the central aisle while they laughed and gestured and called attention to their welcome for the community newcomer. Hank was at his best, looming over the unpretentious public couple with a bedazzled smile.

Feeling grateful for Oak Harbor's protective kindness, Jane joined the conversation. It was hard to believe any member of the community would be after her, but they'd certainly have to stop, now that they saw she and Hank were favored by the mayor and his wife.

"Did you find your sweats?" she asked as she left the store with Hank.

He nodded as he tossed a gold-and-navy Mercantile bag into the back of the car and settled into the passenger seat. "Boss says I can run on the high-school track. You can get shin splints running on the street, and I notice some of the Navy men run at the school if they live in town."

Jane nodded. She knew how much it meant to him that he finally felt well enough to run again.

"In Europe, you have to run in the streets. It's not something people do, there, so they're not set up for it." He grinned. "You're alone at it, and people think you must have some reason. Like maybe you're getting away from a bank you just robbed. The *gendarmerie* are likely to ask to see your passport.

"I was stopped several times by the police," he went on, enjoying his recollections. "And once in a while some tough guy would offer to help me escape from whoever, which was amusing."

Jane smiled at the cultural discrepancy. She knew he was looking for topics he couldn't force himself to talk about, since he'd been told that was one way to check for posthypnotic suggestions. But she also knew he wouldn't have taken the risk of testing these random memories with anyone but her.

When they reached home, Fran was waiting for them, pacing in a way that made Dutch Bulb's kitchen seem small. "I booked an appointment for you, Jane. Friday, two o'clock. Journalist and camera from Seattle."

"They're coming here?" Jane glanced at the poster-size calendar thumbtacked to the wall beside the phone. "Minnie mentioned phone interviews."

Hank stopped on his way across the room. "Interviews?"

Jane wished she had already told him about the calls so he wouldn't have to find out from a hostile Fran.

Fran scowled. "The phone interviewers were following up on tips. This appointment of yours isn't just fishing."

"What kind of tips?" Jane asked.

"Journalists never say." Fran sounded impatiently tolerant.

"This call, what does he want?" Hank asked.

"She," Fran corrected sharply. "She wants to profile Jane for her contribution to northwest growers."

"Was that the truth, could you tell?"

"How do you decide?" Fran snapped.

Jane felt sorry for them both. Fran's thistly nature had its own appeal, but she needed a peaceful life in order to show herself at her best. And Hank was so used to being charming that he didn't know how to react when his basic existence was taken as an offense. Jane was sure they both wanted to be generous, but the best they could seem to do was to stand rigidly, not looking at each other, their shoulders uncomfortable, their mouths flat, their jaws square.

"Let's not worry," Jane said. "The right kind of publicity will help Festival. And if she wants the wrong kind, I'll just clam up."

It was a sensible plan, though none of them felt reassured.

THE JOKER GOES WILD!

Play
this
card
right!

See
inside!

HARLEQUIN
WANTS TO <u>GIVE</u> YOU

- 4 free books
- A free bracelet watch
- A free mystery gift

IT'S A WILD, WILD, WONDERFUL
FREE OFFER!

HERE'S WHAT YOU GET:

1. *Four New Harlequin American Romance® Novels—FREE!*
Everything comes up hearts and diamonds with four exciting
romances—yours FREE from Harlequin Reader Service®. Each
of these brand-new novels brings you the passion and tenderness
of today's greatest love stories.

2. *A Practical and Elegant Bracelet Watch—FREE!* As a free gift
simply to thank you for accepting four free books, we'll send you
a stylish bracelet watch. This classic LCD quartz watch is a
perfect expression of your style and good taste, and it's yours
FREE as an added thanks for giving our Reader Service a try.

3. *An Exciting Mystery Bonus—FREE!* You'll go wild over this
surprise gift. It is attractive as well as practical.

4. *Money-Saving Home Delivery!* Join Harlequin Reader Service®
and enjoy the convenience of previewing 4 new books every
month, delivered to your home. Each book is yours for $2.74*—
21¢ less per book than the cover price—plus 49¢ for postage and
handling for the entire shipment! If you're not fully satisfied, you
can cancel at any time just by sending us a note or a shipping
statement marked "cancel" or by returning any shipment to us at
our cost. Great savings and total convenience are the name of the
game at Harlequin!

5. *Free Newsletter!* It makes you feel like a partner to the world's
most popular authors...tells about their upcoming
books...even gives you their recipes!

6. *More Mystery Gifts Throughout the Year!* No joke! Because home
subscribers are our most valued readers, we'll be sending you
additional free gifts from time to time with your monthly
shipments—as a token of our appreciation!

GO WILD
WITH HARLEQUIN TODAY—
JUST COMPLETE, DETACH AND
MAIL YOUR FREE-OFFER CARD!

IT'S NO JOKE!

MAIL THE POSTPAID CARD INSIDE AND
GET FREE GIFTS AND $11.80 WORTH OF
HARLEQUIN NOVELS — *FREE!*

Jane spent her time until Friday trying to figure out any pattern that might explain all their difficulties. No one theory seemed to make sense of everything.

By the time she went to her room to dress for the interview, she had a kind of plan. If she could find out who was behind the interview, she might be able to use that information to figure out the other unusual happenings.

She knew she would be a better questioner if she didn't rehearse, so she concentrated on her clothes. Wanting not to look too dressed up, she tucked a cream linen shirt into her jeans and crossed the hall. Hank's door was shut.

When she knocked, he turned from the window, oddly subdued. His computer screen was half filled with green letters. Whatever he was working on must have disturbed him. She decided that he needed a distraction.

"Can I interrupt a minute? I need advice."

He sat on the edge of his desk to seem approachable, but Jane sensed he was still preoccupied. She pulled the rocking chair closer and sat down.

"This might be a legitimate interview, you know."

He nodded. "Try to find out."

"Sure. And if it is, what shall I say about Sylvie?"

He answered with a very French shrug. "She won't care. Say whatever you want."

"Where does the money come from?"

"Are you asking for the journalists?"

"In case they ask." It was partly true.

She met his gaze steadily. If he saw jealousy in her eyes, well, that was true, too. And she had a right to her feelings, whatever he wanted to believe.

He sighed. "Sylvie's grandfather was both lucky and driven, and he managed not to lose his fortune during the European war, so his son and granddaughter had it made. I know you think she's sick, but what would you expect? After two generations of recreational wealth, what she is is not her fault."

"I'm not criticizing her." Jane refused to sound defensive. "She won't see the interview, but I want it to be something she'd feel all right about if she did see it."

"Maybe I should warn you." He glanced at the window and spoke too quietly. "Sylvie thought I was a spy when she met me. If you're an American with connections in different countries, all Europeans assume you're CIA. I admitted to having done contract work for the feds before they started treating me like the enemy. She loved it."

"She *wanted* you to be a spy?"

"She's never known one and she wonders what they're like."

He watched her eyes darken. Deciding her reaction was fear, he frowned.

"Look, I know how that sounds here in Oak Harbor. It sounds like she ought to be in a cage. But that's not what it's like in Paris."

Jane decided she didn't want to hear about Paris. "I'm glad you told me." She tried to act like a good sport. "I'll leave it up to you about the cage. You know her, I don't."

He folded his arms. "She's no different from any other European, on that topic. Every time you board your plane and then the flight's delayed, you're suspected. If you're American but not a scruffy backpacking kid, all other nationals are absolutely certain you're CIA."

"It sounds awful, Hank." She pretended not to notice his accusing posture and tone of voice. "Why did you stay?"

"I liked the work." He still sounded on guard.

"I can understand that—I like to travel, too." She wanted to prove she knew what he was talking about. "I'm doing a workshop in Vancouver next week, in fact. It's an interesting city. Want to come with me?"

"They took my passport."

"You don't need a passport for Canada."

"I'm probably not allowed to leave the country."

"Did they say so?"

"No."

There was a total lack of interest in his blank eyes. Bewildered by his rejection, Jane stood.

"When I suggest something that doesn't sound fun to you all you need to say is 'no.' Don't use the government as an excuse."

Without hurrying, he reached the door before she did. His hand beat hers to the carved knob and he turned to face her almost like a host.

"Did I misunderstand? I thought you were putting me on a leash to protect Oak Harbor while you're out of town."

"You're not hurting Oak Harbor."

"I won't hold that remark up to too much light," he said teasingly. Intently he watched the set of her mouth soften as she realized he was trying to repair the damage his black mood had done. "I could use a break, if it won't cause trouble. My staying here caused trouble, so maybe my leaving won't."

Remembering why she couldn't stay to discuss it now, he gripped her shoulder like a coach encouraging a jock. "Good luck with the interview. You look just right. Organized, but genuine."

Soothed by the professional courtesy, she went downstairs, mustering her confidence, to greet the journalists.

Karen Wilcox introduced herself in a clipped way that fitted her gray suit and short brown hair. As a creative type, Karen's photographer, Tim Baker, was dressed casually in a sweater and jeans. His gear bags covered him with straps.

"What works best is for you to just tell us your whole life and I'll do the sorting out later." Karen's smile looked preprogrammed. "Mind if I tape?"

"Taping's fine, but I prefer a more structured approach," Jane said, taking control as she led them to the lounge. "By the time I asked my partner, she'd forgotten what magazine you work for."

"*Seattle*. But this interview is a lot more than local interest. I've got 'do send' agreements from the biggies— *Better Homes and Gardens*, that's eight million circulation. *Flower and Garden*, about two thirds of a mil. And *Horticulture*—smaller circ, but fanatical."

Jane gestured them toward seats. "Why this year, particularly? Our contest hasn't been interviewed before."

"There's this new prize. It's huge. People like to think about that much money riding on luck."

"Breeding new bulbs has nothing to do with luck."

"Oops. Foot in mouth." Karen grinned engagingly. "You're a breeder, I'll bet."

"As a sponsor, I don't enter the contest, but yes. Those tulips are mine." Jane pointed to the pot on the coffee table that was filled with multiple blossoms which opened completely flat to show triangular salmon petals with black hearts.

"Are those tulips?" Karen sounded startled.

Jane nodded. "Species tulips. There are hundreds of different kinds."

Karen bent over the pot cautiously, not offering to touch the flowers. "I've never seen anything except, you know, tulip-looking things."

"Most people haven't," Jane said. "It's a shame."

"What about a tour? Maybe we could get some pictures." Tim interrupted in a tone implying they had gotten into more than they expected.

Jane led them outside to usher them through cold houses, which slowed down early blooms, and through forcing sheds, which hurried summer flowers. She knew their interest might be merely polite, but if it was, they were good at it.

Ending the tour at the potting tables, she pointed out an arrangement of blossoms clenched as tight as fists. Petals on the inner ring showed faint canary streaks, and buds on the outer plants promised a mottled mahogany. Both kinds were out of phase. In nature, the canary should have blossomed and dropped already, while the mahogany wouldn't normally develop color for weeks.

"I did this for the high-school botany class three years ago, when I was new here, and one of the mothers couldn't get over it," Jane said as Tim stroked the velvety petals. "Now she gives a spring party so she can decorate her house with pots like this."

"Charming," Karen said.

"Have I got this right?" Tim sighted through his camera. "For tulips, there's Holland, and then there's Turkey?"

"More or less."

He nodded. "With the big dark eyes, and the luscious bod, you'll do for the Turkish half, except cover up that sandy mop. Maybe a big floppy hat?"

Karen touched Jane's elbow. "It's just how he talks. All he means is, you're attractive. You must have heard that often enough. His problem is he thinks with his eyes and doesn't consider how the words will sound."

"It's all right," Jane said.

"What about the Holland part?" Tim said, not in the least rebuked. "You have a partner. Is she a blue-eyed blonde by chance?"

Jane shook her head. "I don't think Fran's interested in this."

Karen looked at Tim.

"Get someone," he said negligently.

Karen turned back to Jane. "We'll take care of asking her so you aren't to blame." Her smile was knowing. "Which of us is more likely to seem charming to her?"

Jane sighed. "You're both strangers. I'll call her myself."

Fran came to the potting shed without complaint. She seemed to enjoy the photo session, posing obligingly beside simple red tulips while she talked about her trip to Holland. Encouraged by Karen's tactful questioning, she added memories of growing up in a home where spring flowers were the world.

Jane was horrified. Fran never talked cordially to strangers. And usually when she had to let her picture be taken, she was thistly for days.

Could her easy cooperation mean she had arranged the interview herself? Jane wondered. After all, Fran *had* said this call was different from the other interviews. And the most obvious way for her to have known that was to have arranged it herself.

Dreading what she might learn, Jane listened intently. When Fran said goodbye and left the potting shed, Jane decided checking up was worth the risk.

"Did someone invite you here?" She didn't pretend the question was casual.

Karen answered with a woman-to-woman look. "You obviously know your way around, so up-front is best. You know why we're here. We want an exclusive. Will you help us?"

"Maybe." Jane was glad to bargain honestly. "There's a lot I can't say. But I'd like to know how you found me."

Karen lifted both hands shoulder high, palms outward, as if showing she was unarmed. "We got Wandersee's passport number from Customs. Used it to get his social security number. Used that to find out who he worked for last."

Since Karen thought she was sophisticated, Jane decided not to say it shocked her to hear how available private records turned out to be.

"The feds harass Options constantly," Karen added. "So Options was glad to give us a copy of Wandersee's résumé in exchange for a rave write-up saying how wonderful they are and what a blessing they are for America."

"Can you do that?"

"Sure, easy. They're interesting people." Karen paused, giving Jane a chance to pursue that if she wanted to.

Jane nodded.

"Wandersee's résumé lists a Paris mail drop," Karen continued. "No home address in the U.S. Next of kin: 'grandmother, deceased.' So that left nothing to go on except his university."

"It's a blind alley if you call the alumni office, but we're good at digging," Tim said, sighting through his camera at Jane's shelf of culture journals.

"Wandersee's research professor has retired, and so he feels free to gossip now. He doesn't watch the TV, but we told him what Dr. Wandersee said on the news. We thought it was a long shot, and he thought it was impossible, but he looked up Dr. Wandersee's records and gave us your name. The University provided your address."

Jane sighed. "A university never destroys anything."

They both nodded. "Thankfully."

"Yes, I'm glad, too. I was afraid you might be in touch with someone here in Oak Harbor."

"Who?" they asked in unison.

Jane shook her head. "I couldn't imagine."

They laughed as if her answer seemed like irony.

"What can you give us in exchange?" Karen asked.

Thinking carefully about every word, Jane described the call from Sylvie. After a cautious pause, she added Hank's explanation of what the new prize was supposed to mean.

Karen sighed. "Is she weird, or what?"

Tim chuckled. "She sounds interesting."

"That's what Hank—" Jane stopped.

"You call him Hank?" Karen asked to verify. "Is it true the government has him? Do you know where?"

"I guess he isn't free," Jane said as a kind of answer. "But I don't know why not."

Karen pulled a leather card case out of her jacket pocket. "Call when you can talk. Don't try to decide what's important, you won't know what might help us."

Jane nodded. "You've been more than fair."

Karen laughed and held out her hand. "We don't hear that too often."

Wondering if she had given away too much, Jane watched the journalists return to their car.

Chapter Twelve

Jane parked in Vancouver's Elizabeth Park a few minutes before it was time for the ten o'clock coffee, which would launch her workshop. "There's a city map in the glove compartment. Most people go to Stanley Park. It has the best zoo on the Pacific Coast, and the seawall walk is gorgeous when the fog burns off."

They both got out of the car.

"I'll walk around here, to start," Hank said. "What's in the geodesic dome?"

"A garden with tropical birds living free. It's wonderful. That's why I schedule workshops here." Jane stepped onto the raised pathway of four-by-four planking, which connected mock Japanese pavilions leading to the dome. In the lobby, she gave a half wave before she turned away.

The workshop convener swept her into an avidly talking group of women who displayed the hallmarks of small-business owners. Decisive, forceful, they were appealing in a way that put conventional attractiveness beside the point. Some of them were good-looking, but others were only intensely alive, and the difference didn't matter.

Energized as always by their eagerness, Jane memorized names and faces and listened encouragingly to horror stories. Business people everywhere liked to talk about billing dodges and shipping foul-ups as a kind of ordeal humor that showed how much they liked their lives, trouble and all.

When the group seemed ready, Jane drifted toward the presenter's spot. Everyone followed her lead, flocking to chairs at the conference tables.

"Love affairs and corporations run into trouble the same two ways," Jane began. "There's cheating and there's neglect."

The participants were engaged by Jane's startlingly simple rule. Trying it out to see if it could possibly apply, they muttered to each other behind their hands.

"That makes solutions easy," Jane went on. "Your partner mentions bankruptcy? Suggest procedures that work for marriage renewal. Got heart trouble? Look into damage control."

The participants laughed, but it took an effort for Jane to grin. She knew she was offering good advice. Why didn't it help her? After all, she had an accountant among her services and a counselor in her household. Why wasn't that enough?

But she hadn't come to Vancouver to think about herself, she remembered. She straightened and gave her whole attention to her work.

As always when she addressed a lively group, the day flew past. She left the building in a swirl of cheerful women. Walking slowly, she agreed to answer letters, take phone calls, keep in touch.

She spotted Hank leaning against the railing at the crest of the high ground. He looked more comfortable than he had in weeks, his fair hair tossed by the breeze, his easy grin brighter than the late-afternoon sunshine.

The two men beside him contrasted with his golden look. Disciplined black hair. Richly tanned skin. They seemed too entirely at home to be tourists asking about the view.

One of Vancouver's pleasures was the human variety it offered. They could be anyone, she reminded herself anxiously.

Hank shook hands and gripped shoulders affectionately before starting toward the car. They aren't strangers, she thought frantically.

He was waiting in the passenger seat when she reached him. "You have a good manner for that kind of work. No wonder they come away thinking their lives are changed."

She was too alarmed to answer his compliment. "Who were those men you were talking to?"

"Friends." He held out the keys. "I could have introduced you, you'd like them, but I thought your day had probably been long enough already."

"In a city of over half a million, you just happened to run across two people you know who also just by accident look like they could be the ones who held you hostage?"

He had taken off his jacket as the day warmed. She watched his chest expand, stretching the fabric of his shirt.

"They're Canadian citizens," he said slowly. "Brothers. They're business people. They aren't political. They aren't like the Hands of Allah in any way."

The men he had been talking to crossed the parking lot at a leisurely pace. They got into a black Renault with blue-on-white British Columbia license plates.

"Their business and home phones are published in the telephone directory," Hank added in a controlled voice. "I called and asked them to meet me here so you wouldn't think I'd sneaked off somewhere disgusting for satanic rites."

Jane was dismayed by his aggressive answer. "Hank, wait. I've talked myself into thinking someone in Oak Harbor has some kind of grievance against me. It hurts me to have to suspect my friends, but at least I'd thought it meant everything else was all right. Except now this. Do you really think it was wrong for me to mention it?"

Hank leaned back against the headrest and stared at the sun visor. When he finally spoke, his voice was harsh.

"My friends import Italian leather goods and Greek furs. Their parents do the European end of it—I met the parents first and liked them so much I hung around. Eventually I met these sons on one of their visits home. They were having trouble cracking into the business community in eastern Canada. I mentioned that I'd heard Vancouver has a reputation for being open to foreigners from everywhere, though I couldn't swear to it myself since I hadn't been here.''

He blinked slowly. "They decided to follow up on my suggestion. Their move worked out well. The whole family wanted me to see for myself. I promised to call if I ever got to their new city.''

He breathed deeply, hating every word he felt forced to say. "Were you ordered to bring me here in the hope I'd get in touch with someone so the feds could make their life a burden to them because they've been so ill-advised as to remember me? I won't tell you their names, although I suppose you can easily find out.''

"Oh, Hank, you can't mean that," she said, guiltily remembering she *had* been told to watch who got in touch with him.

He slumped in his seat, shifting to brace one knee against the dashboard and lace his fingers across his stomach as if setting himself for the off-pavement segment of a road rally. "Don't pretend this is a posthypnotic suggestion. This is real.''

Jane was too devastated to answer directly. "You have this knack of knowing exactly what to say to butcher me.''

"Don't pretend you were just asking about my day. If you didn't feel guilty, your face wouldn't be so white.''

She bent over the steering wheel, resting her forehead on her clenched fists, letting her long hair sweep forward to hide her face. "I'm ashamed to tell you the truth, but I can't think of a lie that would cover it.''

She gave herself one last chance to think. When nothing came to mind, she sighed. "I guess I care too much about you. I know you said you don't believe in my feelings, but what I feel seems real to me. Whenever the least thing might hurt you, I get scared.''

He didn't answer. He didn't even move.

"You said the terrorists threatened to come after you if they weren't satisfied. When I saw those men outnumbering you, I realized I had left you alone in a strange city where you didn't have any way to call for help if you needed it."

"I've been in strange cities before. You always start out alone. I've had experience handling it."

"I know." Jane straightened up but she didn't turn toward him. "At least give me this—it was the rest of the world I doubted when I saw those men. I didn't doubt you."

He studied her profile in silence. "Whereas I did doubt you."

"I didn't mean it as an attack," she said, discouraged by his readiness to attack himself as well as her.

It took him a long time to think it through. "Let's stay the night," he said at last, tension washing the resonance out of his voice. "No one's looking at us here, provided you'll take my word that the Hakeem brothers are ordinary friends. It gives us some space."

"Sure, let's." She was grateful that he had told her his friends' name. She accepted it as a gesture of trust, but she decided not to mention it since he was so ready to misunderstand everything she said. "You want the city in general so we're anonymous? Or do you feel like something in particular?"

"I feel like a men's shop with a women's shop next door so we can upgrade the packaging for after dark. Then I feel like a French restaurant specializing in nouvelle cuisine, which we don't get at home since I've never figured it out. Then I feel like two hotel rooms with the adjoining door unlocked so we can have a nightcap in privacy without either of us being afraid we're going to misunderstand."

Jane nodded, relieved by the genuine sound of the unexpectedly complete list. "There's a mall in North Vancouver I'm fond of. It's the only place I know I can try on dresses that cost a year's salary while listening to chainsaws logging commercial lumber off the hillside behind the parking lot."

Hank watched Jane adapt to Vancouver norms, muscling into a traffic swarm feeding the Lion's Gate Bridge bottleneck. Like a jammed parking lot, massed cars inched across the high suspension span that crossed the Fraser River to connect central and North Vancouver.

"Is that really a barge of sulfur?" he asked in proper tourist surprise.

Jane spared a very brief glance down to the river hundreds of feet below. A tug scurried up channel, dragging a barge mounded with fluorescent yellow-green powder.

"Seems to be. The Fraser River's tidal so there are miles of docks. The whole Pacific commercial world docks here—look at all the ships out in the roads."

His gaze moved past her toward the hazy river mouth, where a cluster of international freighters rode at anchor. Some wallowed heavily, almost submerged by their cargo, while others waited to be loaded, floating lightly enough to display a vast expanse of rusty bottom paint.

By the time they parked on the roof of the North Vancouver mall, the city's remarkable beauty had pushed their tangled feelings away. Walking downstairs, they separated at a pair of clothing stores.

Jane chose a well-grayed rose color, which paled her complexion while brightening her cheeks. The dress was severely plain, making the most of her trim figure, though it softened into full feminine sleeves that gathered at wrist-clasping cuffs.

"I'm going to wear it out of the store," she said to the clerk. "Would you go ahead and ring up while I do something to my hair?"

"Pin it up, for now, I think," the clerk agreed. "But with your cheekbones, you really ought to cut it right off."

"I used to wear it that way."

"Everyone looks better with short hair," the clerk said with feminist efficiency. "And when you're going somewhere decadent, you can buy a wig."

Laughing, Jane turned back to the fitting-room mirror. Her hair was curly enough to resist flowing in a smooth curtain toward the crown of her head, but once it was anchored, she knew its wiriness would hold securely.

She emerged from the dressing room to find Hank talking to her clerk, who was looking delighted by Jane's delay. A faint stab of jealousy faded when Hank looked up and smiled.

"They're having to tailor me," he said. "But I see you're perfect as you are."

Jane laughed. "I'll just be a second here."

"Taken care of," the clerk said with an admiring glance at Hank.

At Jane's wary reaction, Hank shook his head. "I invited you, remember?"

It seemed to be important to him. Jane suddenly realized how long it had been since he had felt comfortably in control of anything whatsoever. Now was clearly not the time to make a fuss over symbols of independence.

She smiled regretfully. "If I'd known it wasn't going to be on my bill, I'd have wasted more money."

Hank grinned. "We'll make it up on the shoes."

They did. And they made it up on earrings for her newly exposed ears—hammered silver bars with the elemental look achieved by native craftsmen.

As they left the jewelry store, Hank looked her over carefully. "Like this, you'd cause a riot in Paris. I'm not surprised, but I've gotten used to thinking of you in Oak Harbor and jeans."

She tipped her head up, enjoying the whisper of her new earrings against her neck. *"Attention, monsieur,"* she said only half playfully. "I lived in Europe before you did."

He watched her as if she were a different person simply because she had changed her clothes. She decided not to interrupt his thoughts. She wasn't competing with Sylvie—she would *hate* that kind of idle life. But that was exactly the point.

If it takes imported clothes to show him I'm ambitious, she thought with the hint of a chip on her shoulder, then let him look.

He didn't say much as they went to the men's shop. He came back from the dressing room disconcertingly eager for her approval. The not-quite-black suit gave his blond hair the precious complex color of gold bullion rescued after centuries in a saltwater shipwreck. His eyes picked up an added gleam from the wine-and-gray striped silk tie.

She shook her head in a flat-out rejecting way. "No, take it off. All of it. Right now. I'm not letting you onto the street looking like that, you'll be mobbed."

His eyes brightened. "We've never really had a chance to flirt before. I didn't realize you'd be so good at it."

He held out his hand and they strolled through the shadowy tiled mall in the unself-conscious way made possible by big city invisibility. They inspected shop windows, but it was their joined hands they thought about.

A rank of telephones reminded Jane. "Would you mind if I called Fran? I don't have to—I'm not checking in, not for either one of us. It's just in case she worries. Normally I'd come home."

"Have I made myself a tyrant?"

"Sure." She smiled wistfully. "You're as bad as me."

He tightened his clasp around her fingers before he released her hand. "I know it bothers you for me to suspect Oak Harborites, just like it undermines me for you to accuse all Europeans. But we're both trying not to see enemies in every doorway, aren't we?"

She nodded. "And when we do spot shadows no one else would call an enemy, we're frantic for shorter times, now, don't you think?"

He smiled and turned to the phones. "You get hold of Fran, and I'll make dinner reservations. My friends told me about a place that's good and not too touristy."

They stood under side-by-side phone hoods, punching numbers. Hank began talking promptly, but Jane had less luck. When no one answered at Dutch Bulb, she tried Fran. After an endless wait, she called the Amstellens. Bobby answered, since Thelma wasn't home.

"Bobby, this is Jane, will you do me a favor?"

"You bet, shall I come over?"

"No, I'm in Vancouver. Tell your mom, okay?"

"Sure. Tell her what?"

"Tell her I'm staying here overnight, and I want Fran to know, except she isn't home."

"I know she isn't, she's down at the Grange dinner. So's Mom, did you forget? They have to help with the food this month, so I'm eating with vanderPols, they're picking me up in five minutes. If you're still in Vancouver, how are you getting here in time for the Grange dinner?"

Jane smiled. "Isn't it awful—I'm going to miss out."

"Gross. Well, I'll tell everyone why."

"All set?" Hank asked as she hung up.

Ignoring the elevator, they climbed the stairs to the roof parking lot. Jane fought laborious traffic back across the bridge with a calm that proved she was accustomed to it. Intrigued, Hank tried to imagined her back in Oak Harbor and didn't quite succeed.

By the time they reached the restaurant in West Van, evening fog had rolled in from the straits to form luminous globes around the streetlights. They sat at a window table where they could watch the anchor lights on English Bay. When their French Canadian waiter arrived, Hank spoke to him in Parisian French. Their accents were so different that Jane was amused. She glanced around the spacious dining room, and was delighted to find she didn't recognize a single face.

"We should have come here weeks ago," she said. "I'd forgotten how good it feels to be unknown."

"It's a relief at first," Hank agreed. "But eventually you get tired of knowing no one cares about you."

It pleased Jane to hear him defend Oak Harbor. She toyed with her smoked quail, visualizing the Grange dinner where everyone would notice that she and Hank were absent. Warmed by the thought of everyone's protection, she told him about Bobby's reaction.

He laughed. "What's Grange like?"

They were both surprised to find themselves talking about Oak Harbor casually, as a place to live rather than as a source of worry.

The easy mood disappeared as Jane drove to their hotel.

"Do you realize this is our first date?" Hank rested his hand on her shoulder in a datelike way as they crossed the lobby to wait for the elevator.

"You be on a date if you want to, but I'm going to stay on a business trip. I like my work, but I've never had much fun on dates."

"Maybe nothing was wrong with dating—maybe you were just with the wrong men."

Jane laughed over his self-confident answer. But when they stepped into the elevator, his personal energy filled the small space enticingly, and she began to suspect he might be right. She felt like a voyeur, imagining what he would do with any other date. He would smile. Touch. Stroke. Step closer. Bend. He wouldn't be crass about it, but he surely wouldn't ask. She glanced at his profile, imagining.

He grinned suddenly and turned with his entrancing gaze. "I play it case by case."

She laughed, not even trying to deny her thoughts. At the fourteenth floor, he handed her a key and kept one for himself. They stood side by side at their doors, dealing with their locks.

Stepping inside, Jane stopped in shock. Her room was full of flowers. White daisies banked the dressing table. Blue water lilies floated in globes on the bedside tables. The low table between the easy chairs held a bouquet of white roses and blue forget-me-nots. She was still transfixed when the connecting door swung open and Hank appeared.

"They're beautiful," she said. "But I'm not sure what they're for."

He led her toward the chairs and seated her with elaborate courtesy. "What I remember from those natural rock gardens outside Cabin Seven is red or yellow bead-leaf sedums, but when you order over the phone from commercial growers, commercial is what you get."

She was glad to learn that the flowers weren't just part of his standard date, but if they meant he wanted to return to the past, that was worse.

"Point Roberts is only an hour's drive from here." She watched him strip his tie out of his collar with a snap. "We could go there, if you want." She wondered if he would know the reason behind her offer.

He shrugged out of his jacket and tossed it across the foot of her bed before he turned to look into the depths of her eyes. "Point Roberts is a special memory, Sandy, and it always will be. But I don't want to go there. It would just show us how much we've both changed."

"I was afraid you might not know that."

A quiet double tap on the door interrupted them.

"I had coffee and brandy sent up," Hank said.

Room service made space for a brass tray as if all hotel surfaces were routinely buried in flowers. When they were alone again, Hank poured coffee for each of them and brandy for himself.

Jane slipped out of her sandals, curling her feet under her, but she couldn't relax. His arrangements were all so practiced, as if he had gone through the sequence a thousand times. She wished the thought would make her distrust him, but it didn't. It saddened her instead. He had said her new clothes reminded him of Paris. And now, here was this love nest.

At least, she thought it was a love nest. She'd never been in one before, so she couldn't be sure.

"I'm glad we came here, Sandy." He lifted his brandy glass toward her before he swirled it and sipped. "Oak Harbor seems to own you so. That makes it hard for me to think."

Jane had expected such a different conversation that she couldn't imagine what he meant. "They're my friends."

"Which means you chose one another perfectly freely." He set his glass down. "Whereas I showed up on your doorstep like a sopping puppy with an ice storm at my heels. You weren't free—you had to take me in."

Jane was stunned by his humble description which sounded so different from what she had felt. "I was glad to. I told you that."

"Like a missionary. Out to save me."

"You're thinking of my folks." Jane was surprised to hear edginess in her voice. "I'm no missionary. I'm a businesswoman."

"I know what you are." His mouth smiled faintly, but his eyes were analytical. "I'm glad of this reminder, today, of how cosmopolitan you are, when you want to be."

She was offended without being quite sure why. "Does that mean you're comfortable only with city people?"

"I don't know about 'comfortable,' maybe, but I've met people I liked in towns a lot smaller than Oak Harbor." He switched to his coffee, as if keeping his head clear was suddenly more important than relaxing over brandy. "Before I left the military, I was on a mission in Afghanistan and got a little overextended."

Overextended. Jane's heart ached as she thought about what the deceptively mild words meant. "I didn't know we had troops in Afghanistan," she said, wanting him to keep talking in spite of her dread.

"They didn't call me back into the service in order to put me into uniform," he said. "I was an observer."

Jane narrowed her eyes doubtfully.

"Not a spy," he explained before she could question him. "I've never been a spy."

Jane was pleased by his absolute tone. He had sounded so unsure about what he was, when he first arrived in Oak Harbor. The change seemed to show his mind had kept pace as his body healed.

"When it got overly interesting, the resistance hid me for a month, until it was safe for me to travel," he went on, watching her face eagerly, as if hoping his eyes might tell her more than his words could. "During searches, they handed me around from one tiny village to the next. Villages so tiny they'd fit inside a shopping mall." He reached across the space between the chairs to clasp her hand. "You can't believe the courage of people who live in a war zone. It's mostly women and children, you know. Sometimes a few men too old to fight."

He closed his eyes, visiting the past. "You have to overcome your belief that you ought to try to protect them. Women and children are the terrorists and the resistance fighters."

Jane tightened her grip on his hand as she wondered if she would ever get used to his stories. "Is it hard to come back to this other life?"

"Sometimes."

Exactly, she told herself grievingly. That other was the sort of life he did best—feeling warm forever toward kindly strangers who took him in without question and handed him on at the end of the month. "Your letters always sounded like wall-to-wall fun."

"A lot of it was fun. But also—" His eyes filled with turmoil. "I wanted to sound interesting to you. That's what the letters were about. But now, I want—"

He paused. "'Mutual self disclosure' is what people in my business call it. I want us to tell each other the truth about how we feel."

She nodded, her feelings clear in her eyes.

"I was burning out, even before the Hands of Allah got me. I didn't even think about coming home because I've never had one. But I thought about calling you and asking for a date. Like this, except I imagined Seattle instead of Vancouver."

He smiled. "I even looked up the time zones—ten hours difference from Athens, which is where I was then."

"What might have happened always seems sad, so I don't want to think about it," Jane said. "What really happened was your hostage time, and now the federal watch. And for all of that, Sylvie handles it better than I do."

"Sure." He sounded puzzled. "It's easy for Sylvie. She doesn't love me."

"And I do?"

He rubbed his thumb back and forth across her knuckles as if not really aware of what he was doing. "I've always felt that the potential was there, Sandy, I felt it the moment I first saw you. But we had two weeks at the Seminar, which wasn't enough. And by the time I was out of the service, I wasn't sure anymore. From your letters, I thought you'd changed. So I stayed away."

She smiled, but her eyes were bright with telltale tears. "Which kept it a perfect memory for us both."

"But memories aren't really enough."

She drew a quick breath, not trusting her voice. "You seem pretty much in the present to me—the husky voice, the warm hand, the shirt unbuttoning, the heart disclosing."

Understanding instantly, he stood and scooped her up, settling down again with her in his arms. He embraced her, surrounding her. When she slipped a hand behind him, he arched away from the chair, making room for her to hold him possessively.

He tucked her head under his chin and began stroking her hair, dislodging pins until her curls tangled around his throat. "I wish we could go back and do it again. Get it right. Why has it taken me five years to admit how I feel?"

She knew it wasn't entirely fair, but she decided to take the risk anyway. "If you're admitting how you feel, would you use words for it?" she whispered.

He laughed, his chest reverberating excitingly against her temple. "We both know Hank has been in love with Sandy from the start," he murmured. "But it's been hard to know whether that includes me and you."

She nodded, rubbing her forehead against his throat. "Most of the time you seem like Hank."

"You always seem like Sandy, and that's what worries me. Maybe I'm making you over. Not really seeing you. Living with a dream."

Profoundly moved by his confession, she reached up to stroke his cheek. His eyes dark with feeling, he bent slowly, a slight smile easing the set of his mouth before his lips touched hers.

He drew back at last, his fragrant sigh warming her face and spilling into her mouth. He pressed his forehead against hers, looking into her eyes from no distance at all as if determined to see her soul. "Can I count on this, Sandy?"

She nodded. "I do."

His eyes brightened as he gave his whole attention to a bargain-sealing kiss.

Chapter Thirteen

Jane parked in Dutch Bulb's gravel lot, thinking how peaceful Oak Harbor looked after Vancouver's frantic traffic. But when she stepped into the kitchen, she changed her mind. Fran stood in the middle of the room, scowling. Clinton stood beside her, radiating tension in his stuffy way.

"I hope your holiday was worth it," Fran said.

Jane frowned. "Shouldn't we start with 'Hi'?"

"Hi." Clinton was pleased with his ponderous irony. "Someone broke into the greenhouse while you were away."

He expected to shock her, but she thought of the missing storage labels and merely sighed. "What did they take?"

Fran's mouth turned into the upside down V she used when quarreling. "Who knows? What's left is a pigsty."

Jane rushed outside, the others trailing after her.

"The far greenhouse," Clinton called.

She didn't need directions. The open door to her species greenhouse flapped in the afternoon breeze. Jane stepped inside despairingly. Pots were broken but left in place, as if someone had pounded his way down the tables with a crowbar. Her precious experiments lay exposed, their white roots pathetic, their bagged bloom spikes snapped. She walked down the aisle, the heels of her city sandals sinking awkwardly into the sawdust. When she reached the sick bay, she made a pained sound. The glass panel was smashed and the timed grow light dangled from snipped cords.

"I called an insurance adjustor and the sheriff," Fran said crisply. "But I didn't clean up because I thought you should see what you've done."

Jane stared at her partner. "What *I*'ve done?"

"Destruction is a noisy business," Clinton reminded her. "If you had been where you belong, you would have heard it and gotten it stopped."

Jane whirled to frown at her accountant. "Presenting workshops is part of my job."

"Spreading yourself thin?" Clinton asked.

They're upset, Jane realized. They've been dreading how to tell me. They don't realize they sound like vultures.

She took a long breath, determined to stop reacting and take charge of the conversation. "The growth experiments are wrecked, but I can start over. I'll lose a generation of seed from my hybrids, but the bulbs are okay since they didn't turn up the heat. Thank goodness they slashed the greenhouse walls, so it stayed cool in here."

"You can't be thankful for any of this," Fran said.

"I know." Jane accepted the harsh tone as Fran's form of sympathy. "I'll replant with the pots Nyla scrubbed. We can order more pots in time for the decorations we promised for Festival."

"You'd be wiser to heed this warning," Clinton said.

"Is that what people are saying? It's a warning?"

"It couldn't be anything else."

Jane rubbed her forehead. "Explain it to me step-by-step, would you, Clinton? I don't see any sense to this at all."

"What was attacked?" he asked as if obliging her.

Jane saw he was going to lead her through it like a catechism. She wondered if she could bear his tone long enough to find out what Oak Harbor thought.

She sighed. "The experiments."

"The species tulips," Hank said.

"Precisely." Clinton nodded at Hank.

That seemed to be the end of it. Trying to follow his logic, Jane remembered his earlier comment about noise. "Did you hear anything, Fran?"

"No. But Edna says she heard crashes out here last night. By the time she got up to check, it stopped."

Touched to think of the fragile old woman watching out for her neighbor, Jane rubbed her eyes. Knowing she needed help controlling her feelings, Hank turned to the back door to give her something to do. It was half ripped from its hinges, so he stepped outside and reseated it. Jane watched him through the milky plastic walls. When he crouched down at the edge of the woodlot for a better look, she went outside to join him.

"There's been a lot of trampling here." He pointed to the leather-leafed salal that bordered the woods. "Too much for one person."

"The neighbors have already checked for clues." Clinton shoved the broken door aside in order to talk without joining them.

"Anyway, woodland duff doesn't hold footprints," Jane added. "You can tell if people have walked on it, but you can't tell shoe size or distinguish treads. And even if we identified every foot in Oak Harbor, it wouldn't tell us anything because everybody walks back there."

Hank stood. "So how do we proceed on this?"

Jane squared her shoulders. "We repot the bulbs. I'll get into some jeans. And you'd better, too."

Returning to the house, Jane wondered if she should apologize for high-handedly assuming he would help her, but he seemed to take it for granted that she would count on him. He turned to Clinton with a not-too-concerned look.

"Were you here when the sheriff came?"

"I was the one who called him," Clinton said.

"I wanted no part of it," Fran said as her goodbye when they reached Dutch Bulb's patio.

"Can you take a minute to hash through what happened, Clinton?" Hank led the way to the lounge. "I gather it makes more sense to you than it does to me."

The lounge door closed behind them, blocking out Clinton's answer. Jane went upstairs, determined not to give in to her fear. She stepped out of her light blue city dress and pulled on a sweatshirt and jeans. After stomping into her work boots, she trotted back downstairs.

At the back door, she stopped to consider where she was needed most. In the greenhouse, the damage was already done, so time didn't matter much. But in the lounge, trouble might be in progress—she could hear male voices running on.

She went to the lounge.

"I understand you think I attracted this assault, but you're forgetting that terrorists would get me if they wanted me," Hank said as she opened the door. "They're fanatics. Fanatics don't stop with bashing bulbs."

His posture contradicted the defenseless remark. He sat in his favorite spot at the end of couch, his long legs stretched out with his heels resting on the coffee table beside a pot of tiny bronze *persica*. Jane's entrance halted Clinton's pacing, but Hank didn't pause.

"I think this is local mischief. Does the sheriff have any evidence to contradict me?"

"Of course not," Jane answered for Clinton. "If Corny had evidence either way, he'd make sure all of us knew."

Hank tipped his head back to smile at her. "Welcome to the strategy huddle. Clinton says the sheriff's convinced I'm misbehaving myself in some foreign language. I can't contradict since I don't know Oak Harbor well enough to list local people with motives. You're no help because you trust everybody. Where does that leave us?"

Jane saw he wanted to keep it light. Not knowing what might have gone on between them before she got there, she followed his lead.

"It leaves us free to clean up the mess, since there aren't any clues to gather and fuss about."

Hank stood. "Nyla says I have a black thumb, but I'll do anything that doesn't involve the plants."

"Count me out." Clinton spread his fingers as if checking fastidiously for potting soil beneath the nails.

They left the house together, Clinton going to his car while they crossed the yard. Jane stopped at the greenhouse door, shocked again by the destruction.

Hank wrapped his arms protectively around her in a confident way that showed Vancouver had been a turning point for him. "When Fran and Clinton started in, I wanted to hold you. I know how hard this hits you."

She leaned against him, glad for the support he offered without any strings attached. "What makes it worse is, this is the second time. The first time they just took labels."

He stepped away from her as abruptly as if she had kicked and bit him. "Why didn't you tell me?"

It was too much. "Please, Hank, don't pile imaginary wounds on top of this."

"Hiding assaults isn't imaginary."

Her already discouraged posture drooped. "It wasn't an assault, just a nuisance. And it happened while you were downtown with Corny and I guess Maguire."

"What you're too polite to say is, it happened right after I sandbagged you. I've apologized for that, Sandy, and I'll go on apologizing as long as you want me to."

His regret was so dignified she was sorry to have provoked it. "You said we wouldn't fight each other anymore, what with everything else we have to fight."

He clasped her shoulder as she'd seen him do with the others—the Hakeem brothers, Nyla, Bobby. It didn't seem like enough, after the closeness they'd shared in Vancouver.

"Break-ins always feel personal, even when they aren't," he said.

"The other stuff—the tags, the phone calls, the snooping—those aren't really crimes," she said, using the havoc to put distance back into her feelings about Hank. "But this—slashing, breaking. These are crimes."

"All of it's crime," he said in a way that reminded her he knew the rules. "But you're right—there's a difference here. He's losing patience. Whatever he wants, heckling didn't get it for him, so he's trying harder now."

"What could he want?"

"Clinton wonders if he might be trying to get rid of what he calls your 'foreign stuff.'"

She groaned. "Clinton knows perfectly well I brought species tulips to town three years ago, and there was no trouble over it then. Why should it start now?"

"Have you had any experience with violence, Sandy?" His extremely gentle tone was frightening.

She met his gaze unguardedly. "It's always out there, for anybody. When I was a little kid, my parents were sometimes in danger. I can see that, looking back. But I've never even been slapped."

He brushed her cheek as if to verify her claim by touch.

Afraid his tenderness might make her cry, she shifted her attention to her plants. "It drives me crazy—I was pretty close to developing an ice blossom. And now look."

She cleared her throat and flattened her mouth to keep her lips from quivering. "Never mind. I'll start again."

"We can't just accept it and go on." He gazed around assessingly. "If this is the same person who searched my room and stole your tags, then he's working himself up a step at a time. Your guest—no damage. Your greenhouse—theft. This time, destruction without major harm. Next time—"

"I know you're trained to see people's minds. But to a business type like me, this looks like an attack on my experiments as a way to hurt me without hurting Fran."

He nodded. "I'm afraid we're both right."

"Oh, Hank, I hate this. I'm not brave like you."

"I know that. You've brave in a different way." He wrapped his arms around her, letting her cling to him until her usual courage returned. "I'm going to have locks put on the greenhouses. Until we have some clue about who's doing this, we've got to be on our guard."

"They'll just slash the plastic walls if they want in."

"Still." He paused. "And I want you to start using the dead bolts I installed for the house."

"Oak Harbor would die of shock."

Instead of answering, he let her violent words linger, doing their own work. "I'll go put on jeans, okay? Nyla's been training me. I embarrassed her to extinction one day by walking into the Feed & Seed wearing wool."

By the time he came back in his grubbiest clothes, Jane had hauled in a rack of pots and assembled tools. "Would you mind mending the wall slashes? You're tall enough to reach, but I'd have to drag a step stool around."

He picked up the patching tape. "Does this work?"

"They do it differently in Holland, so Fran tells me, but the advantage of a clear plastic fabric instead of glass is, installation and repairs are both homemade. I'll hire some high-school kids this summer and we'll replace the whole thing, but for now, let's make it hold heat."

He nodded and started in. As he moved slowly down the long aisle, his mends made the building weather tight again. When he stopped to pull his sweater off, Jane looked up.

"The striptease is interesting, but we'd better prop the doors open and turn on the exhaust fans instead. These bulbs have to stay cold until they're replanted."

Pots gradually filled the bench as Jane sorted the wreckage. She was able to save plants that had grown only their leaves. But she set aside the bulbs with broken bloom spikes since they would need a dormant period to conserve their strength. Hank watched her trim broken leaves and scoop potting soil in a nurturing ritual that restored her calm. When he thought she had recovered enough control to face their situation, he went back to the analysis that had clearly disturbed her but might save her from added grief.

"Whoever did this isn't as tall as me. That makes it easier." He spoke cheerfully, as if he were only gossiping.

Jane paused to look. "How much can you tell? Was he short? A woman, maybe? Or kids?"

Hank massaged one shoulder while he thought. "You'd probably climb up on the tables, wouldn't you? But our mad slasher didn't, which means he weighs enough that he didn't trust the tables to hold him and he didn't have to risk it because he could reach high enough without. Also, he must be old enough to have lost some flexibility. He didn't bend over and slash close to the ground. A kid probably would have. A pudgy, middle height, inactive man in his thirties would be my guess."

"Well, sir, if some people heard you say all that, they'd know you did it yourself so you could analyze what you'd done and prove you weren't the one who did it, being as how you're taller, skinnier and younger than that." Corny stood in the doorway, looking obliged.

Hank straightened. "Clinton said you'd already been here, Sheriff."

Corny leaned one hand against a crossbar in the exposed two-by-four framing and surveyed the greenhouse with a canny look. "That's what he said to you. To me, he said the two of you're going to contradict me like a hired duet no matter what the evidence shows, so I figured on having my evening's entertainment here and then getting on home to the TV. How I see it is this way. You can't be guilty, Jane, you love those plants so much you call this a mass murder. And you can't be guilty, Hank, because you've been in Turkey, where these flowers came from, so you know bulbs don't scare."

He paused. "So. Now. Get started acting guilty, both of you, because it surely isn't apparent to me."

Jane sprang across the space between them and clasped the sheriff in a grateful hug. "You're the first person around here who didn't act like this is our fault." She pressed her head against his chest. "I'll get you messy with potting soil, but I don't even care."

He gave her a fatherly pat. "Copping is dirty work."

"I was going to come down to your office and talk to you after a while," Hank said. "But I thought I'd help out here first. This doesn't seem like the kind of work a person ought to do alone."

Corny nodded. "Fran's too upset, I expect."

"She hates it," Jane said loyally as she stepped away from him.

"Can't disagree with that."

Hank watched the sheriff's face. "Is there any federal involvement in this?"

Corny met his gaze frankly, but he didn't speak.

"I'll withdraw the question if it puts you out of bounds," Hank said immediately.

Corny offered a homespun smile. "I was thinking more of your young lady, where it might be a sore point."

Hank's slow grin was as unguarded as a boy's. "We used the advice you gave us the other day as the basis for an encounter session. Worked perfectly, like you said."

"In that case, yes, no reason you both shouldn't know an anonymous tip was called in to the Seattle office. According to this John Doe type, you left the country and failed to return as scheduled. It might have caused a stir, except I was able to report that Bobby Amstellen had already notified the Grange supper exactly where you were and why."

"Does John Doe mean a man called?" Jane asked.

"Make that John or Jane Doe."

Hank tried to decipher the meaning behind the shuffling friendliness. "Am I in trouble for crossing the border?"

"I wouldn't call it anything new, especially."

"Should I tell you before we leave town?"

"That would be friendly," Corny said affably.

"I'm doing a workshop at Woodruff's missionary training camp on the Peninsula next Wednesday. We'll stay overnight."

"My folks?" Jane asked. "You didn't tell me you were in touch with them."

It was obvious that he hadn't wanted to tell her now, but he decided to treat Corny as a friendly witness. "I wrote to them about my situation. Their answer came in yesterday's mail. Fran pointed it out to Clinton, and he mentioned it to me while we were talking in the lounge. I haven't had a chance to tell you about it before now.''

"Don't go.''

"They invited me to bring you along.''

"I don't want them dragged into danger," she insisted.

Hank clenched his jaw. "Are you asking me to cancel because I bring danger down on everyone who befriends me?''

She folded her arms across her solar plexus, as if his attack were physical, but she answered without defensiveness. "Please be reasonable, Hank. These attacks against me, sometimes they spill over on you, and I hate that. I don't want them to spread to my folks.''

Clearly surprised by her answer, Hank frowned. "We don't know you're the target, Sandy. This started when I arrived, remember, which probably means our enemy is after both of us. But whatever the truth is about that, I'm willing to share your danger, and from what I've seen, your folks are willing, too.''

"I'm glad to hear you say that, Hank," Corny said. "I met Jane's folks when they visited her here last year. Made quite an impression. Real comfortable people, I thought.''

It was true, Jane knew, her parents were comfortable anywhere. They loved adventuring. They had stopped only because of her.

She remembered the overseas assignment that had persuaded them to settle down. When Jane was six years old, they went as a family to a wildlife research station in Kenya. It ran like a watering hole for English nobility, with a budget that could have fed all Kenya for a year. When they were sure Jane would be petted and spoiled by the researchers and the staff, they left Jane behind and went into the country to help the people who were starving and ignored.

They were warned before they left, and no one was surprised when they disappeared. The staff and guests put themselves out to make Jane's life fun while everyone waited for news. Her clearest memory from that tense time was of a civilized zebra who followed her everywhere including into her cabin at night.

Eventually her parents had trailed out of the beautiful back country. When Jane stopped crying to welcome them, they sat down for a family conference. Jane remembered the porch and the long grassy slope that led down to an unspoiled lake, and the luxury. She also remembered their careful story about meeting angry people who weren't allowed on the pretty porch.

They were always willing to talk about anything, and so she had questioned them over the years. Gradually she had found out how close they'd come to being killed. And it had cured them of too much adventuring—not because of their own end, but because they knew Jane would suffer without them.

Thinking of their unassuming courage, she understood Hank's plan. "You want to work for my folks because they've been through your kind of trouble."

"It could help."

It was odd to remember how devastated he had been in the beginning. During the past few weeks, he had turned into the absolute, glowing picture of health. It was hard to remember that he still needed help. On the other hand, he had always been able to hide his needs.

Chapter Fourteen

Since it was his workshop, Hank drove to the Olympic Peninsula. Banging across the rust-stained ramp off the Keystone ferry like a commuter, he followed the coast highway into the hills. Jane stared at scenery from her childhood world. Hundred-foot-high forest walls lined the road where highway shoulders should have been.

Hank left the highway and drove through a network of branch roads, finally pausing at the crest of a ridge. The scene was almost magical. A meadow surrounded a pocket lake, which glittered like crystal. A group of small cabins hugged one segment of the shore. Chimneys of round local stones jutted above roofs like untidy woodpiles made of three-foot-long pioneer shakes. A rustic lodge crouched against a natural rise.

"Growing up here, no wonder you have such inner resources of peace," Hank said appreciatively.

"*Peace!*" Jane laughed in disbelief.

"The kind of peace I mean doesn't come from what happens to you, it comes from how you handle it." He parked in a graveled area bulldozed out of the slope.

Jane sprang up the steps to the lodge and shoved the door open energetically. "Mom?"

Hank loitered tactfully at the door. Endearingly Jane shed layers of self-sufficiency, relaxing into a kid's eager faith in being welcome. A pair of smiling middle-aged people appeared at the far end of the hall. Jane threw herself into their arms, clinging impartially.

Her mother was taller than Jane, and her sandy hair was silvered, but she had the same active ease which Hank had always thought was purely Sandy's. Jane obviously had taken her intense dark eyes and her cheerful mouth from her dad. The physical resemblances were a jolt. Jane had always seemed to be on her own, but here were people who had claims on her—claims she counted on. Hank felt like an intruder.

Matt Woodruff reached around his daughter to hold out his hand. "Good to meet you, Hank."

Mary Woodruff smiled, and Hank surrendered to the family charm. When they walked downstairs to the dining room, he easily fit into the group of workshop participants assembling for dinner. The missionaries might have been anyone who liked their life. Their remarkable openness was the only quality that set them apart.

Puzzled, Hank turned to his host. Matt Woodruff had been watching him with the same invasive gaze Jane always used when she intended to inspect the inside of his mind.

"We're *inter*denominational, not nondenominational," Matt said. "It gives a framework as well as a flexibility. We hitchhike off everybody's best thoughts, from a Brazilian Catholic to an Indian charismatic or someone down the road."

"I don't know what I expected," Hank admitted.

"Saints? It's pretty hard to spot them on the street."

"Maybe so, but your daughter's a good example of your training."

"Yes, we're pleased with her." Matt gazed down the long table to watch Jane, seated beside her mother. "She does take everything terribly to heart, though, I'm afraid."

"I'd like to talk to you about that."

Matt weighted him with a brief glance. "I usually take a last walk along the lake to end the day."

After Hank nodded, Matt turned the personal subject aside. With the ease of a familiar routine, he introduced Hank to missionaries one at a time so he could learn their names. By the time they left the dining room to the self-effacing staff, Hank had spotted a few personalities he could use in drawing out responses from the group.

He was relieved to find his presentation skills still worked. When he had asked to do the workshop, he'd explained that he didn't know how he might react to the stress of talking about his experience. The Woodruffs had written back assuring him it was all right to come apart because dealing with a crisis would be good training for their missionaries. He had thought their response was flippant, but now he saw it was simply how they looked at everything.

He also saw how subtly they were helping him. On the way to the meeting room, they walked on each side of him and talked to each other across him to keep him from thinking about what came next.

Jane slipped into a shadowed seat near the back of the auditorium, where she wouldn't distract him. She fondly inspected the familiar room. The back wall of gray local stone continued around a corner to form a giant fireplace, where a welcoming fire hissed over sappy logs. Chairs were scattered informally before a rustic speaker's table.

Matt strolled forward with a gathering gaze. Jane beamed at her father. All her life, he had seemed most human when he was most intensely locked into his missionary zeal. She had always loved the sight.

After he had been introduced, Hank lounged against the front of the speaker's table. Comfortably in charge without apparent effort, he avoided the symbols of crowd control.

Watching him warm up the group, Jane realized she had never seen him work. His lingering smiles and committed gaze had always seemed like private mannerisms for individual use. It was a shock to see him pour his personality into a public form which produced a blinding charm.

"The most dangerous mistake you can make is trying to predict how kidnappers will react to you." He let them watch his memory narrow his generous blue eyes as he organized his example. "I learned that the hard way, by getting into trouble from the first moment I was picked up. What happened was, one of my jailers was a woman. Big dark eyes. Intense. I looked at her. That annoyed the men."

He glanced at the fire, inviting them to relive the moment with him. "You're at their mercy—if they have any mercy. You've accidentally done the worst possible thing. Now what?"

He investigated every fascinated face with an uncomplicated gaze. "Fortunately I left my punishment up to them. They blindfolded me. I wouldn't have been satisfied with just making me stop. I'd have insisted on training me."

The room was tensely silent as everyone rummaged in the most unspeakable dungeons of their imagination in order to visualize what else his captors might have done to him.

"Was she beautiful—the woman you looked at?" The female voice was wistfully breathy.

"Exceedingly."

He paused to consider. "All women are."

Explosively relieved laughter filled the room. Hank grinned and scooped them up into his radiant world. The horror was always there for anyone to see, a shadow at the back of his eyes, a hesitation in the way he used his hands. But he listened to questions about terror as if nothing frightening had ever touched him. He turned shock aside with answers gleaned from carefully edited memories that always managed to find some hook into absurdity.

They would have kept it up all night. He was so beguiling, and his experiences were fascinating. But he was accustomed to handling groups. He finally called a good-humored halt. The Woodruffs quickly seconded him, adding routine announcements to bring the trainees back to reality.

"You're really good," Jane said, when the last of the stragglers had drifted away. "But does it confuse you when every woman in the room falls in love with you?"

He laughed and wrapped his arms around her. "Not if that category includes you."

As if his success had earned him the privilege, he nuzzled his forehead into her long hair. It was easy to respond, since he really seemed to want her this time instead of merely needing her.

"Oh, Sandy, wouldn't it be wonderful if we could just put everything behind us and get on with our work?"

"*Our* work! I deal with bulbs and you deal with terrorists, how does an 'our' get in there?"

He laughed again. "We both consult."

The simple answer caught her by surprise. No one in Oak Harbor thought of her that way. She realized she had gotten into the habit of letting Oak Harbor's view seem true to her.

Hank drew away reluctantly, but he kept hold of her hand as they walked upstairs to the family living room. Before they entered, they could hear the Woodruffs recapping the day. Their lively voices proved how interested they were in sharing their experiences with each other, even after working together for thirty years.

When Hank and Jane joined them, Mary poured some unexpectedly dark tea. "This group is headed for South America, so we're pushing maté, the local tea. None of them seem to enjoy it."

Jane smiled as she took her usual seat on the linen-look couch. "Do you ever get tired of being good for people instead of indulging them?"

"No, honey, they indulge themselves—they don't need me for that."

Hank smiled at his hostess before choosing an easy chair in front of the fire. "I'm extremely grateful to you both. I didn't know what would happen in public. But if I didn't try, I was doomed to clip coupons the rest of my life."

"You can't be a rich bum," Matt said. "You don't have the personality for it."

"Thanks." There was a guardedness in his tone that alerted his hosts.

"What worried you?" Mary asked.

"I wish the feds weren't so sure I'm into something sleazy."

This moment was what the trip was really for, Jane knew. He was going to talk unguardedly to people who had been through horrors, too. She was going to have to listen.

She silently promised herself that that's all she'd do—listen. She wouldn't interrupt or even comment. It was their world, not hers.

"I wouldn't make anything out of that," Matt said without any trace of lowering his voice or scanning the room for bugs. "Mary and I've lost our passports a few times. They give them back eventually."

"But once they have a file on you, everything seems like evidence to them."

Mary smiled. "You've found that, too?"

Hank nodded. "The hard way. Someone in Oak Harbor swears I'm un-American and the feds seem pleased."

"Hank!" Jane interrupted anxiously, abandoning her promise to herself. "Have you been hiding things from me?"

"Not really." He looked trapped. "That day the sheriff took me downtown, I told you the feds were worried about community reaction."

"I remember." She also remembered thinking he hadn't told her the whole truth.

"They had an excuse. Someone local had mailed them a tape. It recorded my voice, but just sentences patched together, not a conversation. I was saying the terrorists gave me as much respect and privacy as the feds did. Remarks like that. You could call them disloyal."

"If criticizing particular policies is treason, then we're all guilty," Mary said.

Hank nodded. "I mentioned freedom of speech and of opinion. The feds weren't too happy to hear it."

"Who made the tape?" Jane's voice rang with alarm.

"It's like you always say—I can't believe it of anybody in Oak Harbor."

"What was it for, exactly?" Jane asked tensely.

"Stuff you already know." When no one responded, he gathered himself to answer more fully. "The feds and the Hands of Allah both asked me to do consulting for them when they thought I agreed with their ideas. They both got into physical abuse when I disagreed with them. The feds called it medical treatment, but it felt the same." He frowned, determined to get it right. "Well, no. Actually, it felt worse because drugs are harder to handle than a beating when you're allergic, which they knew I was. Also," he went on as if it were an afterthought, "they both focused on psychological coercion when I didn't give in to bodily torture."

"Psychological coercion?" Jane whispered.

He looked steadily into her eyes. "They make me afraid I'm a danger to you."

Mary shook her head in sympathy. "Yes, that's the hard part—distrusting yourself. Whenever we lost our passports, we used to feel guilty for a while."

"Eventually you allow for that as just part of the cost of seeing more than one side of things," Matt said. "In Africa, I remember we discovered the English residents believed one thing. The German settlers believed one thing. The Dutch believed one thing. Each tribe believed one thing. We were interested, but we didn't exactly *believe* any of it, did we, Mary?"

Mary shook her head decisively. "It's healthier not to settle for limited views."

Hank looked wistful. "You must have been glad to go through it together."

"Yes," Mary and Matt smiled intimately at each other. "Remember the first time we got into trouble together and then had to face it separately?" Mary laughed nostalgically.

Matt chuckled and turned to include Jane and Hank. "That mission was a mess from the start. The people we were trying to help were leery. They had a right to be suspicious of Westerners, given the ones they'd met before us, but things got dangerous."

Mary picked up the story. "When we realized we were prisoners and were going to be taken to different camps, we agreed we wouldn't count on each other—we'd make decisions for ourselves. If we got a chance, we'd help each other, of course, but we'd trust each other to take care of ourselves."

"That was just as well, because it came down to a totally personal decision anyway," Matt explained. "We got to choose whether to die of bilharzia or of thirst."

Hank smiled.

Jane was stunned. It seemed a cruelly inappropriate reaction.

And then her parents smiled with him. She was utterly shocked. Evidently going through such experiences left them with a different way of seeing. It was what Hank believed, but she hadn't expected his theory to be so clearly proved.

"What's bilharzia?" she asked to break into their private world.

"A parasite," Mary answered. "People are the prime host. You get it from drinking water."

"What did you finally do?" Jane asked as anxiously as if the threat were new.

Matt grinned. "Like Hank said, it never turns out to be what you think. That time, I proved you can safely be thirsty a lot longer than I thought you could."

"And my group came upon a clean stream they didn't know existed." Mary shook her head good-naturedly. "Of course, by then, all of them had been drinking polluted water and I couldn't get them to stop."

"You tried to protect the people holding you prisoner?" Jane asked disbelievingly.

"Just like you're trying to protect whoever it is in Oak Harbor who's after us," Hank said quietly.

Her parents immediately looked sober.

"You're blaming yourself about those tapes, Hank," Matt said, "but I think you might want to look at that a little differently. It's possible you're a target, along with Jane. But more likely, someone wants you out of the house so they can get at the usual resident."

Mary nodded. "You're probably protecting her just by living at Dutch Bulb."

"Jane's the one who needs to look at her hole card," Matt added.

Mary looked seriously at Jane. "If you need help, honey, you'll let us know."

Jane nodded, her heart aching. They were so kind to Hank, convincing him his situation wasn't his fault. They were so open about his difficulties, as if anyone of value shared his concerns. As if his worry proved his worth.

They followed up their acceptance by reminding him who he was—a counselor like them. And when they were sure he didn't need to talk about himself anymore, they asked permission to borrow his ideas, and then they started in. Relaxing gradually, they debated methods and exchanged theories as if the three of them were old friends.

It was a jolt for Jane to realize he felt at home. It might be just his charming way, she knew. But she wondered if he still missed his parents and hoped to borrow hers.

Absorbed in her thoughts, she didn't hear her father's question, but Hank's response showed how totally he had opened up to them. "I've tried to go on using hostage rules because my problems here are the same in a lot of ways. But when you're supposed to be safe, it's even harder to keep from imagining the worst."

Matt nodded. "We noticed you were playing both sides on the *Evening News*."

"If you watched that broadcast, then you know what your daughter is to me."

Mary smiled at his abrupt shift to the personal topic. "At the time, we were interested in your reactions because some of our missionaries might be hostages before they're through."

"But Mary recognized your voice when you answered Jane's phone a few days after the newscast, so we were able to add the personal aspect," Matt explained. "Jane used to talk about you quite a bit while she was still in school. We were interested, though her fiancé sure didn't like it."

"He wasn't my fiancé."

"I'm not sure you could convince his mother of that."

All the Woodruffs laughed.

Hank's eyes were stormy as he gazed at Jane. She thought it over carefully.

"I'll say what you did about Sylvie. Joe's a friend—that's all he is. I've known him since second grade."

"I suppose I deserve this, Sandy, but I don't know if I can face it," Hank said, as helplessly as if the Woodruffs were his parents instead of hers.

Jane gave herself a moment to remember how harsh he had been to her about Sylvie. But she also knew what kind of behavior was right for her.

"I haven't done a lot of what you'd call dating," she explained slowly. "But I did spend a lot of time with men, as you'd expect for a person who mostly likes to work. One of them—a local guy here—he started cutting down on his social life. When his mom started getting too cordial to me, I realized he'd stopped thinking we were just real good friends. I got it stopped in time, before anyone was hurt."

"What do you mean by hurt?"

"I mean we talked it over like people who played whistle-punk together as kids. For me that was just a pretend, but Joe really did grow up to be a logger. The last time I saw him, his outfit had landed a big contract on state forest lands."

Her parents watched the quiet fire, giving them privacy. "Is he someone I should meet?" Hank asked raggedly. "No more than any other childhood friend."

Chapter Fifteen

Jane sprawled across her parents' bed after a long, quiet chat with her mother. When her dad came in after his walk along the lake, Jane stayed on to include him in the family talk.

Later when she went to her own room, she was startled to find Hank waiting there. He stood at her window as if he could see into the outside darkness. She couldn't read his eyes.

"I've been on a walk with your dad. He seems to think there's nothing abnormal about my reaction to all of this."

Jane nodded.

Hank continued with what was obviously a list. "The workshop went fine. I was afraid someone might ask a question that would trigger some programmed response."

"They asked pretty much everything, so that's proof you're clear."

"It means I can go to work again. I'll have to negotiate with the feds, but, except for that—"

It was true, Jane reminded herself. She had always known he would go to back to work as soon as he could.

"I can't tell you how grateful I am to your parents. They've provided me with almost a clean bill of health."

"I've always liked them," Jane answered formally.

"That leaves one last step." He looked demanding. "Try a trance on me again. I feel like it might work now. Your folks have been so kind. And here in your room, I'll know it's you, even when you change into a hypnotist."

It wouldn't make enough difference, she knew. "I just want to be a daughter here, Hank, you know? I don't want to be responsible, or mature, or all those things."

He bowed his head, as if he were sorry to ask for what she didn't want to give, but he asked again. "I need your help. Otherwise I'll never entirely trust myself again."

She was slow to answer. "You're good at blackmail."

Remembering what she had wanted the last time, he took off his jacket and sat on the edge of her bed to remove his shoes. Watching her eyes, he lay back against her pillow. The sight of someone else in her bed made her feel displaced. She had to fight for self-control.

"I'm tense about it, Sandy, but it's got to work now that everything else is cleared up."

She smiled in the self-possessed way that made him feel deprived. "It'll work."

She sat on her bed beside him. "Let's talk a few minutes. Something neutral. The future, maybe."

"I haven't been able to plan with this hanging over my head." He reached for her hand, clasping it too tightly as he rested both their hands on his chest.

"Well, if you could have exactly what you want?"

"I want to be in a trance."

Jane laughed. After a moment, he did, too.

"Why not hypnotize yourself?" she suggested. "You won't need to resist yourself."

"I doubt if I can. I'll know what I'm going to do."

She loosened his painfully tight grip on her hand. "That's the point. When it's someone else, you resist because you hate being caught off guard."

She watched his eyes while he considered it. When he stopped looking tempted to contradict her, she started.

"Think of the place you've been—a real place—where you feel most at peace. Describe it to me."

He began describing Cabin Seven, with special attention to the fireplace nook where they had spent so many friendly hours during the Stranger Seminar. Warmed by his choice, she found it easier to go on. As if they were merely reminiscing, she added details occasionally. When she sensed he had stopped looking at his memories and had really gone to Cabin Seven inside his mind, she began to take control.

He didn't notice. He relaxed and began to enjoy himself, apparently forgetting what he had meant for her to do.

It wasn't until drowsiness had a firm grip on him that he realized what was happening. There was a moment of desperation. He tried to clench his fists. When his fingers failed to tighten, his eyes glittered with a wild resistance that came too late. Jane went on talking reassuringly.

All expression drained from his face. His grip on her hand loosened. His breathing slowed helplessly.

She couldn't believe they had accomplished it. She allowed herself a moment for astonishment before she questioned him.

"Think about the last time you were in a trance."

"I never was before," he said in a telltale dull voice.

"Has anyone ever tried to put you into a trance?"

"Yes."

"Who?"

"You."

She smiled at the abject literalness of trance subjects. "Before that."

"Three feds." He searched his memory. "Dr. Conrad. Before that, Dr. Blake. Before that, Dr. Jackson."

"And before that."

His thick blond lashes fluttered against his cheek as he scanned the past. "At the university. In Psych 603. They didn't announce the guy's name. He was a dentist."

"Anyone in between?"

"No." There was no sign of stress in the slight curve of his mouth. Apparently the Hands of Allah hadn't even tried to tamper with him. She wondered if that could possibly be true.

A trance subject was as literal as a computer. She might have used the wrong words for her questions, or she might have overlooked small clues. She would have to ask again, in different words. They needed to be absolutely sure his subconscious mind understood what she was asking.

"Think about when you were with the Hands of Allah," she said reluctantly.

"Okay."

"Your thinking changed several times while you were there, is that true?"

"Yes."

"Describe what happened when your thinking changed the most important time."

"They asked me about movie stars. Charles Bronson. And cowboys. Clint Eastwood. And quotable women. Dolly Parton. Talking about it helped me decide to come back to the States."

"Why?"

"I saw I'd gotten what Europe could offer me and I wanted to come home."

The innocent answer broke her heart.

"Describe another important time."

"I woke up. I couldn't move my hands. I was blind." He was silent a long time. "I'd been dreaming. In my dream, it wasn't chains and a blindfold, it was just you holding hands and teasing me like we used to do at Cabin Seven."

He explained laboriously. "It wasn't you, really, but the dream protected me. It seemed like you came to help me."

She watched him through a blur of tears, accepting the distress that showed clearly now that he was relaxed and couldn't cover his real feelings with a look of gallant charm. He trusted her completely, apparently, could that be true? And if it was, then how could she have tried to refuse the help he needed? she thought regretfully.

No, she corrected herself in order to be fair, what I really don't know is how I can possibly go on with this.

She reached out to touch his face tenderly. He turned instinctively, nuzzling her hand. She closed her eyes to make her grief more private. How can I torture a man I'm in love with? she asked herself.

But she knew that going on would be best for both of them and so she squared her shoulders. Took a deep breath. Looked at the blank wall. I'm a hypnotist, she said silently. I specialize in pain control. His, not mine.

Demanding courage of herself, she continued the cruel litany which might bring him peace. "Did your jailers make you feel helpless?"

"Yes."

"Tell me."

It turned out there were a lot of helpless times. Listening was almost more than she could stand, but not listening was worse. His trance-lightened voice murmured on and on, describing the unspeakable.

When finally he fell silent, she felt destroyed, but she was also sure. No matter how many ways she had asked her question, his answer was always the same. Hungry, thirsty, exhausted, wounded, dirty, threatened—none of it mattered to him. He was convinced violence was over as soon as it ended, and nothing he had gone through had taught him otherwise.

Apparently only one thing had lasted for him—the cure they had worked out together at the Stranger Seminar.

She let him rest a minute while she recovered her shaken nerve. Gently she roused him from his trance and returned him to his own control.

"Do you remember what you've been telling me?"

He nodded.

"Do you see it means you're absolutely in the clear?"

Sitting up abruptly, he struggled with giddiness for a moment. As soon as possible, he braced himself against the edge of her bed and stood.

"I can't believe you'd take advantage of me like that."

She was stunned. "Didn't you ask for a trance?"

"I can't believe you'd set me up," he answered sullenly. "Pretend to be friendly. Take control over me."

"I didn't want to—I've said so over and over."

He glared at her. "What you said over and over was that it would never work."

She wanted to laugh at the absurdity, but she knew she would end up crying if she did. "So you thought you were safe, is that it? You expected to make this tragic parade out of wanting to be hypnotized because there was no risk that it would work. What good is that?"

He started to tell her with so much bitterness that she stopped listening. She simply waited until his harsh, low voice stopped.

"Bobby yelled and insulted me *before* his first trance, not afterward. At least that made sense."

"Is that what you think this is? A childish tantrum?"

Abruptly sick of the whole situation, she wanted it to be over, no matter how. But a hypnotist's obligation included the aftermath as well as the trance itself, so she went on struggling with him.

"I didn't think Bobby was childish. I thought he was normal. I don't think you're childish, either. I think you're overreacting."

His eyes were bitter. "How am I supposed to react, in your view?"

"I won't play games." She decided to protect herself. "Look. I've had misgivings about this from the start, and after you cool off maybe you'll have the decency to remember that. I don't normally do trances for anything but pain control—I told you that, but you didn't pay any attention to my side of it. You didn't care how much it would upset me, you only thought about what you wanted. Now look. I gave you what you swore you wanted, so you don't have a right to feel assaulted. But I have a right to feel betrayed."

"You don't know how it feels. You've never been in a trance. You sit there, smug and out of reach."

It was what he had always resented about counselors. Jane reminded herself he was fighting old battles, but it still felt like he was fighting her.

"Of course I've been in a trance—it's part of the training. But I don't hate people for giving me what I want, and so I didn't abuse my trainer. I'm sure that makes a total difference. So probably you're right—I have no idea how it feels to attack someone who helps me.''

"Self-pity," he said harshly.

"You should talk."

"If you aren't on some power trip, why didn't you just show me how to put myself into a trance?''

"I tried to. That's what the first part was about. But you couldn't do it. You fought your memories."

Watching his angry face, Jane remembered what Fran had said about him. Fran was right—Jane had thought Hank was sick, damaged. But it wasn't true, she had just proved that. So maybe Fran was right about the rest of it, as well. Maybe she had given shelter to a man who expected to wreck her life.

Seeing her problem clearly at last, she realized how simple it really was. "I've put up with everything because you were on the run and we couldn't tell who was after you. But now we know. No one's after you. You're in the clear."

He glared at her. "Apparently I am in the clear, which means you aren't."

Briefly she hoped he was going to discuss it reasonably so they could deal with their feelings, as well as the new facts. But one glance at his face showed her his inflexible rage. She had been right in the first place. Their situation was painfully simple.

"No, Hank, I *am* in the clear, as of this moment, right now. You've interrupted my life for nothing. I'm sick of it. I won't play those games."

His strained smile was rude. "Don't pretend you're sending me away. You heard your folks—having me live in is the only thing protecting you."

"You're discussing this with me, Hank, not with my folks." She kept her voice steady, even though the effort chilled her to the bone. "They know I take responsibility for myself. When I need help, I ask a friend."

The word brought tears to her eyes again. Now that she had helped him trust himself, he could risk telling her the truth about his feelings. The knowledge was unbearable, but she would have to face it. She had thought they were in love with each other. But apparently, to him, they weren't even friends.

Chapter Sixteen

Hank had already finished his breakfast of steak and eggs by the time Jane came downstairs the next morning. Radiating his usual charm, as if their bitter quarrel had left him undisturbed, he wandered outside onto the deck. The missionaries swarmed after him, leaving the Woodruffs alone to finish breakfast and say goodbye.

Anxious not to think about herself, Jane encouraged her parents to talk about the next group of missionaries who would arrive next week. She hadn't been brought up to complain about life's cruelties while eating huckleberry muffins with honey.

They walked her to the parking lot. She hugged them both at once as she had done since she'd been a baby. Hank appeared in a cluster of missionaries. He began shaking hands. At last he crunched across the gravel. His smiling thanks to her parents made it clear he had already said his goodbyes.

Jane stared through the side window, dreading the long drive home beside a man she had to give up, even while she loved him. When Hank settled into the driver's seat, she almost sprang out the other door. She could ask her parents for a ride—they would never ask why, and she could explain later on, when it hurt less.

But it wasn't her way to hide from her feelings, and so she decided to get it over with. No doubt he would go on quarreling, and that would help her face the truth.

He was silent until they passed the crest of the ridge.

"I want to apologize."

"No, don't. When people apologize, they just mean you're supposed to put up with them, horrors and all."

"When I apologize, Sandy, it includes a promise to shape up." His amiable tone implied he had a right to control the mood of their relationship—raving, like last night, when he was annoyed, and polite, like now, when he had cooled off.

She couldn't keep her voice from roughening, but she went on anyway. If he thought his cruelty didn't matter, then it was time for him to learn the truth.

"I forgive you, if that matters, but it doesn't change anything." She pressed her lips between her teeth a moment to steady them. "I care for you more than I've ever cared for anyone, but I can't face rage. I can't go on like this—never knowing when you'll lose your temper. Your self-control. Surely Maguire will let you live on your own, now that we've proved you're innocent."

Disconcertingly, his voice softened. "I know I hurt you, Sandy. You don't have to prove it to me. I also know you won't throw me out over a few minutes of bad attitude."

"No one loses their temper just once."

"Are you sure you're being fair?" When she didn't answer, he sighed. "Last night was the first time I've ever been completely helpless in someone else's hands. I couldn't handle it. It's true I lost my self-control," he said softly. "But I didn't lose my temper. I wasn't angry—I was scared."

She bowed her head. "I've faced rudeness before—no problem. But I can't face it when you strike out at me."

"And you won't have to. Last night, having you in my mind was a shock. But I'm willing, now that I know what's happening. Why shouldn't I be? You've been in my heart for years."

She covered her tear-fogged eyes with a shaking hand and turned away from him.

He drove on quietly, radiating tenderness. By the time they reached Port Angeles, Jane had achieved a kind of calm. Hank had a right to believe he was telling the truth, but his view of what had happened wasn't the whole story. She needed to think it through for herself, but she couldn't do that while he sat inches away in a small car. When she got home, she would be able to analyze their situation properly. In the meantime it would be better for both of them if she set it aside as much as she could.

He parked in the center of town. "Here's where your dad gets his hair cut, do you mind stopping? The Oak Harbor shops all cut for the Base, and I don't like feeling military."

Jane considered waiting in the car, but everyone she knew would surely walk down the street. She wasn't in the mood for hometown conversations, even without the added problem of reddened eyes. Trying to make it clear she wasn't keeping him company, she went inside with Hank.

The barbers were sitting in their chairs, watching traffic with their feet propped up. One of them unfolded laboriously. "I do the downtown cuts."

Hank sat down in the vacated chair and lifted his chin cooperatively. "Just shorten it, I like the style."

It was the style Jane had given him that first night when she was still frightened and bewildered and dazed.

What's changed? she thought resentfully.

Catching sight of her reflection in the mirror wall, she saw one thing had changed. Her mother used to groom her with a few quick strokes of a brush. She pushed her curly, long hair behind her ears. Career women and their children wore their hair short, she knew. Smiling tenderly as she thought of her mother, she wondered why she had let her hair grow to please Oak Harbor.

Reading her face, a second barber stood. "I'm the ladies' man."

Without debating it, Jane climbed into his chair and touched her earlobe. "About to here?"

"Thanks, Sandy." Hank smiled at her as if they had never quarreled and never could.

She had forgotten how much he preferred short hair. Almost forgotten, she corrected herself honestly. But that wasn't the point. She wanted short hair. She wanted to be herself again.

By the time they stood on the sidewalk again, they both had come to terms with the emotional morning. Feeling like a host, Hank looked for some way to lighten the mood for the remainder of their trip home.

He gestured toward a boat broker's marina across the street. "Are you a sailor?"

"I used to love boats, when I had the time."

They crossed the street to a floating dock moored two deep with sailboats. The fortyish man who strolled toward them from the brokerage office was new since Jane's time. Before she could drive him away by insisting they were just looking, Hank took charge.

"We'd like a one-day rental, big enough for here to Whidbey, but don't show us anything that's not for sale."

The broker nodded, sea-going wrinkles deepening around his eyes as he squinted over his stock. "Fiberglass line boat, or one of a kind?"

"I'm a sucker for teak," Hank said.

They climbed over several boats, discussing them in the low-pressure way usual to big-ticket customers. But when they reached the right one, they didn't need a tour. A thirty-foot cutter with a teak deck was weathered to a silver, which perfectly complemented the dark blue hull. Bright brass winches and cleats showed how careful the upkeep had been. An ornately carved name board told them her name was *Bridal Sweet* and her home port was La Push.

"Awful name," the broker said acceptingly. "They put her on the market because they've got three kids now."

Jane smiled, beguiled. "Why not just change the name?"

"You know how folks are about their boats. They love her as she is."

Hank nodded. "Do you rent skippers as well as boats?"

"Sure do. My daughter Carol's got gills. She's only nineteen, but she hasn't drowned anybody yet. My boy

Dave'll take your car over to Keystone on the ferry and come back on the boat with Carol, if you want. Dave's twenty-six, so your insurance won't get after you for letting him drive.''

"We'll need deck shoes." Hank reached for his wallet.

"Not to mention—do you have a sweater like hers? Gets brisk out there," the broker said.

Jane waited on the dock, forgetting her worries as she gazed at the beautiful boat. Hank came back wearing a heavy sweater with a French naval blue stripe. The teenager at his side moved with a sailor's compact grace. Even without gills, she looked very much a part of a water world, her hair as dark and close-cropped as a seal's.

Carol managed people as expertly as she did boats, giving simple directions one at a time. Under her guidance, Hank stripped the cover off the mainsail and unbagged the jib. Jane stayed on the dock to cast off mooring lines. When the boat drifted free, Jane grabbed the backstay and swung aboard. While Hank hoisted sails she took in the fenders that protected *Bridal Sweet* from chafing against the dock.

As *Bridal Sweet* entered the channel, the important moment came. The sails snapped taut. The deck heeled over in a gentle slant. Carol shut off the small engine and they all let their hearing unfold. The only sound was the chuckle of water under their bow.

"This boat's cockpit is rigged for single handling," Carol said. "Go forward if you want."

"Thanks." Jane had always loved the bow, where she could be alone with the oncoming waves. She stretched out facedown to watch the water.

Hank lay down beside her, resting his chin on his folded arms. "I haven't been sailing since my parents died."

He sounded peaceful. Jane wondered if he was.

"I like your folks," he added as a logical next remark.

"Pretty much everybody does. You don't have to be a missionary to catch decency from them."

"They create that feeling. It doesn't just happen."

His possessive explanation annoyed Jane. "I've known them all my life. I know what they are."

He didn't react to the jealous tone of her answer. "My parents had fun together. They were playfellows, fanatics for sports, for days like this."

He gestured at the boat. Curious, Jane didn't interrupt his memories.

"Your parents share everything, not just the romps."

"Work's their fun," Jane agreed.

"I guess that's also true of me. I've been to a lot of resorts. The only one I ever liked was our seminar, which was work. I used to feel guilty about it, but now that I've met your parents, it seems all right to be the way I am."

Thinking about her parents made it hard for Jane to cling to her hurt. She nodded. "They do that to everybody."

"I can see why you didn't marry that guy—Joe, the friend. With your parents for a model, you were never going to settle for less than everything."

He seemed to want a discussion of Joe, but it had already been too difficult a morning. Making a point of it, she closed her eyes to show she was thinking of nothing except the sense of being weightless between sunlight and saltwater. He fell silent with her, as if he had said what he needed to. Companionably, they spent the day sharing the freshness of the salt air and the lulling rhythm of the sea. By the time they reached Whidbey Island, they barely remembered how the day had started with quarreling.

Jane's car was waiting for them, as promised. Mesmerized by fresh air and peace, they drove home quietly. It was dusk by the time they reached Dutch Bulb.

Jane couldn't understand the twilight scene. The street in front of the house was blocked by a yellow fire truck. The sheriff's car added red-and-blue strobes. Neighbors filled the yards and sidewalks nearby.

"I suppose we should have expected it, but I didn't," Jane said in a frightened voice.

Hank parked as close as he could and gripped her shoulder. "Don't let yourself start expecting things like this. I did at first after the terrorists, so I know it's a bad idea. If disaster's going to happen, expecting it doesn't protect you. And it's no kind of world to live in.''

He made no move to leave the car until she seemed to have taken in what he was saying.

She was glad not to be alone as they walked toward the fire. She didn't have to see it to know which greenhouse fed the column of smoke surging upward into the still air. She spared only a glance toward the blackened wreckage of her species greenhouse as she walked down the pathway which opened for her through the crowd. She approached a cluster of uniforms between lines of sympathetic stares.

''Well, now, I had hoped we were going to be talking in the past tense before you got home, Jane,'' the sheriff said.

He lifted his borrowed hard hat and rubbed his forehead. ''Nobody's hurt.''

Jane's eyes closed briefly. ''Thank God.''

''I told Fran you'd feel that way, but she takes a different view,'' Corny said.

''I should think she does.'' Clinton strode up unhelpfully. ''Arson's not Fran's cup of tea. She's gone home, well out of all this.''

''I'm glad.'' Jane turned to Corny. ''What happened?''

''Somebody came sneaking around last night and ran a wick of diesel oil along the greenhouse aisles. Diesel won't explode, the way gas does, so they dropped a match and shut the place up. Baked all night—you know sawdust won't flame. The Klotherspoon kid from down the block finally noticed it on her way home from school. She doesn't sign up for after-school rec, so she gets here before Nyla. Walked past just as flames were breaking out. Figured you weren't doing it on purpose. Mentioned it to her mom. Her mom called, and when you didn't answer, she tried the fire department. Real simple fire, but it did the job. Nothing's left.''

''At least it's spring.'' Jane tried to feel resigned. ''Our stock was down to minimums, anyway. And my experiments were already destroyed, you know, from last time.''

Clinton frowned. "What kind of hell do you live in to find bright sides in things like this?"

Jane shook her head. "My folks say you don't have the right to call something hell just because it doesn't go to suit you."

"Speaking of your parents," Clinton answered. "Whose idea was it for you to leave town so this could happen?"

"Mine," Hank said. "Oak Harbor isn't our whole life, Clinton. Sometimes we have to be out of town."

"That may be, but events add up, just like figures do," Clinton answered in his accountant's way. "You always seem to know exactly when to disappear and drag Jane off with you."

"If I had known we were dealing with an arsonist, I certainly would have urged her to leave town, and I hope I could have persuaded her not to come back." Hank met Clinton's gaze with unexpected coldness before he turned to Corny. "Was this a personal threat, do you think?"

"Could be." Corny surveyed the smoldering evidence. "What I'm not clear on is whether you're supposed to get out and stay out, or whether you're meant to tend to your knitting here. Also, there's the question of whether it's both of you someone's offended by, or whether it's only one, and if one, which."

"It's nothing to do with people, Corny, it's just the species bulbs," Jane said in a labored way. "And it's over now, so we can let it go. They're destroyed. All of them."

Minnie Bostetter hurried up to put a comforting arm around Jane's waist. "Boss just now got home and told me all about this and I didn't know whether to bring a casserole or spare clothes or what so I just came on up."

"Thanks, Minnie." Jane returned the hug. "Yourself was the right thing to bring. The fire didn't reach the house, thanks to Annie Klotherspoon. When we rebuild, maybe we could name the new greenhouse after her."

"Bless her heart, now won't she have such a swelled head she won't be fit to live with," Minnie said.

Bobby Amstellen raced into view, overshooting his mark enough to crash into Jane. "It was neat, Jane, I wish you could have seen, they let me help hold the hose since it was your greenhouse and you would want me to."

"You bet, Bobby," Jane said, her raw feelings steadied by his innocently possessive affection.

Nyla appeared at the edge of the crowd, her hands hanging uselessly. She stared at Jane with tear-flooded eyes. Jane held out her arms.

"Well, how can we put up with this?" Nyla's mouth spasmed tragically. "Who do bulbs hurt, anyway?"

"I know." Jane ran her hand up and down Nyla's arm, trying to give comfort without having any strength left to give.

"Well, if they don't want us gardening here, couldn't they just *say* so?" The ache in Nyla's voice was unbearable.

Jane stroked her hair. The rest of the community crowded forward. A neighbor led Nyla away.

Jane tried to calm herself. Sounding unbelieving, she asked each sympathizer what they had noticed. None of them had seen a thing, and all of them forthrightly accounted for the past twenty-four hours as if supplying an alibi were an entirely natural routine. She knew they were being generous—sparing her the discomfort of suspecting them. But it seemed to take forever, and Jane was so dismayed she could barely endure their kindness.

When the smoke whitened and thinned and drifted away at last, the firemen left and Clinton crossed the side yards to go to Fran's house.

Hank drew Corny aside. "Do you have any theories?"

"Oh, sure, one to fit each of our citizens. I'm obliged to a townful of amateur sleuths for a bunch of clues. Everyone's footprints are all through the woods back there. Half the town keeps a gas can full of diesel on hand to start fires with—mostly legal ones. Everybody knew you two were out of town. Nobody had a motive to burn this building, but we all had an opportunity. How does that add up, would you say?"

"Hopeless as always," Hank said.

As Jane came to join them, Corny changed the subject with a fatherly smile. "Nice looking haircut, Jane. I always did think you were a short-hair type."

Corny smiled supportively and left the yard swathed in evening mist that swirled around his legs like smoke. When they were at last alone, Hank held out his hand. As if she agreed quarreling was a luxury they couldn't afford, Jane gladly clasped his strong fingers. They walked toward the house silently.

The kitchen was invisibly full of the day's excitement. Sooty footprints were everywhere. The sink overflowed with cups. Someone had set up Jane's big reception coffeepot.

Hank led Jane to her private office and closed the door. They sat side by side on the futon couch. "Would you like to just clear out, now that your species bulbs are gone?"

"I'd love to." Jane rubbed her eyes. The firemen had shaken hands with her, leaving her grimy. When she took her hands away from her face, her eyelids were smeared with soot.

"But I can't do that to my friends here. They'd feel like they should have protected me."

Hank could see her point. But her friends hadn't been able to protect her here, and he didn't know if anyone could.

Chapter Seventeen

While workmen cleared the burn site, Jane ransacked her house. Hearing noises he couldn't identify, Hank came down from his study to find the couch cushions stacked on the floor in the lounge. Jane groped slowly along the couch cushions stacked on the floor in the lounge. Jane groped slowly along the crack between the couch seat and the back.

"Did you lose something?" he asked.

She shook her head. "There must be a tape recorder hidden where it picks up what you say when you feel private. It's the only way they could have made that tape you told my folks about. That hate mail someone sent to the government."

"The most likely place for a bug is in the telephone. I already checked."

She finished with the couch and started on her reading chair. "It wouldn't be a bug. People here would use something they can buy openly off the shelves down at Radio Shack."

"They probably took it away when they finished the tape."

"Probably." She finished with the chair and crouched down to look at the bottom of the TV table. "Was there background noise to show where it was made?"

"Not enough to judge. Some thumps. Maybe the kitchen."

Jane started for the kitchen.

"It must have been below my eye level." Hank opened lower doors of the cupboards and felt the bottoms of shelves.

Jane crouched to look under the kitchen table. A dictaphone-size tape recorder was taped inside the brace. She had been looking for it, but even so, finding it was a shock.

The tiny reels were turning as she pulled it loose, but they stopped as she and Hank examined it. "Voice activated."

Jane rewound it and punched play. Trying to think of it only as a clue, not as an invasion of her privacy, she set it on the table while they listened to the community drink coffee and speculate about the fire.

When they heard themselves come to the kitchen and begin their search, Hank clicked it off. "He must have put in a new tape when we left to go to your folks."

"Why would anyone want to snoop on the whole town?"

"It might not be the same person doing both of them."

"We've got an eavesdropper and an arsonist both? You think it's a crime wave?"

Hank put his arm around her. "No. It's probably the same person, getting madder."

Jane sighed. "At least we got this stopped."

Hank wasn't sure that was a benefit since it might make their enemy feel he had nothing left to lose, but he didn't mention his doubts. He also didn't ask her to help him remember what they had talked about earlier when they were within the tape recorder's range. Pretending he believed everything was over, he got on with normal routines.

Jane really seemed to think the tape recorder was the last of the trouble. She spent the rest of the day in the outdoor planting beds, eager to remove all trace of the fire. Some of the plants had been trampled by the firemen, but some were only kicked aside. She tossed hopeless cases into a trash bucket and replanted the lightly injured ones.

She was finishing up the next morning when Thelma arrived, carrying a Festival folder. "These letters."

"Are they piling up?" Jane asked sympathetically, washing cindery mud from her hands in the potting shed before they went into the house.

Then, sitting at the kitchen table while Thelma poured their coffee, Jane read the letters, jotting Thelma's comments on margins so the answers she would write for Thelma to sign would sound genuine.

"Shut me up if I shouldn't mention this," Thelma said when the Festival work was done.

"Of course mention it," Jane said. "Mention what?"

Thelma gave the hallway a guilty glance. "No one listening, I don't suppose."

"Not right now."

"Dirk mentioned goings-on down at the port, which I was sure didn't matter, except he wants you to know, even if he was told to keep his mouth shut, whereas I can manage it, as long as we work on Festival letters at the same time."

Jane ignored the confusion. "It sounds scary, Thelma."

"It is. Started out with a couple of young guys, sport fishermen from out of town, Dirk thought. Asking around where to buy drugs in Oak Harbor."

"Come on, not drugs. Not here in Oak Harbor."

"I guess undercover people hang around a military base. It's this government crackdown on sins, if you believe that. But Dirk agrees with you."

"Why am I supposed to know?"

"You're not going to believe this. I don't. But these young squirts said they heard Dutch Bulb was the place to come. Dirk was flabbergasted. He says to throw them out fast if anyone comes here. It's probably a setup."

"Tell him thanks." Hank came through the back porch with both arms full of grocery sacks. Jane was intrigued to see he had caught the Oak Harbor habit of joining in the conversation before he had quite entered the room.

Thelma stood and began patting over all her pockets in search of her car keys. "I wish you'd run a workshop for husbands, Jane. Teach them how to shop and how to want to. You can use Hank here as your visual aid.''

Hank laughed, sounding flattered. ''It's too late for Dirk, but you might work on Bobby, for his future wife's sake.''

''Now isn't that an idea,'' Thelma said speculatively as she headed toward the parking lot.

''What was that about?''

Hank packed vegetables into the fridge while Jane repeated Thelma's story.

''I suppose it's worth checking into,'' Hank said.

''It's a long way from arson.''

''But it isn't routine, or Dirk wouldn't be sending you warnings.'' He stood. ''I'll go talk to him.''

''Okay.'' Jane went to her office to pick up her wallet.

Hank stood in the doorway, blocking her path. ''I want to go alone, Sandy. If you go, people are going to guess why.''

''No more so than they will with you going,'' Jane protested.

''I'll dream up some port business. Don't expect me back any certain time.''

SHE HAD EXPECTED HIM back at once, Jane admitted ruefully, as the hours crept past. The fire had drawn them together unexpectedly. She could have faced the arson alone if she had had to, but it had helped enormously to have Hank at her side. Now, going to the port alone probably seemed the same sort of arrangement to him, but it wasn't really, because it meant he was trying to take her place in the danger zone. Belatedly, she realized what was wrong with his plan. She wanted a companion, not a protector. For her, love meant going through everything together—including danger, if that was what was delaying him.

By late afternoon, she decided she couldn't wait any longer. She ran upstairs to change out of her work clothes. Tucking a bright silk shirt inside clean jeans, she drove to the port.

Hank's truck was parked behind the service building. Relieved, she parked at the end of the row and sprang up the stairs to the harbormaster's glass-walled office.

"Corny?" she said as she reached the door. "I was only looking for Dirk."

"I expect you were looking for us both," Corny said.

"We were talking over if we should come see you," Dirk explained. "Hank at home?"

Jane shook her head. They were breaking something to her gently. She sank into a chair.

"I see from your face you've figured what this is about. I'm real sorry, Jane, but you know, plain citizens can't interfere when the mischief's federal," Dirk said.

"Tell me everything you can remember," Jane whispered.

Sounding like a friend as well as an effective witness, Dirk said Hank talked to him about leasing moorage if he bought a boat. It was a cover story while he asked about drugs and Dutch Bulb. After he had talked to Dirk, Hank had gone down to talk to the sailors as if he were interested in choosing a slip for a boat he might buy.

Jane gazed down at the busy dock. The harbormaster's office was designed to overlook the entire moorage area. Dirk had watched Hank talking idly for more than an hour. When Hank finally went to the parking lot, three men had forced him into an unmarked government car. Dirk had recognized Hank's attackers as Naval Intelligence, and so he'd called the sheriff.

"They can't arrest him," Corny explained. "Civilians are out of their jurisdiction."

"They can pick up deserters, though," Dirk said. "And that might be what they think. Hank seems military when he's irritated. He was military, you know, and it shows."

"Wouldn't they release him when they find out the truth?" Jane asked.

"Ought to."

Jane saw that meant the worst possibility was the likeliest. "The three men," she asked grimly. "Could they be just plain kidnappers?"

"You're thinking of terrorists?" Dirk asked. "Don't. These guys showed me ID when they first started hanging around, so I'm sure of them."

Jane stood. "Then I'll go to the Base."

"Civilians aren't allowed," Dirk said.

"Hank's there, and he's a civilian."

Corny patted her shoulder to take away the sting before he asked his question. "Are you absolutely sure Hank isn't still in the military?"

She gritted her jaw. "The only thing I'm *absolutely* sure of is that they aren't getting away with this."

She didn't feel as brave as she wanted to sound. She headed north through early going-home traffic, clenching her hands on the steering wheel as she tried to remember everything she had ever known about military routines.

When she drove up to the Base guard post, she rolled down her window as if she didn't mind. The cocky guard asked her to state her business.

Worry for Hank made it easy for her to make demands. "Send for the public relations officer. I'm reporting a serious breach of regulations. I'll start with him."

The guard looked her over consideringly. "Don't move." He stepped inside the guard post and picked up the phone.

"Park in the first bay," he said grudgingly.

He watched until an officer drove up and gestured Jane into his small open jeep. They drove an absurdly short distance and parked in front of a featureless long building. Inside, the officer led Jane to a waiting room painted in two shades of gray. She sat on a functional metal chair and leafed through a magazine devoted to Navy career options, forcing herself to pretend to read.

Her escort came back with a higher ranking officer who led her into the inner office and politely offered her a seat. He looked bored.

"You're holding a civilian," she said firmly ⸺ need to release him at once."

"I can't comment on procedures, ma'am, I'm understand that."

"But I can comment. I won't give your mis⸺ publicity if you can convince me it *is* a mistake ⸺ prove it by releasing the man you're holding."

"The mistake isn't on our side, ma'am. We ne⸺ fere with civilians. It's against regulations."

"Therefore, you'll release the man in questio⸺ you're holding several civilians and don't know ⸺ I mean, he's six-two, weighs one hundred an⸺ pounds, blond, blue eyes, athletic build."

"We have no civilian prisoners."

Jane froze her face aggressively before she spok⸺ a federal detainee under my control."

The officer sighed. "I guess I can't say civilians ⸺ permitted on Base. You're here."

He met her gaze for a while, apparently hop⸺ would look away. Since she had expected it, she ⸺ trouble gazing steadily back at him.

"Start at the beginning," he said when he ⸺ wouldn't cave in to silence.

"No."

He drummed his thumb on the desk blotter ⸺ than a minute, but Jane continued to look sure. ⸺ frowned.

"I assume there's someone I can call to ver⸺ claim."

Jane started to give Maguire's number, becaus⸺ proved he could solve federal trouble for them. ⸺ she had called Maguire before, he had made new t⸺ replace the problem he solved.

Corny seemed like a better bet. He could swea⸺ situation, which ought to rescue Hank. She gave ⸺ number, hoping he would have left the port and ⸺ to his office.

While the officer talked, Jane pretended to inspect the certificates framed under glass on the side wall. After a long pause, the officer described Jane as a policeman would. Disconcerted, she scarcely breathed until he asked for a description of Hank. When he hung up, his behavior had changed. She tried to keep triumph out of her eyes.

"Please do sit down, Miss Woodruff." He stood until she obliged. "The man in question was picked up as a deserter suspected of peddling drugs. The agent recognized him. He was convinced he had seen him on the Base."

Jane realized it was probably true, since Hank had arrived in Oak Harbor through the Navy Base, but she refused to unbend to the smallest extent. "He isn't a deserter. Naturally I'm not at liberty to say what his situation is."

The officer nodded. "I'll have him questioned along these lines. If his answers seem to fit, that will be the end of it. Except, of course, for our apologies."

"I'll attend the interrogation."

He looked at her eyes. She steadied herself by thinking of glaciers.

"You'll consent to remain out of his sight?" he asked.

When Jane nodded, he stood. "I'll leave this door open and he'll be questioned in the waiting room."

Jane couldn't believe her bluff had worked. It seemed forever before she heard footsteps in the hall. Chairs scraped. There appeared to be four people—three questioners and Hank. As soon as they began talking, Jane regretted agreeing to hide. The Navy didn't seem disturbed, knowing she was listening, but Jane felt ashamed of eavesdropping on an innocent Hank. It really was an invasion of his privacy this time, and that was what he had hated about the trance.

The questions were meaningless at first. Hank answered patiently. But when he was asked for his address, an edge appeared in Hank's voice.

"You've already seen my driver's license."

"Live alone?"

"No."

"Someone home to identify you?"

Answer, Jane thought, during his long silence.

"If I give you a name, what are you going to do to the person I mention?" Hank asked at last.

"Call and ask if the whole family's home."

"And if I'm not a family member?"

"What are you?"

There was an endless silence.

Tell them. Jane willed her thought into Hank.

"Who are you living with?"

Hank didn't answer.

"We've been tipped off you're running drugs for your landlady."

"No!" Hank said harshly.

"I'll need some evidence."

"I'm under a federal watch," Hank said unwillingly. "My landlady, as you call her, is really my watchdog. If you aren't going to release me, I wish you'd at least tell her where I am. I can't predict what she'll do if she imagines I'm trying to jump custody."

"Federal watch?" the youngest voice said abruptly. "Now I know why I recognized you, sir."

"Of course," an older voice said. "Marines, isn't it?"

Hank didn't respond.

"Our mistake, sir."

Chairs scraped as they stood. Evidently it was over. Jane realized she'd been holding her breath.

"You're free to leave our jurisdiction, Lieutenant. Your escort is in the office, there."

"If I'm free, why am I being escorted?" Hank asked.

"Your watchdog, I think you called her, sir. She insisted on listening in while we verified her information."

Jane started toward the door. It flew open before she reached it, revealing a white-faced Hank. "You shouldn't have come here."

"Neither should you," she answered.

The ends of his mouth moved. "Thank God you did."

Warning herself they weren't really in the clear until they got off the Base, Jane tried not to react, but her knees seemed to be too frightened to work. She made it back to the jeep by sheer force of will. She sat in the front beside the driver and looked blankly ahead.

When they reached her car, she got into the driver's seat because it was expected, not because she imagined she could drive. Their escort sent them on their way with belated cordiality. Hank responded, but Jane didn't even look up.

"I was so scared," she said after they had passed the gate.

Hank relaxed against the headrest and briefly closed his eyes. "I knew you'd know something was wrong when I didn't get back in time to start supper, but I didn't know you'd come after me. I didn't realize you could."

Jane pulled up to the stop sign before the entrance to the main highway, but she made no attempt to drive on.

"If they hadn't accused you about drugs, I was going to stonewall it," he said. "They'd have sent me somewhere else, which would be to the good. I know you're fed up."

"Come on, Hank, I'm fed up, but not with you." Jane parked on the highway shoulder. "If you're holding a grudge because I didn't let you trample me about putting you into a trance, then say so. Or if you want to leave for whatever reason, you can also say so. But don't invent some patronizing excuse."

He ignored her demand. "When they hauled out that gossip about drugs, I realized that you were the real target of this arrest, just like you have been for everything else."

Finally she saw how it must have looked to him. "You thought they were after you. You were trying to lure them away. You were going back to jail to protect me."

He cupped his hand over hers on the steering wheel. When he realized she was trembling, he loosened her grip on the wheel and tucked her hand protectively between both of his. "We're a lot alike, Sandy. I have protective urges, just like you."

It was such a mild statement to describe the sacrifice he had offered. She couldn't resist her tears.

"Want me to drive?" It was a practical question, but his voice reverberated with a tenderness that made it mean a great deal more.

Chapter Eighteen

After the shock wore off, Jane was able to hear Hank's logic about what had happened. He had gone to the port voluntarily. He had called attention to himself. He was the one who brought up the subject of drugs to check out the gossip going around. The Navy released him willingly once they knew who he was. It wasn't a conspiracy.

One ominous element remained—the drug gossip about Dutch Bulb. They couldn't fit that in with the other attacks. And until they could see the pattern, they couldn't know what might happen next.

They agreed to be on watch and not to wander out of earshot of each other. It wasn't much protection, but it was all they had. And for several days, it seemed to be enough.

At the end of the week, Fran called Jane out of the greenhouses to sign for personal mail. Jane waited until the mail carrier had disappeared before she commented.

"This is from Paris. We don't order from there, unless you set up something new while you were in Holland."

Fran shook her head. "Contest entry?"

"Three feet by four? That's a weird shape for a bulb."

Fran laughed in her abrupt way and grabbed a knife to slash the strapping tape. Both partners pulled up the cardboard flaps to peer inside. The carton was full of bulbs in carefully labeled net sacks. Jane scooped out a layer of dormant bulbs, looking for a packing slip. Under the bulbs,

a brown paper package was covered by a loose sheet of red
paper that was covered in aggressive lettering in white ink:

!! WARNING !!
!! THIS PART TO BE OPENED ONLY BY !!
!! *ADDRESSEE* !!

Jane lifted out the warning page. The package was addressed to Henri Wandersee.

Jane had to remind herself to breathe. All her nightmares came together in a surge of devastating fear. The
Hands of Allah, the extra-legal powers of government,
unnamed terrorists—they were real, and even her parents
had believed they were involved in her relationship with
Hank.

She hadn't known what to expect, but she hadn't
expected this. If the package were merely personal, it would
have been marked "personal." But this one carried a
warning rather than a request for privacy. There was really
only one thing it could possibly be—a letter bomb.

"What on earth?" Fran reached for the package.

Jane grabbed her wrist. "Don't touch it!"

Fran frowned at her, suspecting possessiveness.

"Letter bombs have to be addressed *only* to the person
who's supposed to die," Jane explained in a horrified
voice. "Otherwise, it might be your business partner who
opens it and gets hurt."

Fran's face flushed as she stepped back abruptly. "I'll
call Corny."

Jane hurried upstairs and tapped on Hank's open door.
He looked up from his computer in a distracted way.

"Would you recognize a letter bomb?"

Warned by Jane's white face, Hank sprang across the
room and clasped her hand, enclosing her wrist as well.
They raced down the stairs with matching strides.

"Sheriff says don't touch anything." Fran hung up the
phone as they reached the kitchen.

Hank stood over the package, gazing at it silently. In a surprisingly short time, they heard car doors slam. Far too many feet crossed the front porch. Corny led the way down the hall, followed by a pair of Navy airmen. Behind them came Maguire. All Jane's internal processes froze at the sight of him. It proved that Corny was reporting to Maguire, as Hank had suspected.

"If it *is* a bomb," Corny began in his homespun drawl, "I figure let's use kids who're young enough to think getting blown to bits is fun."

"And if it's *not* a bomb," Maguire picked up with his sophisticated copying of Corny's accent, "I'm left with a natural chance to say hello again, Miss Woodruff. And Dr. Wandersee."

Jane didn't even pretend to respond, though Hank was polite, as always. But everyone's real business was to watch the servicemen peer into the box. They dug into their briefcases and scanned the package with electronic gadgets. Finally they stepped back.

"I'm not sure what it is, sir, but bomb it's not."

"Tell you what," Corny said in a bargaining tone. "The rest of us've got families or fiancés or whatever and all you've got is parents. You open it."

The airmen laughed.

"Take it on outside just in case?" Maguire added.

Their grins widened as they picked up the carton, being careful not to tip it as they crossed the cluttered back porch. They set it delicately on the patio picnic table and reached inside. Very slowly they lifted out the inner package. They glanced at each other and then leaned over it to begin their delicate tampering.

The kitchen was utterly silent as everyone watched them pull wrappings back. Reaching inside, they unwrapped again. Abruptly the taller of the airmen threw his head back and collapsed onto a picnic bench so he could laugh more thoroughly. The other one grinned in a way Jane had always associated with rude remarks.

"It's explosive, for sure, sir," he called.

He picked up the flat contents and came back to the house, leaving his partner to follow with the packaging. He stopped just inside the kitchen door. Pausing dramatically, he turned the object so they all could see.

It was a portrait. The gilt frame was studded with rubies and pearls, which picked up highlights in the painting. The artist's subject was a stunningly beautiful woman whose teasing smile evoked a smoking sensuality far beyond mere canvas and paint. Her hair was the complex red of a maplewood fire, and her leaf-green eyes gleamed arrestingly above the faint suggestion of a Middle Eastern harem veil, which did not conceal her face. The veil was the only garment in the full-length portrait.

"If you've moved on, sir," one of the servicemen said, "I'd be pleased to take this off your hands. Our rec room could use brightening up, which this would do."

"You can keep the frame, sir, if those stones are valuable," the other airman added generously.

Hank laughed at last. "I guess I'll keep the whole thing, sorry. She's a good friend, and not the sort you forget."

"For sure." The airmen nodded like resigned good sports. "There's this letter, also, sir."

Hank scanned quickly through three pages of crackling parchment before handing the letter to Maguire. "It's personal. In French."

Jane watched Maguire's eyes move back and forth as rapidly as if he were reading English. He paused to smile at one of Sylvie's jokes.

Jane was shocked. She turned to Hank. He was watching Maguire with a careful self-control, which showed how bitterly he resented the invasion of privacy.

"The letter's to both of us," he said to Jane. "It explains that the bulbs are a gift to you."

Maguire handed him the letter. "I anticipated trouble, Dr. Wandersee, and apparently I found some, although as usual with you and Miss Woodruff, it's not the kind I looked for."

Hank looked assaulted. "The gifts are just friendly."

With his usual perfect timing, Clinton looked through the kitchen door. His face flushed as he noticed the painting. After a pause of indecision, he stepped to the side for a better look.

"People I know let it go with a greeting card, but I can see you're a man of parts, Hank," he said ponderously.

"When I came over to do your books, Fran, it sounded like quite a party going on out here and now I see why," he added.

Absurdly Clinton's comments made Jane want to cover the painting, even though she hadn't felt the need to protect its explicitness from the other men's eyes. Sharing her irrational feeling, Hank picked the painting up and carried it into Jane's office. When he came back, he closed the door.

Needing to join him in taking action, Jane gathered the scattered bulbs into the empty packing box. All the men stood more idly once the portrait was gone. Jane decided Clinton was no worse than the rest of them.

Maguire casually introduced himself to Clinton and led the way down the hall. Corny dismissed the bomb squad by thanking them on the way to the front door.

When Fran left, shaking her head, Jane looked at Hank. "Is it Sylvie?"

He nodded.

"From what you said about her before, I thought she was the same sort of thing I had with Joe."

"You've never fully explained to me about Joe," he answered predictably.

When she didn't answer, he frowned. "Is this the sort of thing Joe did with you?"

"He'd never even *dream* of having a portrait done, not even with his clothes on."

"If he did, would he feel free to send it to you?"

"Why are we discussing Joe? It's Sylvie who sent all that skin." Jane sat down at the table and propped her head in her hands, wishing she didn't feel like crying.

Hank sat down opposite her and reached for her hand. She shut her wet eyes, sure he would accuse her again of pretending to feelings he didn't believe she had. She couldn't bear it.

She was surprised when he explained instead.

"When you were in France with your folks, you were probably too young to notice how different it is. Sylvie doesn't understand American relationships. Exclusiveness. Jealousy. That whole line. She can't believe in it. She thinks Americans are weird."

"Weird!" Jane repeated too loudly. The men in the hallway turned to look. "If Americans are weird, what's she?"

"She's European. She's loyal to her own place. She's afraid I might blame her world for what happened to me. She wants to remind me I have good memories to balance the bad. If she said so in words, I'd argue back, of course. So she sent this portrait, which can't be argued with."

"The letter says that?"

"Not exactly, but it's how she thinks."

"The harem veil is supposed to show that the Middle East can give you pleasure sometimes," she interpreted painfully.

"Exactly."

"Pleasure, but not love," Jane added.

"That's it."

"And the bulbs?" Jane asked sadly.

"The same sort of thing. She knows you care about me, because you took me in. So you might hate the world that held me hostage. She's reminding you of the other side, too."

"The bulbs I like best come from that region, so I can't hate it as a place."

"I'm glad you understand."

Jane wasn't glad.

Still, making room for Sylvie's view of life started her thinking about her own. After the portrait was stored in the attic and the bulbs were put into quarantine in the basement, Jane spent two frustrating days trying to make sense out of the past few weeks. When that seemed hopeless, she decided to accept the past without explaining it. It left her free to ask what she wanted next.

She sat at the desk in her private office, leaning on a legal pad. Dividing the pad into columns, she labeled one side "work" and one side "personal."

Then she paused to think. After a while, she realized she was staring at a pot of *turkestanica* hybrids on a corner of her desk. They had escaped the fire by being in the house. She had worked through several generations to produce the green-streaked reverse on their dainty white bells. The color was still unstable, ranging unpredictably from almost lemon to a green darker than lime. She hoped to stabilize the variations since she loved them all.

Reminded by the tulips, she added a third column to her legal pad and labeled it "bulbs." Staring at the three topics showed her the problem. She ought to have a column labeled "Oak Harbor" and another column labeled "Fran."

Thinking of Fran's fury over the recent complications, Jane laid down her felt pen. Her mind shied away from the web of danger, and so she used an indirect approach. As if she had stored her memories on videotape, she saw Fran again as she was in the beginning—frank, friendly, cheerful, ready for anything. She replayed Oak Harbor—warm, folksy, kindness personified. She had meant to analyze. Instead she sat transfixed by happy memories.

Footsteps in the kitchen called her back. Hank had come in from his afternoon run, his face pleasantly flushed.

She beckoned. "I need a business consultant. I know you're usually expensive, but could you tailor your fee to my partnership's income?"

"Sorry. My charges are based on my worth, not yours."

She looked rueful. "That'll bankrupt me."

He laughed and slouched into her conference chair.

"I've been thinking about Dutch Bulb. I bought this partnership to test my theory about women entrepreneurs.

I think women understand you better if you're working along with them instead of telling them what to do. A lot of them resent authority, and if you're an outside consultant, you're just one more boss."

"Makes sense."

"It's worked perfectly, this time. Fran makes better management decisions now, and Dutch Bulb is coining money like a counterfeiter's printing press."

He smiled.

"But one success doesn't tell you much. It could be personal. Or an accident. I need to do the same thing several times before it's proof."

He nodded, his eyes intent.

"So. I think it's time to dissolve this partnership and try again somewhere else."

Dispassionate intelligence gleamed in his eyes. "You don't mind seeing the tulips all go back to red? Clinton really likes that Holland centerpiece you put in the lounge after the species bulbs burned. I want to punch him every time he looks at it."

"It'll never go entirely back to red. Not now that Sylvie's prize has made our contest international."

He touched the green-streaked creamy *turkestanica* stars. "What will you do if you sell out here?"

"Leave."

He inspected every detail of her face.

"Moving on for business reasons isn't the same as running away," she explained. "No one will be hurt by it."

His neutral gaze was disturbing. "I have to notice that you settled in a small town like the one where you grew up."

She paused, wondering if there was any truth to his observation. "I like a small town near a big town—like Oak Harbor and Vancouver. It's what I'll choose again."

"But why here? California has small towns near big towns, and it's a gardener's paradise."

"How long has it been since you got yourself current on California taxes?" Jane plunged into a mind-bending account of numbers and percentages. She followed up by reciting footnotes to California business law, quoting loopholes with a confidence that showed she had memorized the fine print.

When Hank laughed, she stopped, but she didn't smile.

"Is this really how you think about it?" he asked.

She nodded.

"If you leave Oak Harbor now, you'll never know who was after you."

"If I leave now, with some reason to go, all this will stop. People will forget."

His eyes darkened. "You're afraid to know, aren't you?"

She drummed her felt-tip pen on her legal pad. "At first I hoped it was someone on the outskirts, someone I hardly knew. But with what we already know, it has to be a friend, Hank. Why should I insist on figuring out which one? I forgive them, whoever it is. But I'm tired of it."

He watched sympathetically.

"Am I acting like a coward in disguise?" she asked edgily.

"No. What you say makes sense to me."

Her quick smile showed how important the consultation was to her.

"Why don't you throw a party?" he asked to endorse her business plan. "Show people you aren't running. Use Fran's house, so it's not just business. Tie it in with Festival."

She nodded. "People remember a great party."

She dragged her calendar closer and began looking for a party date in order to hide her distress. His reaction showed he agreed that her enemy was a friend. His suggesting Fran's house for the party showed he suspected Fran.

Instead of protesting automatically, as she had when he searched Fran's house, this time she considered it. The attacks didn't show a clear pattern, but one element was clear: their enemy knew everything about their schedule and a great deal about their pasts.

In Oak Harbor, that included everybody, she insisted loyally. But Fran knew more about her than anyone else.

Chapter Nineteen

"Can we trade consulting gigs?" Hank asked. "I've been thinking about the future, too."

Jane nodded. He watched her face grow sad, as it always did when he mentioned his predicament.

"I went to see your Doc Brussel."

"Is something wrong?" Anxiety made her eyes enormous.

"No. But I want to make some plans. And before I commit myself, I need to be sure I'm not carrying around some sort of permanent damage from all this mess." He smiled. "Doc says I'm in better shape than I've ever been in my life."

"He doesn't know what you've been all your life," she objected logically.

"That's the advantage of a small town. People can tell you what you're like whether they know or not."

She laughed uneasily.

Encouraged by her response, Hank stood up, pulling her to her feet. She cooperated hesitantly as he led her to the futon couch. When he sat down, she looked confused. It wasn't until he beckoned that she realized why he had moved. Smiling slightly, she sat beside him.

"I'm tired of acting like I never want to touch you except when you're frightened." His quiet voice was coaxing. "I want to hold you now." He put his arm around her shoulders as if to demonstrate.

She scooted closer to him on the couch. "It's been rough on both of us, hasn't it?"

With his free hand, he brushed her short hair away from her ear, as if wanting her to hear more clearly. "I'm not asking for any kind of commitment. I can't talk about the future, because I won't have one to offer in return until the feds release me, if they ever do."

She looked at him with no pretense of hiding her feelings. "The government doesn't worry me too much, Hank." She paused. It was hard for her to tell him, but she needed to.

"Can I tell you what really worries me?" she asked, trying to keep it from sounding abrupt. "I can't fall in love with you and then be a good sport and wave goodbye when you decide to take off again. And we both know you will. Even if you don't go back to Europe, you won't stay in Oak Harbor."

"I like Oak Harbor," he said slowly. "But you're right— I'll leave eventually. I doubt I'll ever stay anywhere forever."

He ran his fingers along her jaw and touched her mouth before lowering his hand to snug her body against his.

"And you're not staying in Oak Harbor, either," he added when she wrapped one arm around his waist. "You just told me so."

She sat up abruptly so she could see his face. He grinned as if he had won an argument. "All I'm asking for is the chance to court you. Just to see, the way anyone handles the sense they're falling in love. No promises on either side. No damage meant. Do you like me enough to try that?"

"Oh, Hank, *like* you!"

He laughed, enjoying her extravagance. "Okay. But look. We wander around here together. When you see me, your face lights up. I can't tell you what that does to my feelings. But you turn on the very same radiance when Corny walks through the door. And when you see Boss. And Dirk. And Bobby. And your parents. And I haven't seen you greeting Joe, but it's the same, I have no doubt."

He watched her eyes darken, interested that it pleased her for him to admit his jealousy of Joe.

He couldn't tell her what he really wanted. He wanted her to feel the devastating loss, the emptiness he felt whenever she left the house, looking back over her shoulder with an all-purpose friendly grin. He couldn't tell her that, so he told her as much as he could.

"I want us to see if we can feel truly special about each other."

She had a glow he had never seen before. "Hank, don't be absurd, you aren't special. You're utterly unique."

He let the words echo inside his mind, to be sure of what she had said. And then he smiled as if he had won a marathon. "Convince me."

She released his hand in order to lock her arms around his neck. He bent his head for the kiss that would seal their bargain. Catching excitement from his urgent body, she clung to him more tightly. When she relaxed against him at last, he moved on, trailing kisses across her throat, nuzzling her sweatshirt aside as sensually as if it were made of silk.

When he sensed the first hint of reserve, he straightened and smiled into her eyes. "Let's take our time. We've spent five years getting this far. Another five minutes won't hurt."

She smiled wistfully. As if wondering whether their bargain was real, she stroked his face. He closed his eyes and moved under her hand, murmuring luxuriously.

"It'll be easier if we don't have to hide our feelings," she whispered.

He studied her eyes, needing to be sure she wasn't simply accommodating him. "I'm glad you think so, too."

THEY DECIDED TO HOLD their party the weekend before Festival began. Everyone agreed it was a great idea. They called it a new tradition.

The universal enthusiasm gave them another excuse for feeling happy as they walked across the side yards to Fran's house. It was their first shared experience as host and hostess, and so they had planned carefully. They dressed modestly, hoping not to seem like exotics in the hometown gathering. Jane's copper silk dress brought out bronze tones in her sandy hair, and Hank's charcoal jacket brightened his eyes by contrast while paling his hair to gold. In spite of their best intentions, they looked disconcertingly expensive.

They lingered in the kitchen talking to Fran until the guests began to arrive, and then they separated. Hank had prepared the food, which gave him a perfect reason to stay with sandwich trays and snacks. Corny had agreed to tend bar, so Fran and Jane were free to enjoy their guests.

Jane drifted through the quickly filling rooms, pleased that everyone was there—the business community, the town government, the school. Even the bomb squad had sent their names so Jane could include them on Dutch Bulb's list. It was going to be a party to remember, as planned.

Hank appeared in the dining room doorway, his height making his golden head visible above the crowd. He lifted his arm in a beckoning gesture. Jane worked her way toward the front door.

Dutch Bulb had invited all the breeders and retailers who were close enough to make the drive seem worthwhile. In a businesslike way, the off islanders had organized van pools. They had also organized a donation campaign. They trailed across the yard carrying pots of their best species bulbs as party thank-yous.

"Heard about your fire," DeWaard said.

"These aren't a drop in the bucket against your loss, but they stand for the help we'd like to give," Maas added.

"Just back order us, we're good for anything peculiar as soon as you're built back up enough to ship," Veitvek said.

Each one of them had something kind to add as they walked through the door with pots of remarkable blossoms in their hands, but Jane couldn't really hear. She bit her lips, to start. When that didn't help enough, she ran a quick finger along her lower lids. And finally she frankly lifted her hands to cover her eyes.

She wanted to duck the greeting line and hide in the bedroom until she could calm down, but everyone who was close enough to know what was happening crowded forward to watch. Surrounding Jane indulgently, they blocked her way to keep her included while they admired the odd gift blooms. By the time she could retreat, there was no longer any point to embarrassment, because she had given up and wept openly while her shoulders were patted sympathetically by everyone in reach.

Feeling awkward, she went to the kitchen, knowing how red her eyes must be. She moistened a dish towel and blotted at her feverish cheeks.

"These little things might as well be water lilies, spread out flat like that, and next to nothing for a stem," Minnie said as soon as Jane showed signs of recovering.

"It's a *kaufmanniana* hybrid," Jane said damply, touching the orange petals. "I was going to stay out of trouble with whoever has it in for us and keep the party decorations just goblet shapes and clear reds."

"Then I'm glad these growers betrayed you," Minnie said. "Most of us love these beautiful stars and those twisted petals there by the coffee urn."

They clearly did. The guests toured the amazing display, which had turned Fran's house into a conservatory.

Clinton's voice interrupted her reverie. "I see from your smeared face that you think of this as fitting in, Jane, but you've had quite an impact on Oak Harbor. I've just been having my ears scrubbed out with foreign words from *chrysantha* to *acuminata*. Of course I'd heard the technical terms 'double' and 'fringed' before."

Jane couldn't keep herself from laughing. She looked up at Clinton, hoping he had intended a joke.

"Our dealers are so kind it breaks my heart," she said. "You see what they did because of the fire."

"Everyone sees." He adjusted his gray bow tie.

"I wish we'd had the party at your house." Fran emerged from the storage porch with an armload of bottles of sparkling waters. "Those blossoms look like they've got a disease. Oh, I know," she said quickly, before Jane could answer. "I could just look somewhere else, if it was only me. But whoever burned your Turkish greenhouse isn't going to like this."

Blood rushed to Jane's face and then drained away too fast. "I've done my best about that, Fran—I'm giving up on Turkish bulbs so Oak Harbor can stay pure Dutch. But what can I do about this? Everyone likes these Turkish bulbs."

"Not everyone," Fran said.

"Oh, Fran. I'm sorry."

More sorry than you know, Jane added silently, forcing herself to face Fran's bitterness, along with everything it implied.

"I want them out of here the instant people are gone." Fran stalked away. Clinton hurried to help carry her supplies to the bar.

With half of her mind, Jane heard Nyla explaining a black *hageri* dwarf to an admiring group. Jane stared at the compound bloom, trying to preserve her own calm while she thought about Fran's attitude.

Even if Fran isn't our enemy, the partnership's over, she decided sadly. Partners have got to trust, and neither of us does that, anymore.

Maguire detached himself from a noisy group near the buffet and crossed the kitchen to interrupt Jane's dreary thoughts. "Great party."

With his usual mysterious knowledge of everything about her, he handed Jane a glass of ginger ale, not something alcoholic. He clinked it with his glass of Irish whiskey on ice. "This means you're pulling out? Thought you might."

Jane gazed at him in abrupt despair. She had invited him because she didn't want him to attend as the mayor's guest. She suddenly saw there was a great deal more she didn't want to know.

"Do I need permission to leave town?"

Maguire smiled in his unnatural way. "We can protect you anywhere."

Protect. Jane gave herself a minute to deal with the reality instead of the dungeons that sprang fully equipped into her mind.

"Maybe I don't need protection."

"That'd be nice," Maguire answered noncommittally.

"I'm a little hopeful. I'll get rid of these bulbs, to make things easier."

He scanned the room casually, dividing his attention between the tulips and the noisy guests. "Hang on to them for a while. Let's see if anyone gets annoyed."

"You're expecting more trouble?"

He met her gaze expressionlessly. "Aren't you?"

Chapter Twenty

When they got home from the party, Jane stopped in the middle of the kitchen. The door to her office shouldn't have been ajar. Through the gap, she saw chaos.

Springing across the room, she slammed the door wide open. Drawers had been pulled from her desk. Files scattered. Publicity posters had been stripped from the walls, leaving shreds dangling from thumbtacks.

Jane stared, bewildered. Warm with pity, Hank wrapped his arms around her.

"I wish they'd been satisfied with just greenhouses," she whispered in a wavering voice.

"They're amateurs, try to remember that. Pros would have slashed pillows and upholstery and knocked the desk apart to find false bottoms to the drawers." He rubbed his jaw against her temple comfortingly.

"I'm scared." She burrowed her face into his shoulder.

He kissed her forehead undemandingly. "The kitchen seems to be okay. You wait here while I do the tour."

Instead she reached for his hand so they could investigate together. Feeling out of place in their party clothes, they checked the public office. It looked like a tornado had struck. In the lounge, the mail had been tossed around the room. Jane folded her arms suddenly, trembling as if she were cold.

"I really believed it was just the bulbs," she said.

"It might be just the bulbs. If we get rid of all those pots people brought to the party, that might end it."

"We can't throw out gifts!"

"Good. I wondered how scared you are."

"Just ask, don't test. I'm *totally* scared. But it doesn't change anything."

Finishing their damage tour, they checked their bedrooms. Their angry visitor hadn't gone upstairs.

"Maybe there wasn't time," Jane said.

He held her close, as if his warmth would make her situation easier. "Do you know who it was?"

"Fran practically had hives over those party gifts."

"But when would she have had time to trash your house?"

"She was in and out all evening, restocking supplies."

"It would have been easier for almost anyone else."

"That's true." Jane knew he was giving her an out in case she wanted to defend her friend. "Someone who left early, do you think? Did you keep track?"

"No. I was enjoying the party." He led her to her bed and sat down, his arms sheltering her.

"It could be anyone," she whispered against his shirt. "As always."

"I hope it's Fran. I trust her not to hurt you."

"No one would hurt me."

He disagreed, but he didn't tell her so. He kissed her temple before he disentangled himself.

He stood to look down at her with a self-mocking smile. "I want to comfort you, but I only know one way, and now's not the time for that. You'd think I was protecting you, and I'd start raving that you don't feel what I want you to, and our enemies would have what they want."

She nodded. "Us, separated and confused."

"Will you be afraid to sleep alone?"

"Sure. But it doesn't matter. What about you?"

He didn't answer. He just bent to cup her face in both hands as if he could print a feeling of safety on her mind by exposing her to his warm skin. He left reluctantly. She didn't want him to go, but they both knew he was right to leave.

She didn't expect to sleep, but she changed out of her party clothes and crawled into her bed.

She was astonished to wake up with sunshine in her eyes.

Hank made breakfast while Jane got to work on the mess. Sitting on the floor in the official office, she sorted the paper snowstorm into preliminary stacks.

"There's a pattern," she said as Hank joined her, carrying plates of scrambled eggs and muffins. "If you have a Dutch or English name, your papers are here. But if your name is Moen, for example, or Khoury, your file is gone."

Hank sat down cross-legged beside her and sipped his orange juice. "So they're after everyone they associate with the species bulbs. Does it still sound like Fran?"

Before Jane could answer, the back door slammed. Footsteps crossed the kitchen and paused.

"Jane!" Fran's voice was harsh with hysteria.

"Down the hall!" Jane called, glad to get it over with.

"What *is* this?" Fran stopped in the office doorway to stare at their breakfast party.

"I wish I knew." Jane was surprised at how real Fran's shock looked.

Fran's naturally square jaw became more visible. "When I signed partnership papers with you, I never meant it to mean arson and break-ins and this."

Wrestling with nostalgia and loss, Jane took the plunge. "You're right. We'd better dissolve the partnership."

Fran gasped. "I meant this stuff's a mess. I didn't mean our partnership!"

Jane searched for some way to give Fran an out. "But you've never liked the species bulbs and that's my part of the business. I couldn't believe it last night when you loaded the gifts onto a cart before people were hardly out of your house."

Fran didn't cry easily. The whites of her eyes reddened first, and then lines etched her forehead and cheeks. Her mouth quivered distressingly before it turned down hard at the corners.

"*Of course* I tried to get those bulbs out of my house fast! I was scared they'd do this to *my* place." Fran's breath came in unrelieving gasps. "But why did they do it to yours?"

"Don't you know who's doing this?" Jane asked.

"Of course not." Fran sniffed unashamedly. "Do you?"

"No, but you know everything about everybody."

"I don't know about this." The horror and grief in her voice were too genuine to leave room for doubt.

Overjoyed to be able to cry with Fran, Jane stood to wrap her partner in an apologetic hug. "I've been afraid you knew and wouldn't say." It wasn't quite the truth, but it was all Jane thought their friendship could stand.

Fran shook her head vigorously enough to set her corn silk hair flying. "If I knew who to accuse, every cop on the coast would be standing right here in this room."

"Have you had your breakfast, Fran?" Hank asked.

"I'll settle for juice."

It was the first time Fran had accepted anything from Hank. All three of them saw it as a turning point. When Hank left to get Fran's juice, the partners righted chairs and sat down in more dignity than Jane's picnic style had allowed.

"We really do need to separate," Jane said.

Fran wiped the tears from her cheeks. "I knew Hank was trouble. From the minute I heard about him, I've been dreading you'd get the itch to leave."

"Is *that* why you've been so angry at him?"

"What did you think?"

"I'm not sure I thought," Jane said, ashamed. "I think I was just worried." She shut her eyes tightly to clear the tears. "But it *is* time to split. Not because of Hank. The real problem is, I've gotten so jittery because of all this. You have, too."

It took Fran a long time to nod. "All right. It's true. But please stay involved as a silent partner so we'll keep in touch."

"I'd love to."

Being able to trust Fran helped Jane get on with her work. She was doubly glad since there was barely time to clear up after the break-in before Festival began.

She dressed carefully for the first official event, her camel skirt topped by a small-check jacket in casual and cream, which brightened her brown eyes and emphasized the soft colors in her hair. Assigned to inspect door passes, she drove to the school for the new bulb contest.

She stood in the cafetorium door, greeting observers and checking credentials from strangers. When enough people had arrived to crowd the room, the mayor's wife drew the Canadian judge they'd selected aside, so she could have a moment to compose herself.

Miss Barton, a private grower from British Columbia, had sixteen international patents to her credit, and no involvement in growers' politics. It was the kind of background Jane had looked for—she could not possibly give offense, even in a crisis-ridden small town.

The woman herself was even more reassuring than her reputation had been. Small boned, straight spined, she moved with a birdlike quickness. Her practical walking shoes and thick Scots tweed contrasted with her fragile look to make her seem an ideal choice. She looked as if she had been ripped from an English garden of three hundred years ago.

News of the Canadian judge had attracted a photographer from the *Vancouver Sun*. And Jane had also checked credentials from the Seattle *Times*. But she was caught off guard when a pair of late arrivals turned out to be the team of journalists who had interviewed her a few weeks earlier.

Karen Wilcox flipped her head to rearrange her dark short hair. "Let us crash, okay?"

Tim Baker flashed his charming smile. "We'd have gotten ourselves invited if we'd known the judging was a closed event."

"How did you find out the right time?" Jane asked.

"Could you not ask?" Karen said.

The leak could have come from the Seattle *Times*, Jane decided. Not wanting to scare herself, Jane nodded and let them in.

For all the hopes and money riding on it, the judging was brief. Several digital wristwatches chimed the hour. A hush fell. Minnie moved forward with her sweet smile, Miss Barton at her elbow. When they reached the display tables, Miss Barton went on alone. She looked intent, as if nothing else existed except the handsome contest blooms.

She walked clockwise along the tables, pausing before each plant. When she reached the end, she turned on one practical heel and glanced back along the colorful display.

Nodding once to prepare her audience, she returned to a clear white Darwin. Its globular shape was kindergarten simple. Its translucent petals were evenly blotched at the base with black. Silently, looking gravely at the blossom, Miss Barton held up three fingers shoulder high. Cameras clicked and whined. She ignored the sound.

She cut across the room to stop before an orange *greigi*, its huge petals freckled in mahogany. Concentrating on the flamboyant tulip, she held up two fingers in a V.

After the cameras, Miss Barton lingered to heighten the drama. When she held up her hand the next time, a breathless grower would suddenly feel unreal. Some cherished hobby would be plated in gold for good, thanks to Sylvie's gift of the huge new prize.

Her heart speeding up sympathetically, Jane imagined how it would feel. Suppose she had entered her green-black turkestanica. Or suppose one pot held her *sylvestris serpentine*. Or her ice blossom—suppose it hadn't been destroyed. The real thing wasn't the money, she knew. It was the prize itself. Imagine the whole world of patent tulips knowing your name, she thought, recognizing your work.

With unexpected showmanship, Miss Barton walked tormentingly slowly toward her last choice. Crossing the hopefuls off by passing them, she stopped in the far corner of the room. She gazed down at the tiniest of tulips, a *chrysantha* hybrid, which made up for its thimble size by glowing a nearly fluorescent antique gold. She held the pot up in her garden-roughened hand, respectfully presenting the first bulb ever to win the Hands of Allah Prize.

The watching room applauded. And then the crowd flocked forward to gaze upon the tiny bloom, which had earned its breeder fame in the world of competitive bulbs and enough prize money to fund a lifetime of painstaking experiments.

When Jane looked up from checking her list to identify the winning gardener, she realized she needn't have bothered. The winner was the only person still standing by the back wall. An amateur from Sumas, Mrs. Roosma was too overcome to stand without support.

"I only started with spring flowers at all because I was so homesick when we first moved here years ago," she apologized to Jane, her round blue eyes anxious in her round face. "I don't know why I entered your contest, I certainly never dreamed to win. If I'd dared suspect how it would turn out, I'd never have come here to watch. I just wanted to see the other blooms and maybe get new ideas from them."

Jane smiled. "Yours is beautiful."

"Well, yes." Mrs. Roosma glanced furtively toward the crowd which blocked her view of her own bulb. "I did think my plant deserved to win. I'm the one I have doubts about."

"Come on over here and let everyone talk you into feeling pleased with yourself, do you mind?" Jane clasped a steadying hand under Mrs. Roosma's elbow.

As they approached, Miss Barton strode protectively toward the shy woman who was almost twice her size. Her hands outstretched in a peer's welcome, she drew Mrs. Roosma into the center of the crowd. Beginning to explain what the younger woman had accomplished, she left some sentences unfinished in an encouraging way. Mrs. Roosma finished them automatically, and finally she began to talk more smoothly. Once she was started, not even the noisy journalists could shut her up.

Eventually the crowd was ready to supervise the pinning of ribbons for second and third place. Thoroughly excited, they admired the tiny trophy for first—a pair of hands held up in a tulip shape. An Indian artist had carved it from local cedar and promised an annual supply.

Jane felt pleased with the show's success. It had all worked beautifully. The letdown reminded her that it had been a long day.

She came home to an empty house.

Hank's truck was gone. Trying to believe he was just running an errand, she checked the fridge door. No message. Struggling against alarm, she hurried upstairs. His worktable was undisturbed and his closet was neat. Nothing was out of place but Hank.

He's gone to the grocery store, she told herself, not believing it. She went to her bedroom to change into jeans.

A sheet of paper lay in the middle of her bed: "Come to the port."

Terrified, she tried to think. It was Hank's writing. It might be nothing—just an ordinary, hurried note.

It didn't look hurried.

If he'd been kidnapped, they could have forced him to write it in order to lure her to join him.

She thought of calling the sheriff, but there might not be time. Panicked, she stopped trying to think. She left for the port at a dead run.

Chapter Twenty-one

Never run on a dock, Jane reminded herself as she ran down the cleated ramp, it's too dangerous. She raced along the floating pier toward the visitor's dock. Never wear heeled shoes around boats, she recited dutifully. She stripped out of her sandals as she ran. She slowed down when she was close enough to inspect the visitors.

There were two of them. The large Grand Banks cruiser was a more likely choice for a kidnapper, but it wasn't readying itself to put out to sea. The cutter looked familiar—dark blue hull and weathered teak.

She had just recognized it as the boat they'd sailed home from the Peninsula when a blond head appeared at the hatch. Hank came out of the cabin, looking happy. Catching sight of her, he smiled easily.

"Are you all right?" she gasped.

He looked contrite. "Oh, Sandy, I'm sorry—I should have said 'good news' on my note."

"Worry? Me?" she answered, trying to make light of it. She knew it was a sign of his recovered health that he could set trouble aside so easily. She decided she needed to work on it, herself.

"I got new name boards," he said.

"She's yours?" Still shaken, Jane went to the stern to look. Reaction and all, she smiled. "I needn't have asked."

The new name boards read *Cabin Seven*. Oak Harbor was listed as home port.

"I know we're leaving, but we can ship her anywhere. You're keeping money in Dutch Bulb, so we can claim this as home port in a lot of ways, wherever we are."

He watched her think about it. "I can't invite you aboard. You're co-owner, it says so on the registration. You'll have to step aboard without being asked."

"Co-owner?" Jane said faintly.

"I'd like to talk about it."

Swamped by the violent change in mood, Jane stepped aboard. She climbed down into the cabin, and he followed her. A blue ice chest in the galley held a picnic. Zipped-together sleeping bags covered the double bunk. It looked homey, in an on-the-move way.

"Dutch Bulb's been fun, but Fran's your partner there, and I wanted a place that belongs just to us." He watched her face.

She wasn't sure how she wanted to react to what he apparently had in mind. "It's a wonderful boat."

He put his arms loosely around her. "I want you to have a safe place, where there haven't been any emergencies."

She nodded. "I'm awfully tired of disaster."

"I'm going to turn myself in, Sandy." His voice was sure. 'I'm going to ask for an exit interview and whatever that provokes, I'm going to get this business with the feds shut down for good."

"No! *Don't!*" Jane locked her arms around him in a rib-cracking hug. "We can put up with Maguire. If he wants to follow us all over, so what? We're used to it."

"We can solve the threats to you by leaving. I want my trouble cleared up, too."

"No, Hank, please. I'm afraid of them for you."

"Don't be afraid."

"Remember the last time you said that to me?"

He nodded. "That first night. Neither one of us knew quite where we stood, or why, or what was happening."

"Suppose you turn yourself in and they don't let you go?"

"I want to be free. I don't care what it costs."

She caught her lower lip between her teeth. "I care *terribly*."

"Thanks." He waited.

She stepped into his arms as if they could hold each other and deny the world. After a few moments, she relaxed. She didn't feel joy. She felt more than mere delight—she felt they had come home.

They had already faced so much, and they had no way to guess how much was still to come. But for this moment, in this private place, their world belonged to them.

"I'll go now and get it over with, if you want me to." He tightened his arms around her.

She thought of the picnic cooler and the sleeping bags, which indicated the opposite. "Don't go."

"You're sure?"

She nodded.

His gaze incandescent, he eased down onto the bunk. He stretched out and waited for her to join him. When she nestled against him, he coaxed her leg over his so not even their own bodies would keep them apart.

He pressed his forehead against hers with an intimacy she remembered. "Oh, Sandy, how did we manage to wait for this?"

She was mesmerized by the fragrance of his breath against her face and by the pressure of his chest against her breast as his breathing quickened.

"Why are we still dressed?" she whispered.

"That's up to you. I need to be sure you want me."

She smiled wistfully. "You know I'm in love with you."

He nodded, his confident acceptance more touching than any false claim of tactful uncertainty. "We both know we're in love. But there's still the question of what to do about it."

"Is that a question for you?"

He drew away from her and sat up, lifting his arms above his head, his elbows crooked, his hands loose fists. She stripped his sweater slowly upward, pausing for a last electrifying look before she shrouded his head. Pulling the heavy knit along his arms, she reversed body and sleeves as he peeled out of it. Responding to his quickened breathing, she grabbed both sides of his collar and opened the snaps down the front of his Western shirt.

When she touched his bare chest, he stroked her shoulder, giving her one last chance to turn back. Instead she ran the backs of her fingers tantalizingly down his belly. He smiled and peeled her jacket off so he could unbutton her blouse and lift her camisole over her head.

After a pause to look, he reached with luxuriating hands to trace her breasts. When she shuddered, he pulled her against him so their skin could touch.

They clung together, savoring that touch for a few moments and then got to work on shedding the rest of their clothes. She unsnapped his jeans and he lifted himself so she could ease the denim past his hips and down his long legs, tugging his deck shoes off as she went. He reciprocated by unfastening her skirt and lifting it away. He gazed at her gold briefs as if they were a complex puzzle.

Glorying in his reaction, she waited until he cradled her to remove her last garment before she reached out to return the favor, helping him out of his briefs.

Moving slowly, they lay down again—at first satisfied to gaze. But helpless craving quickly led their hands to touch and stroke. They smiled and eased into each other's arms to move and cling. Their bodies adjusted instinctively, solving the problem of arms and legs by locking around each other with single-hearted agreement. Like the old friends they were, they found each other's rhythm easily. They moved with an outward tenderness which belied the fire storm bonding them within.

At last, absorbed by the fulfillment of their senses, they lay against each other peacefully. Their sensitized skins cooled slowly as they shared a pillow. Jane reached around him to tuck the second sleeping bag against his back.

He opened his eyes drowsily. "With the terrorists, I used to have this fantasy. You'd lie on me to keep me warm while you stayed cool enough to sleep."

She stroked his face. "I don't mind if you cover up."

"You'll be too warm to sleep."

"That's all right, provided I get to pester you."

His laugh echoed fascinatingly inside his chest. "Absolutely. Pester me."

"I may not be very good at it."

"In that case, you'd better start practicing."

They both laughed happily.

Honestly unsure, she braced herself on one elbow so she could lean over him. She slipped her forearm beneath his head to cradle him. Encouraging the gesture, he nuzzled his cheek luxuriously against her breast. She stroked his temple. His eyes held nothing but glory even in their farthest depths.

Watching his reactions intently, she started to explore. When he groaned and closed his eyes, she moved on top of him. He reached to help, opening passion-blind eyes so he could guide her.

"I want to look at you while we do this."

"I have to hold you."

"I know. I want that, too."

THE NEXT MORNING, they left *Cabin Seven* reluctantly. They stood in the port parking lot between their cars. Their hair was jeweled by drifting mist. It was time to say goodbye.

"I have to go now, Sandy, or I never will."

She touched his mouth. Neither of them knew whether she was hushing him or stealing a kiss.

His truck was already loaded. There was no reason for him to come back to Dutch Bulb.

"If you sense the least danger, I want you to move down here to the boat. That's what it's for."

"I'll be all right. Will you?"

"I'll call tonight." He kissed the top of her head.

She lifted her face.

He kissed her fiercely, then tore himself from her arms, climbed into his truck and drove out of the parking lot. He didn't look back.

Jane drove home in a tangle of feeling. Already lonely, but still elated to be able to touch him freely at last.

She trusted work to solve the loneliness. It left her free to dream about the rest.

When she parked at Dutch Bulb, she remembered what it might have meant for them to be away overnight. Feeling wary, she toured the house. Everything was functioning and secure.

She thought about it while she changed into a sweater and jeans. Their enemy must not have realized they hadn't come home last night, since all their recent absences had led to an attack. So anyone who had known the house was empty ought to be in the clear. Who did that cross off?

She stared into space, going through the list. Fran had spent the day in Burlington with a friend from kindergarten days. Minnie and Boss had gone to Seattle to visit a niece. Thelma was in Langley on Festival business. Clinton had gone with Thelma because Dirk had a conflict—a night meeting with the Port Authority. Nyla was on an overnight camp out at Deception Pass with the high-school marathon team.

But Corny had been home. And Edna. She smiled at the thought of her fragile neighbor as an arsonist. Her smile faded slowly as something tugged at the edge of her mind. What? A worry of some sort floated just out of reach.

Arson had suggested it. But why? She frowned.

The bulbs! She looked at the pot of budded *tarda* on the kitchen window ledge. The Hands of Allah prize wasn't a Holland bulb!

Why didn't I think of it before? she asked despairingly.

She knew why—that kind of thinking had gotten shoved aside by her fears for Hank. And then there had been the night.

She gave in to it, knowing his bare skin again, his husky love-soft voice, the soulful depths of his emotional eyes. With that memory to support her, she could face anything, she told herself. To prove it, she went to the phone.

"Corny? I'm afraid Festival might be attacked." She had imagined it was going to be hard to explain, but a couple of sentences did the job.

"We'll lay on some private security for the contest bulbs."

"Fran would peel apart."

"No, now, I'm just going to mention it to a couple of those former high-school football heroes running to fat lying around under their cars. It'll do them good."

Satisfied that she had done what she could, Jane got started on the rest of the day.

Her first job was at the high school, where she was supposed to supervise while the contest display was moved. The art teacher was waiting in the main hall. An enthusiastic woman, Miss Crabtree was sure the display should be based on color values rather than on prize rankings. As she unlocked the display cases set into the walls, she insisted it didn't matter which flower had won which prize.

"I hope you're right," Jane said. "If everybody feels that way, we'll get through Festival."

Miss Crabtree stared at Jane as if she suspected irony but she decided not to dig into mysteries that didn't belong to her. The hockey team clattered into the hall, carrying pots. They were followed by the journalism class, who had written descriptions of each entry. The mob seemed out of control to Jane, but when the class bell rang and everyone else disappeared, she discovered she liked the display. Relieved, she checked the office on her way out of the building.

"You'll keep the display cases locked, won't you?" she said to the office assistant, a grandmotherly volunteer.

"Yes, dear, even if those locks are such a joke I could break in myself," Mrs. Vandervleet said accommodatingly.

"It's a lovely display. Banquet guests will see it Friday, and everyone can look Saturday after the parade."

"I'll put it in the school bulletin that you're pleased," Mrs. Vandervleet answered.

Jane pulled her appointment calendar out of her purse as she left the school. She was glad to run late since it shielded her from emptiness. She didn't get home till dinnertime. She stood in the ktichen, feeling confused.

I've forgotten how to cook, she thought. She made herself a sandwich and took it to her office. She spent the evening frowning over balance sheets, getting ready to pull out of her active partnership. When her plans looked workable, she checked the time. Hank hadn't called.

Knowing how distracting math could be, she went over the whole set of figures again. By three o'clock, he still hadn't called. She went upstairs.

He wouldn't forget, she told herself.

They might have shipped him to the East Coast on a redeye flight, she added.

She knew that wasn't the likeliest explanation. It took courage to face the truth. Hank had a lifetime habit of pulling away from everyone who loved him, and he had told her he was leaving even before he asked her to spend the night.

Her mind paused. Had he asked her to spend the night? No, she didn't think he had. He had made it easy, but she had volunteered.

It took her a long time to move beyond that thought. I'm not sorry, she decided. No matter what happens because of it, I'm glad about the night.

Without undressing, she stretched out across her bed and stared through the dark window.

What if he doesn't call? she asked. That could be just his way—love and move on, she admitted. But what about the boat? Surely he wouldn't have bought the boat and coregistered it with her if he intended to leave.

Yes, she thought, half smiling in spite of hovering tears, that's *exactly* what he'd do. If he really meant to go, he'd leave behind a thank-you present which would break her heart forever.

She buried her face in her pillow and let her feelings take control.

After a long, blank time, she drew back from grief and took another look. If he's in trouble, he can't call, she thought, beginning to feel panicky.

Was there any way to know? she wondered. She could try phoning Maguire. Or the Base.

If she called, he'd find out. And if he wasn't in trouble, if he had just wanted to walk away, he'd feel hounded.

But one phone call to check. Would that count as hounding? She decided it was the kind of question she should sleep on before answering.

She couldn't sleep.

At dawn, she was relieved to get up and start the day. Skipping breakfast, she went to the potting shed. She distracted herself by making last-minute adjustments to the banquet centerpieces that the driver-education class was due to pick up right after lunch.

She didn't consciously decide to do it, but as soon as she could pretend the sheriff might be awake, she phoned. Her blend of worry and explanation was garbled, but Corny seemed to understand, regardless.

"I don't think we're quarreling," she ended lamely. "And maybe I just misunderstood. But in case he faced more than he thought, from them, could you help?"

"I could probably check."

"Would you?" She went back to the greenhouses and vowed not to think.

She knew the news was bad when Corny drove into the parking lot instead of phoning. She went out to his car. He got out and leaned on the door. "You got him out of the Base that once because he was crosswise with some lower-ranking busybodies. But I can't advise you to try it again. Maguire isn't really down-home, no matter what he pretends."

Her pulse deafening, Jane clenched her hands. "I've never believed that folksy act of his."

"Good." Corny reentered his car and slammed the door.

"Please, Corny. I love him. Help me rescue him."

"He's not being tortured, you know," Corny said gently.

"Tormented. Not tortured. Maybe it's not the same."

But it seemed the same to Jane. Standing on the sidewalk to watch Corny drive away, she added it all up. Apparently Hank was at the Base, since Corny had warned her not to go there again. Evidently he was being held in isolation, which explained why he hadn't called. She couldn't bear the thought of his imprisonment. And Corny had comforted her instead of offering help. That must mean there was nothing the law could do.

Her heart breaking, she remembered how Hank had counted on her when he was with the Hands of Allah. He was surely counting on her again, and this time, she had given him every reason to.

Oh, Hank, I'll manage somehow! I *promise* you, she thought despairingly.

By the time she got back to her house, she realized there was one last possibility. Rooting frantically through the box of business cards in her desk drawer, she found Karen's card. Not daring to put her hope into words, she stepped into the kitchen and picked up the phone.

At first she thought Karen's number was going to ring forever, but finally an answer tape clicked on. "Karen, I need help. I need it badly. In exchange, I'll tell you *everything*."

Karen's machine had a four-minute cutoff, so Jane had to call back twice. When she had it all said, she felt a little better.

"You've *got* to help us, Karen, *please*," she ended, pleading. "Nobody else can save him, but surely you can, can't you?"

Chapter Twenty-two

Jane knew she had done everything she could to help Hank so she made up her mind to trust that she had done enough. It left her with nothing to do but get on with Festival. For the banquet, she put on the dress Hank had bought her in Vancouver. The memory gave her a pang, but she could live with that. She needed her memories of him to give her strength.

She drove to the school feeling official and entered the cafetorium with a determinedly cheerful look. Board members served as table hosts, so she stood beside her labeled chair. Clinton left his assigned spot and marched toward her.

"What's this rumor about you leaving Dutch Bulb?" His face was oddly bright, as if his feelings were disturbed.

Jane struggled to remember that Oak Harbor still thought her most important worry was her partnership plans. "Fran and I've agreed. Would you run up official figures? I'd like to pull out just enough money so I can buy into another business. I'm staying on as Fran's silent partner."

"You're not leaving?"

She was puzzled by his strange tone. "I'll live somewhere else, but I want to keep hold of Oak Harbor. I love this town, and I'm *so* fond of Fran."

"I'm glad to hear you say that, Jane." Bernice, from the Dutch Café, entered into the discussion as a matter of course. Jane was glad, even though Clinton's posture as he returned to his own table warned her he would find time later to give her some of his usual advice.

Sad, worried as well as amused, Jane watched her news spread outward from Clinton in gossiping rings. Guests raised eyebrows in astonishment and then looked over to frown at her, or smile regretfully as they caught her eye, or shake their heads emphatically to change her mind. In response she nodded, and shrugged, and ran an apologetic finger under her eye to stand for tears, showing how much the community meant to her. For a moment she struggled against real tears as she thought how much Hank would have enjoyed the homey drama. But she owed it to herself and to Oak Harbor to make the scene stay manageable, and so she struggled to maintain her smile. By the time coffee was served, the news had reached the farthest corner of the room.

Leaving Fran to face the talk, Jane ducked out. She planned to come back and check on Corny's guards after everyone else had gone home, but while she waited, she wanted to be alone. She wanted to think about Hank and her, to hope for the future.

She went home to change into her usual sweatshirt and jeans and to try to while away a couple of the endless waiting hours in the greenhouses.

When the town seemed quiet, she drove back to school. The building was dark, except for the floodlit front doors. A van was parked under a streetlight. Jane parked and walked over to tap on the driver's window. Floundering noises answered from the darkness inside.

"Norrin?" she said as a sleepy face peered around the driver's seat. "Everything okay?"

"Oh, hi, Jane." He rumpled his already sleep-touseled hair. "I was just sitting here in the back talking to Viola. Leo's in the other parking lot. Real quiet around there, too."

Jane nodded. "I'll just walk through."

Since she had the use of a passkey during Festival, Jane unlocked the front door. She crossed the dark entry and groped for the light switch. Light flooded the main hall.

Even before her eyes adjusted, she moaned—not with shock but with despair. The glass cases were broken. The species contest entries had all been ripped from the shelves. The hall floor glittered with glass slivers mixed with torn leaves and wadded petals and trampled, mangled bulbs.

Numbly she walked into the mess to get a better look at the prize winner's area. The devastation was total except for the third prize winner—the white Darwin bulb was still in place. Of course, she thought.

But she didn't have time for bitterness. Footsteps approached rapidly from the dark side hall. Jane pressed herself into the shallow recess of a closed classroom door, trying to sort out the echoes from the footsteps themselves. They seemed to be approaching the main office.

All the lights went out. Terrified, Jane dashed for the front doors.

The mess underfoot betrayed her. Slipping on damp plants, she crashed to the floor in the midst of glass shards and potting soil. She struggled to her feet and took off from a crouch, like a sprint runner.

A large shadow loomed outside the glass front doors. She saw she had run the wrong way. Spinning, she tried to escape farther into the building. She fell once more.

There wasn't time to get up again. She lowered her forehead to the cold floor and waited hopelessly, thinking only of the broken glass catching in her hair, and the fragrance of damaged leaves.

The lights came on. She sat up slowly, hoping she would have the courage for whatever she was about to face.

"Well, now, Jane, the janitor was sitting up here tonight to help out, and when he called and said he heard someone out here busting up the school, I never thought he was asking me to come toss a net over you." Corny's friendly voice was such a surprise Jane couldn't answer right away.

"Oh, Corny. Was that you outside? I was scared it was some monster who was going to— I don't know what." Jane was relieved until she saw his stern face.

"Are you arresting me?" she asked in disbelief.

"Let's start with some first aid, you could use it. While that's going on, we can chat to keep your mind off it."

Jane looked at her hands. They were bleeding slowly. Glass slivers glinted in some of the cuts. They began to sting when she saw that she was hurt. She stood.

"Will you let me question the security guards first?"

"Might go better if we both ask," Corny agreed.

By the time they reached the street, Leo and his date had joined Norrin and Viola in front of the school.

"Well, now, boys," Corny said. "A guard and his date isn't the same as a guard."

"Yes, sir," both guards said, looking at Jane.

"I must not be the only one who went inside the school tonight," Jane said before guilt could shut them up. "Did you see or hear anything?"

"Yes, ma'am. Sheriff, here, drove past before he went to bed. Thelma and Minnie had chocolate with Edna after the banquet. Checked us on their way home. Who else?" Leo said.

"Nyla hung around till her mother came after her. Clinton came by and told us how to do this sort of work. Dirk stopped after his last check on the port," Norrin said.

"Did they all go inside?" Corny asked.

"The one's with Festival passkeys did."

"That's everyone but Nyla," Jane said.

"Was Dirk here last?" Corny asked.

"Yeah."

Jane's heart sank. She decided not to notice what else they said.

"How long have you been asleep?" Corny asked.

"We weren't clear asleep," Norrin insisted.

Corny shook his head. "Viola, you drive Jane's car home for her. Norrin'll follow you in his van and take you home from Dutch Bulb."

Jane protested, but Corny pointed toward his car.

"It couldn't be Dirk," she insisted. "Anyone could have gone inside after the kids fell asleep."

"I didn't suppose it was Dirk. You're the one we caught in the act." Corny opened the passenger door for her. "Hold your hands above the level of your heart, slow that bleeding," he added as he settled into the driver's seat.

"If you're arresting me, I have to ride in the back."

Corny's homey smile helped. He phoned ahead to Doc Brussel as he pulled away from the curb. Jane crossed her wrists on top of her head and leaned back, visualizing Cabin Seven with its magical peace in order to compose herself. Self-hypnosis wasn't likely to help with the real pain—it wouldn't help her stop wishing she could go to Hank and strengthen herself from his comfort and understanding. But it would help with the medical ordeal Doc Brussel would put her through.

The doctor was waiting for them in his home office, his night beard a white smear across his jaw. "You're getting to be as bad as your friend Bobby," he said encouragingly as he seated Jane in a comfortable chair and anchored one of her slashed hands under a bright light.

He showed no signs of listening as Corny talked to her about the night's events. The school janitor had heard glass breaking. He'd phoned the sheriff and said he wasn't a hero. After everything quieted down, he'd felt ashamed so he started out to look. Before he reached the display cases, he'd heard a desperate groan and so he went to the main switch and turned off the lights. He couldn't say why he had done that.

"The groan was probably me," Jane said.

"Is this hurting you?" the doctor asked.

"No, I took care of the pain the same way I fix it for Bobby. It doesn't work quite as well on yourself, but close enough." Jane watched him pick glass out of her hand, imagining how it would feel without autohypnosis to help.

It was broad daylight by the time the doctor finished bandaging her hands and pushed his glasses up onto his forehead. "I figure you want your fingers free. But you've got some pretty deep cuts there, so keep them clean."

Corny drove Jane home in silence. She got out and leaned down for a last word. "Now that it's over, I guess I can stand to know. Who's been doing all this?"

There was no hint of confidential information in Corny's gaze. "Over, is it, you figure? That's a relief."

Chapter Twenty-three

Jane felt empty. It seemed she had lost every battle she had ever fought. She hadn't rescued Hank from prison after all. She hadn't saved the species tulips. She was going to have to leave Oak Harbor under a cloud.

She couldn't bear any of it. And especially, she couldn't face it without Hank.

But she stood on her patio to think it through again. She had said she couldn't fall in love with Hank and then wave goodbye, but that's what she had been forced to do. It hurt unbearably, which made everything else seem minor in comparison. She could do the rest because she had to.

She sighed and crossed the side yards toward Fran's house to say goodbye. She walked into her partner's kitchen as bravely as she could. Fran was sitting over a cup of coffee finishing her breakfast.

"Your hands." Fran reached for the coffeepot to pour a cup for Jane.

Jane sat on a bar stool and labored through the story. After Fran's face turned bright red, it was even harder to talk, but Jane managed it.

"Festival's finished except for the parade," she ended sadly. "I hate for it to end this way, but my going now won't leave you in the lurch. I'll clear out and think things through."

"Are you allowed to leave? You're under suspicion."

The question sounded harsh, but Jane reminded herself that Fran's prickly nature would never change and that she didn't really want it to.

"Right." She stood. "I'll check."

The morning fog was just beginning to pull back as she crossed their side yards to Dutch Bulb. Stupefied by physical shock and grief, she sat down at her desk, concentrating carefully.

She signed a check for Nyla. Writing a note describing where Sylvie's bulbs were stored, she asked Nyla to take care of them.

She signed a check to pre-pay for extra work and wrote a note asking Betty to pack up and store her things as well as Hank's. She didn't tell why. She wasn't going to give their enemy the satisfaction of knowing they had been driven out of town. She and Hank were both ready to go— that was all anyone needed to hear.

Lining up the notes and checks on the kitchen table where everyone would find them, she went upstairs and drew a bath. She removed her clothes and sank into the tub, carefully keeping her bandages dry.

As she had hoped, the fragrant warm water relaxed her. She leaned her head back and closed her eyes, hoping to be able to think.

I'm not going to run, she said meditatively. I'll say a proper goodbye. I'll go downtown and watch the windmill dancers one last time. That can't hurt anyone.

Feeling somewhat restored, she dressed in linen pants and a nutmeg sweater with extra long sleeves to help mask her wounds. Brushing her hair, she thought she heard banging noises beyond the parking lot. Puzzled, she listened curiously.

When the racket kept up, she went outside. From the patio, she saw a hazy figure through the fiberglass walls of the new greenhouse where the party-gift plants had been stored.

Oh, dear God, no, I forgot about them, she realized as she started to run. She jerked open the greenhouse door just as a pot crashed into the brace above her head, showering her with soil and broken leaves and clay shards.

"I've worked on you for years." Clinton hefted another pot. "I finally get you almost presentable, and the whole thing comes apart."

He threw the pot. Narrowly missing her shoulder, it sailed through the open door and broke on the grass. He looked around for another pot, but Jane saw that he was surrounded by better weapons—shears, trowels, stakes.

Horrified, she forced her mind to track. "I had no idea I was getting it wrong, Clinton. But it's stuffy in here. Let's go outside." Away from weapons, she added silently.

He adjusted his canary-yellow bow tie, leaving a thumbprint of soil on one side. "Very well."

He stopped her in the potting shed. It was full of shovels and hoes and even a pick. Shocked by the sight of the tools she had never thought of before as dangerous, Jane retreated behind a service cart.

Clinton picked up a hammer, which was generally used to break up cracked pots. "You've attended Festival parades. You know Oak Harbor doesn't use Turkish costumes."

"That's true."

He slapped the hammer shaft rhythmically into his palm. "This foreign element. First the man himself, and then this loathsome prize."

"I could cancel the prize."

"What good is that now? Those party favors in there prove you've infected the town."

"People only brought them to be kind."

He pounded the hammer on the potting table, raising a cloud of dust. Jane saw that it was dangerous to contradict him.

"I destroyed one batch of plants, and you get more from Paris. They disappear. I think you've learned your lesson. More are given. And others win the prize."

In spite of the unreal evidence in front of her, his claim was too much for Jane. "Clinton, stop it. You didn't snoop and slash and burn. You *couldn't* have."

He threw the hammer at her in a sudden sweep. It was simple to duck, but she couldn't escape the murderous glitter in his eyes.

"You've always underestimated Oak Harbor." His voice was almost unrecognizable.

"No," she insisted unwisely. "I love Oak Harbor."

"Then you must be glad that I've got this under control at last. Wandersee's in a ward for the criminally insane. The false tulips are destroyed. You're on your way out of town. Next year's Festival will be normal. I told you I'm going to be the director, and I won't preside over anything but Dutch." He picked up a stake-splitting maul.

Shaken, Jane tried to see the real man behind the perfectly familiar face. "Nobody could get this angry about a *bulb*."

His laugh was frightening. "No, not about a bulb."

He paused dramatically. "I'll admit I fell for you. Who wouldn't? Even an alley cat like Wandersee responds."

When Jane drew her breath angrily, he lifted a hand to hush her. "I know—he only meant to use his body to pay for his room and board, but you've got something and, well, being around it on a daily basis, not even he could resist."

"Get out." Forgetting she was defenseless and he was armed, Jane started toward him in a rage.

She was too furious to hear a car drive up, but Clinton hesitated and turned. Running feet crossed the parking lot, Clinton frowned as he peered at the sound through the crisscross lath screen wall of the potting shed. Jane sprang for the maul.

Caught by surprise, Clinton let it slip through his fingers. Letting go suddenly was as good as an attack. It sent Jane reeling backward to trip over the service cart.

Clinton lunged inexpertly for Jane, but a big hand grabbed his shoulder and spun him aside. He crashed against the potting table and sank to his knees.

Hank leaned down to wrap an arm around Jane's shoulder and help her to her feet. "Are you all right?"

"Oh, Hank, he called you an alley cat," Jane gasped.

Hank frowned. "Is that the worst?"

"What could be worse than that?"

He shook his head, scanning her quickly in order to see for himself that she was all right. Abruptly he pushed her sweater sleeve back to expose her injured hand.

"It's nothing." She tried to cover the wounds. "It happened last night."

Frowning, Hank released her and crossed the potting shed in a single stride to loom over Clinton. Hank's posture was both ready and relaxed.

Hank's behavior was so out of place in Oak Harbor that Jane finally saw him as he really was. She and Clinton hadn't done much damage because neither of them knew how to fight effectively, but Hank knew. Dressed simply in a sweater and jeans, he looked like what he really was—a powerfully athletic man with aggressive confidence in his physical strength.

Dazed, she saw at last what Oak Harbor had seen from the first. And not just Oak Harbor, she realized, shocked by the click and whine of a camera.

Smiling, Karen walked over to her. "You promised you'd make it worth our while to spring your man. I'd have been satisfied with the interview he granted us down at the Base. But these action sequences will make the *Evening News.* We'll put Oak Harbor on the map."

"You will not," Clinton said with surprising dignity, from his seat under the potting bench. "That's an invasion of this town's privacy."

Realizing no physical attack could wound Clinton half as much as an invasion from the outside world, Hank moved back to stand beside Jane. She wrapped her arms around him, relaxing at last. "Oh, Hank, I can't believe you're here."

He smiled as he embraced her protectively. "I'm feeling a little unreal, myself."

For a few moments, they simply held each other, not needing words. But at last they remembered they weren't alone. They drew apart reluctantly contenting themselves with holding hands. "Calling Karen and Tim was a brilliant thought," Hank said in a pleasantly husky voice. "The feds were going to hang on to me until they discussed every word in my journal, but the intelligence community can't stand publicity. So when your media friends here set up a clamor, the Base was glad to let me go with nothing but a forwarding address."

"So, what's your address going to be?" Karen asked.

"Our boat."

"We'll drive you down," Tim offered.

The sheriff's car drove into the parking lot, followed by a second car, which no one recognized. Corny and Maguire got out of the cars and came toward the potting shed.

"Edna, next door, called me when the battle began," Corny said. "I radioed Maguire, as I'm required to do. I've been living for the day I could tell you that."

"We knew," Jane said.

"Well, then," Corny said affectionately. When he turned to Clinton, his voice was still amiable, but it wasn't warm. "I'd like to discuss your rights with you, down at my office."

"I know my rights. My family set up this town."

"Things keep changing." Corny gestured toward his sheriff's car.

Clinton stared at Jane as if he still had a great deal to say. Everyone waited.

The intimidation of Tim's waiting camera was finally too much for Clinton. Protective of Oak Harbor to the last, he left without looking back.

Jane gazed around in disbelief. "It seemed like a battlefield, but it's just a potting shed."

"To Mr. Clinton Jarvis, it's a beachhead for change," Maguire said. "Cutting your hair pushed him over the edge."

Jane looked at his face. He seemed to mean it. She laughed almost hysterically. "My *hair*."

"I was hoping it was something that personal. Otherwise what we had pointed to him cooperating with something international. You've got some fairly nasty groups here in the Northwest. The woods make too good a hiding place."

"International? *Clinton?* He hates even Seattle, and that's only fifty miles away."

Maguire laughed as if she had made a successful joke. "The drug rumors down at the port gave us our break. Mr. Jarvis told some Seattle boaters he wanted to buy cocaine, but he didn't know how that's done and they got scared government agents might be checking them out. They reported him to the harbormaster, a friend of yours, Mr. Amstellen."

"Dirk tried to warn me of something," Jane remembered.

"We sent in a string of boaters—innocent-looking youngsters on noisy holidays. Mr. Jarvis was going to have to deal with strangers, because townspeople would just laugh if he approached them. We expected him to try again, and he did. Our undercover kids asked him where to go. He tipped them off to try Dutch Bulb."

He shook his head as if the simple trap shouldn't have worked. "Our undercover kids were wearing wires, of course, and Mr. Jarvis has a distinctive voice. It wasn't enough, in itself, because it didn't connect him to the violence, and you've taught us we can't put a watcher on someone in a small town. Fortunately you figured out where the next hit would be and told the Sheriff. We decided hiding a stranger where he could watch the school had to be worth the risk. You were right—what you told Sheriff Postma—Mr. Jarvis did wait until their dates distracted your guards before he went inside the second time. By the time we realized what that meant, he was gone and we couldn't find him. We should have known he'd wind up here.''

"I don't want it to be true."

"I'm sure you don't."

"He won't be punished, will he? He hasn't broken any real laws, just courtesies.''

Maguire's unnatural-looking smile was contradiction enough, but he went on with the words anyway. "Assault with a deadly weapon. Arson. Destruction of public property—the school.''

He lifted one hand in a casual wave as he left the potting shed. "It's been a pleasure, Miss Woodruff.''

Jane rubbed her forehead in bewilderment. "I can't believe it happened, and I can't believe it's over."

Karen laughed. "So what comes next?"

Tim casually led the way toward their car.

"We've worked well together on this, so we're setting up a joint consulting service," Hank said as he followed Jane into the back seat of Karen's car.

Jane looked at him guardedly. But then she remembered how he had reacted to her parents' working together.

They both reached out to hold hands.

Karen smiled.

"I need her help," Hank explained. "The Hands of Allah asked me how to launder money, and I didn't know. They had to settle for publicity."

"I've never understood money laundering, either," Karen said as if they were simply talking like friends.

"It's nothing mysterious," Jane said. "You funnel money as income through a business where it can't be checked out. A service is ideal, because no one can say whether you actually performed whatever you were paid to do. A commodity isn't good, because you need warehouse inventory to match your income."

"You're saying your consulting partnership would work, but Dutch Bulb wouldn't?" Tim said.

Hank and Jane both laughed.

Tim drove into the port parking lot and stopped by a TV van. "The town's full of media for your Festival, so this was easy to arrange on short notice."

Hank met Jane's doubtful gaze. "We owe them."

She nodded. "Oak Harbor won't mind."

They got out of the car to face the good-natured mob.

"Is this going to be a wedding trip?"

Hank gazed amiably at the smirking journalist before turning to Jane. He spoke in his private voice. "When the Base locked me up without phone privileges I realized I left without fully explaining myself. You have a right to know I'm old-fashioned about my feelings. After my workshop, I asked your dad if he thought I was right for you."

"I don't care what he said."

"I do."

She reached for his hand.

"What do *you* think about it, Sandy?" he asked soberly. "I'll be satisfied with what you've given me, if that's where you want it to stop. But it would feel good to me for your mom and dad to read the words over us."

"I can marry you," she promised. "But if we go to my folks for it, there's the ferry ride to the Peninsula with a thousand journalists. I can't face that."

"Let's forget the ferry and just do the rest."

Their arms around each other, they walked down the dock.

"Hey!" one of the journalists yelled. "This is supposed to be a press conference!"

Hank smiled good-naturedly but he didn't stop. They took off their street shoes and stepped aboard *Cabin Seven* in their stocking feet. She turned on the small engine and took the wheel. Hank cast off the moorings.

By the time *Cabin Seven* passed the breakwater, some of the journalists had managed to rent powerboats. Smiling noncommittally, Hank opened the stern deck locker and rummaged inside. He straightened up holding a yellow flag.

She laughed. He took time out to grin before balancing lightly against the channel chop as he clipped the signal flag to the halyard and ran it up.

"Surely even journalists will respect that," he said.

She shook her head. "I doubt they believe in yellow fever quarantines, but maybe they believe in honeymoons."

"Your folks don't know when to expect us."

"Let's anchor in that first cove." She changed course and cut the engine back to trolling speed.

In the small bay's shelter, he went forward to rattle the anchor chain through the guide.

By the time she had the engine off and the wheel lashed, Hank was already below, arranging their bed. They undressed quickly and slipped into the sleeping bags, curling together in the trusting way of lovers who know their eternity will be perfectly easy and forever sweet.

A loudspeaker clicked on under their bow. Hank groaned.

When the enterprising journalist's questions rang out across the water, she laughed. She pulled the top sleeping bag over their heads to shut out some of the noise.

"It's no worse than a small town." She tightened her arms around his bare body.

"It's not too much worse than terrorists," he added, entwining their legs so they could press together more completely.

Delighted with their bad jokes, they snuggled deeper into their nest and gazed into each other's eyes and smiled contentedly. It took a long time for the tactless journalists to give up and trail away. It didn't matter.

Sandy and Hank heard nothing beyond their own quick breathing and hammering hearts and love whispers.

HARLEQUIN
American Romance

COMING NEXT MONTH

#321 A CAROL CHRISTMAS by Muriel Jensen

The children wanted a family to belong to. It was their last Christmas together. Housemother Carol Shaw wanted to make it special for Frank, Docras, Kathy and Candy—children who'd never had a family and faced an uncertain future in foster homes. Help arrived when baseball pro Mike Rafferty came to St. Christopher's. Mike brought excitement into all their lives. And then the snow came, bringing with it Carol's dearest wish for her charges. Mike, Carol and the children were going to celebrate the holiday as a family, with joy and love.

#322 MRS. SCROOGE by Barbara Bretton

All Patty wanted was a father of her own. Normally, chemistry didn't present a challenge to ten-year-old genius Patty. But man-woman chemistry was a different thing, and it had Patty stumped. Patty thought she only had to find the perfect father, introduce him to Mom and the rest would take care of itself. But Mom and Murphy O'Rourke weren't showing any signs of chemistry. Maybe chemistry was like magic—somehow, suddenly, it just happened. So maybe Patty didn't have to worry, for the most magical things happened at Christmas.

#323 DEAR SANTA by Margaret St. George

Flash and Amy wanted to be a family again. Their dad's job kept him in Los Angeles. Amy and Flash lived with their mother in Aspen Springs, which was supposed to be a great place for kids. But Amy and Flash knew where they all belonged—together. It wasn't easy convincing parents too stubborn to admit they were in love. So Amy got a pencil and paper, and wrote a letter to Santa....

#324 THE BEST GIFT OF ALL by Andrea Davidson

All Spence wanted was a mother to love. Spence Carruthers had a room full of toys, a live-in grandfather who knew all about fishing and a father who'd forgotten how to count his blessings. Mark Carruthers had run so hard and so long from childhood poverty that he'd lost sight of what he had here and now. Leah helped Mark remember. Leah brought the spirit of Christmas into the Carruthers' home. To Spence it was warm and comforting—like a mother's love.

Especially for you, Christmas from HARLEQUIN HISTORICALS

An enchanting collection of three Christmas stories by some of your favorite authors captures the spirit of the season in the 1800s

TUMBLEWEED CHRISTMAS by Kristin James

A "Bah, humbug" Texas rancher meets his match in his new housekeeper, a woman determined to bring the spirit of a Tumbleweed Christmas into his life—and love into his heart.

A CINDERELLA CHRISTMAS by Lucy Elliot

The perfect granddaughter, sister and aunt, Mary Hillyer seemed destined for spinsterhood until Jack Gates arrived to discover a woman with dreams and passions that were meant to be shared during a Cinderella Christmas.

HOME FOR CHRISTMAS
by Heather Graham Pozzessere

The magic of the season brings peace Home For Christmas when a Yankee captain and a Southern heiress fall in love during the Civil War.

Look for HARLEQUIN HISTORICALS CHRISTMAS STORIES wherever Harlequin books are sold.

HIST-XMAS-1R

Indulge a Little
Give a Lot

An irresistible opportunity to pamper yourself with free gifts (plus proofs-of-purchase and postage and handling) and help raise up to $100,000.00 for **Big Brothers/Big Sisters Programs and Services** in Canada and the United States.

Each specially marked "Indulge A Little" Harlequin or Silhouette book purchased during October, November and December contains a proof-of-purchase that will enable you to qualify for luxurious gifts. And, for every specially marked book purchased during this limited time, Harlequin/Silhouette will donate 5¢ toward **Big Brothers/Big Sisters Programs and Services**, for a maximum contribution of $100,000.00.

For details on how you can indulge yourself, look for information at your favorite retail store or send a self-addressed stamped envelope to:

INDULGE A LITTLE

P.O. Box 618
Fort Erie, Ontario
L2A 5I3

ONE PROOF OF PURCHASE

To collect your free gift you must include the necessary number of proofs-of-purchase, plus postage and handling, along with the offer certificate available in retail stores or from the above address.

CHAR-2

Harlequin®/Silhouette®